***A note from the author*:**

Proceed with caution! This book really isn't for you. *The Book of Joe B: A Love Story* is *not* a typical Christian novel. Some purists might find it offensive and vulgar, though it certainly isn't my intention to upset anyone. This book, a modern-day retelling of *The Book of Job* from the Old Testament, was written to encourage mainstream readers who might not otherwise open a bible to seek out the original story. It is not intended to be a substitute for God's Word but exists only as a humble signpost back to it. To this end, many liberties – perhaps, too many – were taken in order to make the story relatable and accessible to modern readers. Please be assured great effort was taken to keep the bible's narrative structure, themes, and messages intact despite giving it a whimsical and lighthearted tone. Facts may have been changed in order to build the story, but a foundation of God's Truths remains. I hope Christian readers will recognize this. And I hope they'll pass this book along to their unsaved family and friends. You know the ones; the nice, carnal people (whom we love) that spend their time playing Fortnite, going on Facebook, posting to Instagram, watching sports, Netflix, YouTube or porn, while ordering-in food, and, of course, taking selfies instead of taking some time to get to know the living God. This book is for them. See, it's really not for you. Yet, I hope you'll read it, regardless. I tried to get the message God was telling me onto the page without screwing it up too badly. Did I fail or succeed? I'm not sure. Write a review on Amazon or B&N and let me know. But be kind -- remember you're a Christian!

~Michael Winn

(March 2019)

The Book of Joe B: A Love Story

This book is a work of fiction. Names, characters, places and incidents are products of the author's imagination or are used fictitiously. Any resemblance to actual events or locales or persons, living or dead, is entirely coincidental.

A MW Publications Trade Paperback
First Edition 2019

ISBN: 978-0-9840269-7-5

MW

Michael Winn Publications

Book Layout by Michael Winn

Cover by
Michael and Tina Winn

Printed by IngramSpark

THE BOOK OF JOE B:

A Love Story

MICHAEL WINN

MW Publications | Long Island, NY

For Evan and Kim

“And said, Naked came I out of my mother's womb, and naked shall I return thither: the LORD gave, and the LORD hath taken away; blessed be the name of the LORD.” (Job 1:21)

1

Joseph Bustamante parked, stepped out of the little car, and patted the bulge in his jacket to make sure it was still there - it was. Had he lost it, not only would he be out five thousand bucks, but the most significant moment of his life would swirl down the toilet. He slid a hand into his pants pocket. With considerable effort, out came a quarter between nimble fingertips. He examined it, rolled it, and walked it between knuckles, a skill he'd learned as a kid. He stood at the side of his Mini Cooper at the car-lined curb. People strolled by, oblivious to his dilemma. He started to feel ridiculous standing next to it looking like a boy with a Radio Flyer wagon - friends already ribbed him about his toy car. But, hey, it had been a thirtieth birthday gift from his mom, and he appreciated the thought and the sacrifice she'd made. You couldn't return a car for being the wrong size and color like a shirt. So, he'd put the seat back as far as it would go and had come to love it. Joe palmed the quarter and fanned his fingers upward and outward, the coin finding a bed in the soft cleft of his hand. He could've been a street magician. Sleight-of-hand came easy. He was a big guy. His shoulders were big. His chest was big. His hands were big. A quarter to him was a dime. He wasn't keen on wasting one if he didn't have to, though. He checked his watch - twenty to... They only ticketed from eight in the morning to six at night. What were the odds a traffic cop would mosey down the sidewalk to check the meters in the next twenty minutes? Joe looked left and right.

He loved this old village. It had been originally settled by Uzbeks upon coming to the US having escaped the Russian Empire that took control of Uzbekistan during the mid-1800s. American yuppies became keen on the location during the 1990s and revitalized the area. The restored buildings were an architectural hodgepodge of brick and stone, all connected, extending along each side of the street. Unusual looking. Most of the structures skinny but tall, squished together like the bellows of an accordion - pretty cool. Joe started to work the quarter back into his pocket and took two steps, his lead shoe stopping with a skid. He turned around, returned to the meter and slid the coin into the slot. With a turn of the knob, it dropped with a chank; the needle going from red to 2 hours; the VIOLATION flag gone with a snap... Naturally, Joe had paid. Joe always did what's right. There was no way around it. He'd parked before six and the rule says that costs a quarter. If you try to rationalize your wrongdoing, you're asking fate to kick you in the butt. Besides, Joe had never gotten a parking ticket in his life and didn't want to start tonight, especially tonight. If you follow the rules, good things will follow… He patted the pocket again - still there. Silly to keep checking. But he hadn't been this nervous, hmm...since never. It wasn't a scared type of nervous, mind you. Just an excited, bubbly kind of feeling. He walked in the direction of Steeples resisting an urge to skip.

He was three blocks away. The whole main street was only six blocks long. Still, there was no shortage of places to blow your paycheck. There were coffee houses with live folk music, a smoothie shop, a chocolatier, an antique shop, two nail salons, health food stores, a bookstore, a craft beer house that sold eleven-dollar drafts, bistros with tiny, circular tables, a Mexican Cantina, and a Sushi joint with square dinner plates and tables set so close together it was like eating with strangers. Regardless of the crowds, Joe felt at home here. There was no meanness. No hotheads. Certainly no crime. Even having come to Steeples for Happy Hour every Friday - Frappy Hour, they called it - for the past six years, Joe had not once witnessed a fight or even an argument. He never saw a drunk stumble or anyone panhandle. All you saw were well-to-do folks milling about. Yep, this night was no different. Joe strode by professional men and women in casual attire with moods to match. Of course, this micro city had a name, but the name's not important. Most people called it Little Uzbekistan or, more simply, The Village, and Joe had never heard anyone utter a bad word against it. He secretly referred to it as The Land of Uz, and he loved coming by after work for a beer.

The closer Joe got, the more he wanted to trot, to run, to sprint. He concentrated on keeping his stride and demeanor controlled, though. Everyone else meandered like they had a written guarantee to live to one hundred and he didn't want to stand out. He moved in the direction of the setting sun and was sorry he'd left his sunglasses in the Cooper. He used a big hand to shield his eyes. The tomato red ball was dipped halfway below the horizon, saying goodnight with long, magenta streaks.

He stopped at the intersection of Island Avenue and stared at the illuminated don't walk hand. A machine voice said wait...wait...wait. So he did.

Joe wondered if Rebecca was already there. That wouldn't be good. She didn't like to wait. Of course, nobody likes to wait, but it bothered Rebecca more than most. Bothered her in a scary way, actually. Like people made her wait on purpose. But, so what? Everyone has pet peeves. Boy, did he adore this woman. He walked past a shoe store and The Library. Of course, it wasn't actually a public library, anymore. A lot of things in the village had been refurbished and turned into something else. Steeples, where Joe was heading if the pole would ever let him walk again, used to be a church a hundred years ago but now it was a bar and grill. The Library was an upscale wine and cheese place. On a corner, a few blocks back, the old post office was now a dance club called Stamp.

The traffic pole told Joe to walk...walk... walk. So he did.

The sidewalk ahead was packed, but it wouldn't bother him. He hoped Rebecca wasn't there already, though. Not tonight. He wanted everything just right, so he'd remain collected, despite the risk he was about to take. Joe worked his way through the throng of people, hands tucked in pockets, looking at his shoes. Darn, they kept the village super-clean. Not even a gum wrapper on the sidewalk. Unusual for a bustling little town. No trash to trip on but impossible to move without bumping into a doctor.

Two miles west of where the main drag ends were two huge hospitals, curiously set right next door to one another. Between the village limits and the hospitals was an endless string of medical buildings and rehab clinics. Seemed everyone who came by, especially on a Friday night, was a doctor or at least called themselves one. Even though he'd studied a surprising amount of anatomy and physiology, Joe wasn't a doctor. Not even close. Unless you consider a middle school phys ed teacher almost a doctor, which most people don't. Still he loved his job, actually won an Excellence in Leadership Award the prior year, and working with the kids was a joy. At the school, they called him Joe B because there'd been another gym teacher named Joe. The funny part is, the other Joe came five years after, but somehow, he became the default Joe and he, Joseph Bustamante, became Joe B. The name stuck and spread even after the second Joe moved on to a different job, go figure.

He raised his head to catch his reflection in the window of a Polish bakery as he passed. Rebecca was too pretty for him, of course. His lips were thick, his nose and brow were thick, and even his skin was thick like animal hide. Worse, Joe had a habit of his big face getting overly concerned when he noticed the bad stuff in the world, his heavy lips puckering into a perfect little O. That inclination, along with a thick brow and a double-helping of eyebrows hanging over soft, sensitive eyes, made people - well, his mother, anyway - say Joe resembled a reluctant gangster, a movie mobster hampered by a conscience, like a young Chazz Palminteri. This may or may not be true. Though his mom had said this forever, Joe still hadn't bothered to google the actor so he'd forfeited the right to object.

So, Joe wasn't a doctor and didn't look like a doctor, but he did dress like one - an off-duty, thirtysomething intern just out of med school, maybe. This special night he wore a navy sports jacket over a white polo shirt and khakis. He'd slicked his hair straight back using a copious amount of gel and smacked his cheeks with after shave. It didn't matter how he looked, though. He felt good. That's what's important. And it didn't matter if Rebecca was too pretty for him. Seemed to Joe, most gals were too pretty for their men. People were the exact opposite of peacocks.

Joe went on the five broad granite steps of the converted cathedral coming to the heavy, dark wood doors. He paused for a full breath. Not that he was worried. He was a decent catch, and that ain't boasting. Not only had he never gotten a parking ticket, he'd never earned a speeding ticket, either. Never been in a fender bender. Never a fistfight. Never cheated on a girlfriend or his income taxes. Never stole or done drugs. Heck, he'd never gotten drunk, not really, and felt sorry for his friends who had that particular need. Moreover, he'd never been out of work. Never been sick, not seriously, anyway. No big family problems and no money problems. Joe never lied or cursed. And because of the way he chose to live, he had never been down on his luck or unhappy. But he couldn't take all the credit. Joe knew he was blessed. Each night before bed, he dropped to his knees and thanked the Almighty for his good fortune… Yet despite all this, something was missing. Something was off. And Joe knew what it was. Yes, somehow true love had eluded him. That feeling of loss for something he'd never had created a hollow space, a longing inside him. For years, maybe for his entire life, there'd been a hole in his heart the size of a crater. But soon, those feelings would be no more. For that hole would get filled tonight!

He removed the ring box from his pocket and opened it. Before his eyes was a brilliant, clear 1.7 carat diamond set in white gold. A pinkish light shimmied on the stone. He snapped the box closed, returned it to his pocket, and smiled.

He'd saved five thousand dollars for the ring. Not easy on his salary. Of course, he could've dipped into his holdings - an investment portfolio consisting of exactly one stock - but he'd promised his mother never to touch what she called the Nest Egg. Her father, Joe's grandfather, had invested in a neighborhood, storefront business, Pillbox Accoucheurs and Dispensing Chemists, LTD, sixty-five years ago. He'd liked their ointment for cankers and scrumpox. Moreover, they had a liniment on the drawing board that promised to treat milk leg and a syrup to combat female weakness. Grandpa, to Grandma's great ire, purchased three hundred shares, a considerable stake in the upstart company. The business grew modestly and the stocks gained value accordingly. Except for a brief mention at Thanksgiving dinners, the investment was all but forgotten. After her grandparents passed away, Joe's mom inherited the shares. His mother, in turn, gave them to Joe on his eighteenth birthday with explicit instructions never to touch them. Little did anyone expect that five decades after the company's launch, their research into deplumation would pan-out in a most unusual way - designer eyelashes. With its name changed to Pillbox Pharmaceuticals and a newly minted pink Starfish pill that promised - and delivered - thicker, longer Cleopatra lashes, the company's profits skyrocketed. The original shares, having split again and again, their number increased exponentially. They were now valued at more than three million dollars. Joe, however, always remained discreet regarding his finances. Nobody knew, not even Rebecca, the only exception being Joe's yearly donation of the dividends to Happy Campers so a few disadvantaged kids could go away for the summer. Otherwise, he liked being the millionaire next door, one of the wealthiest men in Uz. Having the Nest Egg was a huge comfort. It would always be there if things went sour. No matter what happened, he'd always be able to provide for her.

Rebecca would say yes. She'd have to. Joe already had their futures mapped out. He and Rebecca would get married and have seven sons and three daughters - extra boys to look after the girls - and a whole lotta pets. He'd rise early every morning and make their children French toast, burning it as was his custom. They'd all laugh it off, and everything would be forgiven.

He pulled the door open wide. Music and murmurs came out as he stepped in. There was nothing to fear. Nothing could go wrong. This is how relationships clicked. You met a good girl and courted her with flowers and dinners out. You got to know one another. Eventually, the man bends a knee. Joe had followed the playbook with Rebecca. He'd bought a beautiful ring. Everything was good to go. Besides, Joe B was a good

⸙ 2 ⸙

"Why do you always leave it on top of the bar? Put it back in your pocket. It drives me crazy," the first said, his voice an odd falsetto.

"Why? What's it to you?" the second responded, calm, goading his little friend.

"Because you're going to lose it. Or someone is going to steal it."

The wallet lay nested on fanned-out bills. A group of friends were seated in a line of barstools. All wore white jerseys; two wore ball caps, the group part of a company softball team, The Angels. The first two in the line were having the playful little argument. The other sons-of-guns watched with mild amusement, enjoying the show.

The first continued, "You're gonna get up and go to the bathroom or leave tonight and forget to take it. Either way, somebody's going to snatch it."

"I don't like reaching into my pocket every time I want a drink. Besides, you're being paranoid. We're in a good place. Nobody's going to steal it."

"How can you know that?"

"'Cause I have faith in humanity."

"In people? Really?"

"Yeah. The way I see it, most people resist tempt-"

A single, sharp clap came from behind. The group turned to a well-dressed man they hadn't seen approach. He took a moment before he spoke.

"There isn't a man or woman within this establishment or on the face of this entire, corrupt planet who wouldn't steal your wallet given the chance," he said.

The certainty within his tone, the boldness of his interruption, silenced the group. The Angels turned and waited for an explanation that was not forthcoming. The stranger stood confident, patient. He had sharp cheekbones, intense blue eyes, and the full, tousled hair of a male model along with a tailored, cream-colored suit to match. He rested an elbow within a cupped hand and gripped his chin. He sported an enormous designer wristwatch. Silver rings on nearly every finger caught the light and flashed.

"Where did you come from?" a gravel-laden voice from behind the bar said.

"Oh, I've been roaming about, here and there," the visitor replied, his voice a song. "What's your take on this moral question, Barkeep?"

The bartender didn't answer. Instead, he climbed atop the wooden stool kept behind the bar next to the cash register and crossed his arms over his chest. He was short and squat with a barrel chest and bulging, hairy forearms coming out of rolled-up shirtsleeves. Though there certainly wasn't any comeliness to attract anyone, if you looked past the thinning, auburn hair, bulbous nose, and ruddy complexion, you'd notice the intellect, compassion, and wisdom within his pale, unblinking eyes.

The accuser disregarded him and addressed the teammates.

"If you were to choose any person in this room and left them alone for even a minute, your wallet, my friend, would be a memory. Don't confuse lack of opportunity with virtue. It's not any incorruptible morality or great love for others or the law that keeps the human animal honest, but merely worry of being caught, exposed, and punished. It's the fear of being walloped and thrown into the outer darkness by our good barkeep that keeps the beasts at bay, nothing more. Look about, you'll not find one honorable man - not one."

One of the white-shirts tittered though nobody thought the conversation was funny. After a moment spent studying the outsider, the bartender spoke.

"Have you considered my favorite patron, Joe B?"

The interloper snapped his neck around to look upon Joseph Bustamante speaking with the young hostess at her station. Though they were too far away to hear the conversation, it was clear to all Joe wasn't bragging or flirting or telling tales. As his huge smile revealed, he was simply happy to be here, waiting for a table, excited about the possibilities that lay ahead.

The bartender lowered his stubbly chin, and continued. "There's no one like Joe B. The man is a stand-up guy. Completely blameless and honest and decent… And he's a good tipper."

This last part made the group laugh, and all hoped the discussion would end on a high note. The visitor, however, turned back to face the bartender, features contorted, jaws clenched, and eyes ablaze. But just as quickly as he'd become angered, his countenance morphed into one of bright eyes and a large smile showing bleached-white teeth. He patted the two teammates on the shoulders, emitted an amiable chuckle, and leaned forward.

"You're hedging your bets," he said, addressing the bartender. "Is Joe B a do-gooder for no reason? Since he has it all, he has too much to lose. He's only honest and upright because he's received good fortune upon good fortune. Take away his job and he'll rob banks. Give him a drug addiction and he'd swipe the wallet right out of your hand. If he were facing death-"

"No such thing will ever happen to him," the bartender said, and cautioned the stranger with a single raised finger.

The visitor stood erect and stepped backward. Despite being rebuked, or maybe because of it, his voice became defiant, the vocal equivalent of a sneer.

"So, he's a good tipper? Only because you give him buy-backs. Stop the freebies and I'd wager that Joe B will curse you to your face."

Silence followed. The break in the discussion seemed to extend to the entire restaurant. The clinks of forks on plates, clacks of billiard balls, raucous laughter, and even the piped-in pop music went dead.

"Alright," the bartender said. "It's in your hand. We'll see what he truly believes. We'll see what's inside Joe B's heart."

* * *

When the young hostess eventually escorted Joe to an empty table, he was thrilled. When the server came by, he ordered a draft beer and a Pink Lady. Though he'd planned for a more intimate setting in a darkened far corner, this one, a virtual bullseye at the center of Steeples, was better. If a man was going to propose to the woman he loved, he shouldn't be ashamed to be seen doing it. Anyway, he was glad Rebecca hadn't arrived yet. It gave him time to settle in, buy her favorite drink, comb his hair with his fingers, and mentally rehearse the poem he'd written. He'd actually penned two, one that rhymed and one that didn't. He preferred the rhyming poem, though he suspected a refined woman such as Rebecca would appreciate the latter. Joe shut his eyelids and began inwardly reciting:

"I can't promise a mansion
Or European vacations
I won't predict perpetual bliss
Or anything close to perfection
There are too many unknowns
In a world that can't be controlled
So a lifetime of love is all I offer
But these words are a pledge
For my love is forever assured
If you'll wear this ring as my wife
We'll weather all storms together..."

"There you are," a voice cracked over the noisy room. "Sorrrry. First, a customer comes in at five minutes to closing and wants to try a sample of every shade of lipstick ever invented and then doesn't like none of them. Then on the way over here, I step in dog doo. Almost slid and broke my ass. Brand-new pumps, too. Took forever to scrape it off. Whatcha doin' with your eyes closed and mumbling to yourself?"

Joe opened his eyes to a vision. Rebecca stood before him in all her loveliness. She donned a silky burgundy blouse with a pussy-bow and a beige skirt. Her dark hair was put up like a princess's. Oversized sunglasses sat on top of her head like a tiara. Joe rose from his seat, kissed her on the cheek, and pulled out a chair. They made small talk about their work, the dog excrement occurrence, and Rebecca's sister, Jennifer, who was, in Rebecca's words, an emotionally unstable psycho who needs to get a life. Joe listened and nodded politely despite feeling edgy, perspiration forming on his upper lip. The ring box tucked within his pocket started to pulsate like a second heartbeat.

"Rebecca," Joe said. "I have something to say."

"Is this for me?" Rebecca said, lifting the Pink Lady from the table, sipping. "You know, I don't blame the dog."

Joe tilted his head, waited.

"It's not the dog's fault he pooped on the sidewalk. It's the owners' fault for not cleaning it up. People are such eff-ing slobs," Rebecca explained. She then went on, in great detail, how the human race would be better off if we were all more like dogs.

Joe found himself getting short of breath. His chest went tight. Either he'd propose soon or have a heart attack.

"Rebecca, darling, I have something to say," he interrupted.

"O-kay," she said cautiously. "But let me go first. There's something I need to say. I should've told you sooner, Joe, but I've been avoiding it, and now it can't wait any longer."

Joe looked, his mind fogged and mouth dry. He took a gulp of beer.

"There's no easy way to say this, so I'm just gonna blurt it out," Rebecca said. "I'm seeing a doctor."

Joe's heart swelled with worry and fear. He swallowed a gasp. He fought back tears. He shook his head no. He had to force the words from his throat.

"Is it serious?" he said.

"Who knows?" Rebecca replied. "Who can tell with these things? He's taking me to the Bahamas."

Joe clasped Rebecca's hands on the tabletop and massaged her knuckles with a big thumb. He wondered why the Bahamas. He'd read something about clinics in the Caribbean but thought they were for tummy tucks or something. He looked into Rebecca's pretty face, her eyes. There was so much to love about her - Rebecca sneezed whenever walking into sunlight, she liked to cook more than she liked to eat, and, bless her good soul, she phoned her grandmother almost every Saturday morning unless she was busy. Rebecca was amazing.

"W-what's wrong with you?" Joe said, wanting to cover his ears.

"Nothing's wrong with me," Rebecca said, annoyed. "I just think we have different priorities right now. And these different priorities are going to take us in different directions."

"Not a chance! I love you, Rebecca. You're priorities are my priorities. I'll come with you to the Bahamas. I'll be at your side the whole time."

"What are y-"

Joe slid his chair back hard and dropped to one knee. He fumbled to remove the ring box and he opened it."

"What? Joe, don't do this!"

People noticed. A small crowd formed a semicircle. Some nudged others. More joined in. Onlookers at the rear stood on toes for a better view. Joe's mind groped about in the dark to find the words. When he thought he grabbed them, he began.

"Rebecca, I can't promise a mansion or a...or a second mansion…"

"Oh my gosh. Get up, Joe. Don't!"

Several people whipped out phones and began recording the special moment.

"I also can't promise vacations… To France or anywhere… Unless you consider the Bahamas trip a vacation. That I will promise... But I won't predict perpetual bliss or...something else…"

Joe paused, closed his mind and tried to visualize the napkin he'd originally composed the poem on. A man tried to rescue him.

"Alright buddy, you got it," he yelled. "Keep going. You're nailing it!"

Somebody else clapped. Joe was emboldened by the support even as the verses slipped further from memory. No matter, he'd cut to the end.

"So a lifetime of love is all I offer…"

The crowd applauded. Someone went awwwww…

Joe smiled sheepishly, his face reddened. Rebecca's face reddened, too, as she recoiled into her chair and looked about, wide-eyed and aghast.

"So, please take this ring and be my wife," Joe said, presenting the opened box.

"No, Joe! I can't believe you did this. Why would you? Are you stupid? I can't marry you," Rebecca said, sitting up and hiking the strap of her handbag high onto her shoulder. "Joe, I met someone else, Dr. Richard Spiera. He works near here. I told you when we first met that I didn't want anything serious. And I meant it."

It took a moment for comprehension to kick him out of his lovesick stupor. Joe closed the box and returned it to his pocket. Before turning away, someone booed and a few others grumbled. One even made a snide remark in Rebecca's direction that shouldn't be repeated.

It took great effort for Joe to slap a palm on the tabletop, rise from the floor, and slide onto his chair. At first, he couldn't speak. When he could, his tone was hushed, barely a whisper.

"Why didn't you tell me sooner?" he said.

"Joe, I told you eight months ago when we first met that I didn't want anything serious. I told you that, after Tony, I wasn't ready to commit to any one person. You knew this could happen."

"Knew what could happen?"

"That I could find somebody else," she said.

He looked down at his self-twiddling thumbs. It was true. She'd been honest from the start. But weren't they in love? Didn't love count for anything?

"Look, Joe. You're a great guy. You're just not a great guy for me… I want the mansion and the vacation in France. Do you think I want to sell cosmetics for the rest of my life? And, no, I don't want ten kids and thirty dogs and cats and chickens. But there are women who do. And you'll meet one. You'll find someone who is right for you - the perfect fit."

Rebecca stood, lifted one of Joe's hands and kissed the back of it.

"The right one will be lucky to have you," she said. "Take good care of yourself, Mr. Joe B."

She weaved through the throngs of people talking, drinking, and others reveling in Frappy Hour, and was gone, taking his plans, dreams, and ten children with her.

Naturally, Joe appreciated Rebecca turning his proposal down gently. He was especially thankful for the kind sentiments she'd expressed while dumping him. To be truthful, however, something in her words seemed as ephemeral as the smell of perfume she'd left behind. Her predictions about his future didn't heal but only poured salt into an existing wound. If anything, the hole within his heart, the one he had before birth, seemed larger and more painful now. With Rebecca gone, the chance of finding true love seemed stolen, destroyed. He hoped it wasn't true. Because if it was, what would become of Joe B? How would he ever know joy?

Joe paid the bill and walked out, The Land of Uz darkened now, the streetlights inadequate, the faces of passing strangers shadowy, unapproachable. He kept hands in pockets and gazed towards the pavement as he made the trek back to his car. At the car, he saw a small flyer had been placed on his windshield and expected it to be an advertisement for a local business or bar. After snatching it from beneath the wiper blade, Joe examined the piece of cardstock with the checkboxes and the scribbled signature and determined what it really was - a parking ticket. He turned to the meter as if to argue, but the device stood silently accusing, a red VIOLATION flag raised behind its glass face.

3

Joe arrived home to find his mother, Gladys, sitting on a sofa within a darkened room, the TV on with no sound.

"Ma, you alright? Why the lights off?"

He switched on a lamp, leaned over, and kissed her on the forehead.

"Just sitting here, thinking," she said. "How was your date?"

He hadn't told his mom he'd intended to propose to Rebecca. He'd planned to drop the bomb when he got home. Had Rebecca said yes, she would've hugged him, uncorked a bottle of prosecco, and called her church friends.

"It went fine, I guess," Joe said.

"You shouldn't have to guess," Gladys said.

Joe looked at the TV. An old black and white western was airing. Eight hundred channels came with their cable TV package and this is what Gladys Bustamante had chosen to watch, without audio, no less. The scene showed a saloon.. There were card players and a player piano. He imagined it wouldn't be long before a fracas broke out, punches thrown and bottles shattered over heads.

"The one with the mustache is holding a gun under the table," Gladys said. "Why does there always have to be a bad guy?"

This confused Joe. All the men had mustaches. Gladys pointed towards the screen for clarification. Joe and his mom often communicated without spoken words.

They sat and watched together. His mom was a little thing, a child's doll compared to her son. She was also older than people expected upon meeting her for the first time. She'd been told she couldn't have children, but then conceived at age forty-three. By the time Joe reached high school, the other kids mistook her for his grandmother. Now, in her late-seventies, she certainly looked the part. Her hair was white and her bones seemed hollow like reeds. Her wrists were knobby and brown blotches stained the back of her hands.

Over the years, people razzed Joe about still living with his mom in his mid-thirties, but he took it with good cheer. He loved his mom and enjoyed her company. They ate dinner together, watched late-night movies and college football, and played gin rummy. Why would he be in a rush to live alone? Who knew? Maybe his mom was his one true love. They'd journeyed through life together for a long time.

His dad died suddenly when Joe was thirteen. Joseph Bustamante Sr., a burly, boisterous man with a huge gut along with a huge appetite for food and life, had been tinkering with the family's old lawn mower. Apparently, he'd suffered a heart attack in the morning heat and keeled over. The Bustamantes were renowned for having the nicest lawn in the neighborhood - thick, hunter green, unblemished even by a single dandelion - and this gave Joe Sr. a social station he took great pride in. Neighbors often solicited advice, and he was happy to give it... Joe Jr. got off the school bus to find his father face down in his beloved grass. There was a lovely funeral, burial, and a small reception back at the house with a lot of whispering relatives and deviled eggs. But something felt wrong, like they weren't respecting his father's secret wishes. Prior to the funeral, Joe beseeched his mother to have his dad cremated so his ashes could be scattered over the lawn as fertilizer. His mom said no. Joe took over lawn care duties after his dad's death, keeping it well-manicured to this day. The small lawn in front of the little house may no longer be the nicest in the neighborhood, but it was still pretty darn good in Joe's opinion. And he was proud to keep his father's legacy alive.

"Did ya eat?" Gladys asked. "I'll make something."

The house smelled of meatloaf. Joe loved his mom's cooking but his appetite had left when the love of his life had walked out.

"Yeah, Ma. I ate. I'm good," Joe said. "Think I'm gonna turn in early, though. Going fishing tomorrow at dawn. I'll be quiet."

He rose from his dad's recliner and headed for the staircase.

"Joe, wait," his mother said. "I have something to tell you."

He returned and sat on the couch next to his mom, and waited. Her eyes were glassy, faraway, while her mouth incongruously formed a sweet and sorrowful expression. When she didn't speak for a long time, Joe pulled her hands into his.

"Ma, what is it? Tell me."

"Joseph, don't be upset, but I've been seeing a doctor," Gladys said.

Joe wasn't sure what to say. His dad had died so very long ago and his mom had never dated. It seemed odd she would take up with someone new so late in life. He wondered if he'd have to move out.

"Well," Joe said, fidgeting, gripping and squeezing his knees. "This is news. I understand. I really do. It must get lonely without dad. I just want you to be happy."

"What?" Gladys said, brow furled, eyelids scrunched. "I'm not dating a doctor. Your father was enough of a pain-in-the-neck, why would I want another man? I'm sick."

Joe shook his head no. Gladys continued, matter-of-factly.

"I've been feeling weak and dog-tired for a long time. So, I finally went to see Dr. Ford and she sent me to a specialist, Dr. Mudgil. Joe, I have cancer."

Gladys let this hang in the air for a moment. Joe's lower lip quivered. Then his entire body shook. His mother pulled him downward, his big face pressed into her bony shoulder, and he wept, wetting the flimsy cotton of her nightgown.

She tried to comfort him by telling him everything was okay, that she had to have her lymph nodes removed but that the prognosis was good. Joe heard yet didn't hear. He'd stopped listening at the word cancer and couldn't stop crying. His mom explained that she'd be leaving tomorrow to move in with her sister.

"For only a little while," she said.

"No. I'm here. I'll take care of you," Joe insisted.

"You work. Your aunt is home all the time doing nothing except tending to her bees. And she's closer to the clinic. You can come see me on weekends."

This was true, and it made sense. Joe didn't like it, but it made sense.

"You sure?" he said.

"I'll be fine. As long as I don't get stung by those damn bees," Gladys said, and smiled.

They talked so long the movie ended and the credits rolled. They talked a little about her medical diagnosis but mostly about old times. By the end, Joe felt better, encouraged. His mom was strong, They'd be alright. Joe offered to cancel his fishing trip to take her to Aunt Edna's.

"Not necessary. Your kooky aunt is coming to get me," Gladys said. She then retold the familiar joke about her sister having bees in her bonnet, and Joe laughed as if hearing it for the first time. Gladys became serious.

"Do you want to know the worst part about the chemo treatments?" she said. "All my hair is going to fall out."

"It'll grow back, Ma."

Gladys ignored this. She was far away again, staring through the TV set.

"Do you know what your father said to me the first time we met?" she said. "We were at a dance hall that's probably not there anymore… Your father swaggered over to me right in front of my girlfriends and said, 'Hey, doll. You've got a big nose.'"

Joe's mouth hung open. He'd thought he'd heard all his mother's stories, but this one she'd saved...as what? A painful memory? Gladys continued.

"Yes, that's what the suave Mr. Joseph Bustamante said - you've got a honker, baby, but the most beautiful hair I have ever laid eyes on… And we danced the rest of the night. Your father was very light on his feet for a big man." She ran her fingers through her hair. "It was silky and chestnut then. I wish my nose would fall off instead of my hair."

Joe stared into his mother's face. It was true. She did have a large nose, long and thin with a downward bend at the bridge. Strange he hadn't noticed before. She'd always just been Ma, not Ma with the schnoz. Joe hated she'd let this mean idea manifest.

"I think you have a fine nose," he said, and he pinched her nose between a forefinger and thumb. "Dad didn't know everything."

Joe didn't know how to interpret her smile. It was a small, perplexed but affectionate simper like he was an exotic and quirky bug. He kissed her on the forehead.

"Heading to bed?" he asked.

"I'm going to stay up a little while more," she said.

Joe retired to his bedroom and removed his suit pants and unbuttoned his shirt, leaving his clothes in a pile. He knelt beside the bed and clasped his hands. He thanked the Lord for all he had and asked that his mother be cured quickly. He also asked that Rebecca find happiness with her new boyfriend and that someone special would come into his life, as well.

He laced his fingers behind his head as he lay on the bed looking up at the ceiling. Moonlight came in between the slats of the open window blinds casting silver stripes about the room, making a jail cell. A spider, the size of a nickel, was on the ceiling directly above. It didn't move. Joe studied it for what seemed a very long time. The spider's patience was unnerving.

For some reason, he suspected it knew whether his mother would live or die. The spider and he remained locked in a staring contest until Joe realized he'd forgotten to brush his teeth. Frustrated, he rose and hurriedly tried to put on his bathrobe but it tore at the rear seam - he tossed it aside. Naked as the day he'd came from his mother's womb, he went through the hallway and into the small, green tiled room. His mind went numb like a foot that had fallen asleep. By impulse, instead of reaching for the toothpaste, he grabbed the can of shaving cream from the cabinet behind the mirror. He pumped a large, foamy, white blob into the palm of one hand. After inspecting it for a full minute, Joe proceeded to vigorously rub and work the shaving cream into his scalp as if it were shampoo. He then pushed his hair back at the hairline, took a twin-blade razor and pulled it over his scalp, front to rear, the razor plowing lines through the shaving cream, making a soft scraping sound as it went. Joe turned the faucet on high to repeatedly rinse the foam and the black, silky ringlets off the blades and into the basin. It took longer than he'd imagined. When finished, he washed his head clean, patted it dry with a towel, and returned to bed. Sleep fell upon him like a piano in an old cartoon. He slumbered as motionless and dreamless as a dead man.

4

The alarm clock came on and played a peculiar song on an oldies station - the illuminated digits indicated 4:30. Joe thought he'd set it to sports talk but must've done something wrong. Instead of box scores and banter, he heard a long-forgotten black man crooning in a raspy, mournful voice backed up only by a single trumpet with a mute. The music crackled as if an old vinyl record was being played on a one-hundred-year-old Victrola. Joe turned it off.

He shaved and showered, feeling funny about not cancelling the fishing trip. But what was he to do? His friends had already chartered the boat and were expecting him. Besides, Joe's mom would insist he go. He dressed quietly by the light of a small lamp, not wanting to disturb his mother, who he assumed was asleep in the next bedroom. It surprised him to find her seated with eyes shut where he'd left her. The TV was still on, its illumination flashing over her darkened form. He leaned over and touched her shoulder.

"Ma," he whispered. "Ma, wake up and go to bed."

The oddness of the request struck him after he'd said it. Regardless, when she didn't rouse, he gently shook her shoulder. A thought occurred to him that she might be... Joe shook harder.

"Ma..."

Gladys's eyes opened and went wide with terror. She sprung to her feet and let out a shriek that rattled the loose glass of the china cabinet in the dining room.

"Joe! Joe! Come quick! There's a maniac in the house!" she shouted.

He tried to hug her but she slapped his face and boxed his ears in a flurry of blows.

"Ma, Ma, it's me!"

The assault ceased and Gladys's facial expression morphed from fear to puzzlement to amusement.

"Are you trying to kill me? What did you do?" she asked. "What happened to your hair?"

She caressed her son's face as an apology. Joe bowed his head for inspection. Gladys reached up and ran her fingertips over his pale, smooth pate.

"Why?" she asked, though she already knew because she knew her son. Her smile was broad with amazement

"You were worried about your hair falling out," Joe said. "I want you to know you're not alone. I'm going to shave my head until yours grows back."

"Joseph, you're crazy," Gladys said, and laughed heartedly.

"Crazy about you," Joe said. "We're going to get through this."

"So this is what I can expect? It feels like a baby's butt."

Joe laughed, joining in this impromptu celebration of family. "Do I still look like Chazz Palminteri?"

"Now you look more like Kojak."

Joe smiled and hugged his mother despite having no idea whom she was referring to. "Sure you don't want me to stay home?"

"Go fishing with your friends. Bring home dinner, but you better wear a hat or you'll freeze your tuchus on the boat - both of them," she said.

An unexpected peace came over Joe. His mom's humor was still the same. The way she talked and the way she cared about him, too. No disease could steal any of that away, unless he let it. Joe's mom with cancer was still his mom, and that was a comfort.

They exchanged goodbyes, and he promised to call later in the evening. He watched her head up the stairs, step by slow step, to bed. He felt good. Renewed. This would be a good day. Maybe he would catch something. Each new day comes with certain promises, certain gifts, if only you are willing to receive them. Joe packed a rucksack with bottled water, wrapped sandwiches, and an abundance of junk food for his friends. He retrieved his father's fishing pole and tackle box from the garage and loaded everything into the Mini Cooper. Though the sun wasn't showing itself yet, a pretty saffron glow from the east foretold its arrival. The weather would be perfect, Joe was sure.

* * *

Eli and Bill were already on the boat when Joe arrived at the docks. Zoe would come afterward. No surprise here. Zoe's invariable tardiness was a running joke within their group - though Eli didn't find it funny.

They'd all chipped in and chartered the same boat as usual, All My Glory, an outing they did as a ritual once per year. Taking it in now, along with a mouthful of the dock's stench of fish guts and low-tide muck, he thought the boat was too beat-up and larger than needed. There were many smaller, sleeker and newer charters to choose from - Joe wondered why Eli was locked on this one. The vessel had proved itself, however. Merely finding it still afloat at the end of yet another season with the canal's frothy green water lapping its sides testified to its sea worthiness. All My Glory certainly didn't live up to its name, though. The boat was a thirty-two foot trawler with peeling paint and splintering wood. On board, it would look better with a well-maintained main deck and comfortable cabin for the guests. There was also an open railed second deck, topped by a blue canopy, where only the mates were allowed and, climbing metal rungs from there, a small, enclosed third deck with large, tinted windows on each side. Presumably, this is where the captain steered the boat. Nobody, it seemed, not even the mates, were allowed access to the upper room. Going out on this particular boat was surely an adventure, an act of faith. For even after taking many trips, Joe had never seen the captain, go figure.

"Hey, buddy," Bill said, as Joe stepped off the short, shaky gangplank and onto the deck.

"What's up, dude," Eli said.

They were standing next to one another leaning over the rail. There was the usual exchange of fist bumps that felt awkward, like they were appropriating a greeting from a younger generation.

"What's with the cap," Bill said, snatching it off Joe's head before he could object.

"What the..." Eli said, and swallowed a weird inhalation of a laugh.

"Holy... Did you get into a fight with your barber?" Bill said.

Joe thought about coming up with a story to avoid the subject, but then he told them about his mom's diagnosis and his pledged support. His friends expressed concern and wished his family well. The truth, as it often does, seemed to kill the fun, but the group soon recovered and the two friends teased Joe about needing simonizing wax and being blinded by the glare. Joe flipped the cap back on.

The three amigos caught up regarding their respective jobs and complained about how bad their favorite pro sports teams were performing. Eli complained about Zoe holding up the boat.

"Doesn't she realize we're already on the clock?" he said.

Joe smiled. Eli complained about Zoe so often, Joe assumed he must have a crush on her. When Zoe finally arrived, Eli made sure he met her at the gangplank to hold her hand as she boarded. They'd make a cute couple, Joe decided. Eli was short and chubby, a wad of baby fat beneath the chin, with curly, dark hair and heavy eyeglasses. Zoe was taller, Asian, pretty, and slender with an elongated torso as the cutoff black tee shirt and bare midriff revealed.

"Nice of you to join us," Eli said.

Joe couldn't tell if he was being sincere or sarcastic. No matter. Zoe offered only her usual sideways smirk as an apology. If they ever did become an item, Eli would have to change his wardrobe, loosen up a bit. For even now, on a fishing trip, Eli wore a dress shirt buttoned to the collar. But more than the clothes, while Zoe always seemed at ease, holding back laughter, privy to an inside joke; Eli always appeared concerned, brow furrowed and lips pursed by constant fret, certainly not in on the joke. And then there was Bill. Bill was the joke, or at least the jokester, a guy who always had a quip or comeback. He was tall, thin, with a pronounced Adam's apple, large teeth, and even larger gums. These features, in conjunction with blonde, thinning hair, didn't prevent him from being viewed as a lothario, primarily by himself. The three were Joe's BFFs and he loved them dearly.

"Hey, big guy," Zoe said. "What's with the hat?"

"Joe B is having a no-hair day," Bill said.

The mates untied All My Glory from its moorings and the boat rocked freely. Soon, the engine rumbled and the four were enveloped in a pungent odor of diesel fuel. The boat maneuvered away from the dock and chugged through the canal at slow speed. The pace quickened as they entered the bay and headed for the inlet. They'd be in open ocean soon, though the captain needed to navigate around a long, wooded strip of land first. Barrier Island was known for its beaches, campgrounds, and little seaport town with its many eateries, souvenir shops, and live music. During the summer months, it was jammed. This day, with the tourist season nearly over, nobody was swimming, and only a scattered number of people fished off the pier. Joe thought it a nice place for a couple to go for a three-day weekend. Perhaps, he would, someday, if he ever got married, which suddenly didn't seem as certain as it used to. But at least he had his friends.

They were all on deck, enjoying the sunrise, the sea breeze washing over their faces. Joe took it in with full breaths. While at the dock, the air had smelled fishy and stagnant. But, now, as they headed for open water, the spray was briny and invigorating. He could taste its life; feel the mist renewing his mind and spirit. The boat slowed, coasted through the wide break between the rocky jetties that formed the inlet. Fishermen were casting from atop the boulders and one stopped to wave. Joe waved back, using his cap. The ship motored onward. The bow of the vessel cut a rolling, white divide through the tranquil, turquoise sea. Joe thought about the legend, as he always did, while moving through the inlet.

According to local lore, many fishermen, surfers, and whale watchers had seen something in the water near or just beyond the lines of huge, slippery rocks. As far as Joe knew, nobody had ever reported the creature coming into the bay. What exactly it was is open to debate. Its description - shark, whale, or serpent - varied between each account. But all agreed it was enormous, the reported size ranging from forty to one hundred feet in length with a purplish, barnacle-covered back broad enough to play tennis on. Yes, The Land of Uz had their very own sea monster legend. But unlike the curiosities at Loch Ness and Lake Champlain, this one had no name and no grainy black-and-white photos offered as proof. Moreover, there were no memorabilia shops feeding the imaginations of tourists and no marine biologists or amateur enthusiasts out looking for it, either. The sightings were quietly passed from person to person as tales at the docks, and more often, within the pubs near the docks. The tragedy of two teen boys who'd taken a skiff out onto the ocean to never return was attributed to the monster. Joe didn't know if he believed the legend or not. It was just something he thought about when out on the water.

As the trawler cleared the inlet, the unseen captain pushed the throttle and the boat moved at a surprising, almost alarming speed. The engine groaned. The wind grew cool. The bow skipped on the water's surface like a stone. For a short while, gulls followed above, wheeling and screeching as a portent, and then disappeared.

They'd charted All My Glory for eight hours. The first two would be spent venturing far into the ocean. The next four would be spent fishing for striped bass. The last two hours would be spent coming back to shore. During the excursion, they'd lounge and talk and joke around and eat meatloaf sandwiches, and of course, drink beer. Unfortunately, whether or not they had a good time was up to the fish. If two brought home a striper each, that would be a good day. If all four caught one, that would be a great day. But if they got skunked, Joe's friends would curse this day throughout the winter months. Sad.

The trawler traveled on. How far out they'd venture was astounding. No land to be seen in any direction. No ships, either. A little scary. The vessel, which seemed so large while tethered to the bulkheads back at the dock, soon seemed insignificant, a tiny, bobbing toy in contrast to the ocean's vastness. Some people liked being cut-off and isolated. They called it freedom. But Joe considered it a healthy smallness, a good way to foster proper perspective.

For reasons known only to him, the captain cut the engines. This spot, one of an infinite number, would be where they would drift and fish.

* * *

"So…what'd she say?" Zoe finally asked, practically singing.

Zoe taught English and world culture classes at the middle school where Joe watched chubby tweens fail at climbing the peg board. They'd been buddies since she'd locked her keys in her car on her first day of work. Joe wished he could see through her mirrored sunglasses to search her eyes for the reason she was asking. Did she already know answer? Women can be perceptive. Was the rejection carved into his countenance, sewn into the inflection of his speech? Regardless, he was happy to get it done with. The question had been the elephant on the deck since they'd started fishing two hours ago. The three knew of his plans to propose to Rebecca the prior evening. Zoe had held out asking as long as she could.

"Rebecca said no," Joe replied, matter-of-factly.

"Get out of town!" Zoe said, genuinely surprised. "Why?"

"Does it matter?" Eli said. "She shot him down. Ain't that enough?"

"Of course it matters," Zoe said, and let out a burst of air to show her indignation. "Did she say she wasn't ready? Or that you need to know one another better? Or she wants to go back to college? Or that she wants to get her career started first?"

"Maybe she told him she's gay," Bill offered.

While the others leaned on the railing, poles in hand, lines reaching far out into the sea, Bill lounged behind in a low, canvas deckchair, shirt off, drinking a beer. He often drank more than he fished, but he usually took the most home.

"Actually, she said she's met someone else," Joe said.

"For real?" Eli said. "Rebecca hooked-up with another guy?"

"Probably a woman," Bill said. "She secretly hated you all along, Joseph. It's because you have a Johnson. I run into this all the time."

"Shut up, dummy," Zoe said. She waved a hand in the air as a token threat to smack his face. "Can't you see Joe B is hurting?"

Bill poured beer on to his chest and rubbed it in like tanning oil.

"I'm fine," Joe said. "Really. I've always believed when one door closes another will open."

Eli's laughter was scornful, bitter.

"Who told you that fairytale," he said. "The tooth fairy? While he was riding a unicorn? On his way to meet Bigfoot?"

Joe, Zoe, and Bill stared at Eli. He tended to over-explain his points making him appear condescending. Even his jokes went on too long and turned sour. Joe would never tell him, but deep-seated negativity and pessimism was probably why Eli, himself, wasn't married.

"I think that's a good outlook, Joe B," Zoe said. "There's somebody for you. There's someone for all of us."

Eli tilted his head down, pouty. Joe hadn't thought about it, but it was weird that no one in the group was married. Well, technically, Bill was married for almost five months, but the divorce was finalized years ago. Strange that none were in a relationship now.

"You know what you should've done? You should've opened your big mouth and swallowed the ring right in front of her. That's what I would've done," Bill said.

"You would've eaten five thousand bucks?" Eli said.

"Darn right, I would," Bill said. "It would be worth it to see her face. To let her know how she had steamrolled my heart."

"What if she called you the next morning to say she'd changed her mind?" Eli said.

"She'd get the ring back between twelve to eighteen hours later," Bill said, offhand.

Zoe shook her head in disgust.

"Look Joe, you sure you didn't do something wrong?" Eli said, turning his face away, tone low, ashamed by his own accusation.

"What do you mean?" Joe said.

"I mean, people don't get dumped for no reason. Did you, you know, forget her birthday or borrow money and forget to repay?"

"No, of course not," Joe said, indignant.

"Well, then did you get caught texting another woman? Or come home with a different perfume on your clothes?" Eli added.

"Are you crazy?" Zoe said, angered. "Joe B is the most honest and decent man I know. Aren't you, Joe?"

Joe didn't respond. He wasn't sure what she meant. Does not cheating on your girlfriend make you honest and decent? Are those things decided by what you don't do? It's like when you ask someone if he thinks he's going to heaven when they die. Invariably, people respond Yeah, I'm a good person. And then go on to itemize the things they didn't do. I never killed nobody. Never stole anything big. Never cheated on my wife or income taxes any more than most people. Never hurt anybody on purpose. Strange.

"Jo-Jo, was Rebecca wearing a hood at the time she gave you the boot?" Bill said.

Joe stared at Bill blankly, more confused.

Bill expounded upon his theory. "I'm telling you, Rebecca's batting for the wrong team. It's a Freudian thing. These mixed-up girls love hoodies. On their shirts, sweatshirts, sweaters, coats, you name it. Reminds them of their private parts."

Joe's lower jaw fell open. Zoe bent over, reached into the water of the five-gallon bait bucket on the deck beside her and pulled out a live eel. The creature was a foot long, green, slimy, and squirmy. She tossed it with a flick of the wrist toward Bill. It landed with a wet smack on his belly. Bill shrieked, swatted the eel off and sprung to his feet, the deck chair toppling. What the… Get off… Get off… The beer bottle he'd been holding dropped and rolled away, its contents pumping out onto the deck. Joe and Zoe laughed raucously. Eli laughed with his eyes, mostly, with a hand cupped over his mouth. Bill's expression showed his horror and shock and he struggled to catch his breath. Thankfully, he soon recovered and joined in with good-natured laughter of his own.

"That's not cool, girlfriend," he said. "Do that again and I'll drop one down the crack of your-"

All froze as Joe's line went taut and the tip of his rod bent.

"You got one, Joe," Eli shouted.

"And it's a big boy," Bill said, his face stone serious.

Joe let out a bit of line, like his dad had taught him, and gave a sharp yank to set the hook. He gripped the handle hard, pulled backward. The rod bowed into a letter C. Joe's shoulder muscles strained. His heart thumped. Sweat dripped from his forehead and stung his eyeballs. Zoe stood at his side with a net, hopeful, waiting. Joe's hands hurt.

"Give it more line," Bill said. "More!"

Joe went to release more line, but it went slack... There was a period of silent mourning over the loss. Other than sea robins, skates, and other garbage fish, this was the first fish they'd hooked during the trip.

"It's gone," Eli said. "Must've been a monster."

"Too bad," Bill said. "Would've been good eatin' for all of us. Forty or fifty pounds, probably."

Joe reeled in the line. It took about a million turns.

"Aww," Zoe said. "She took your bait."

This was true. The bait and hook were gone. The fish had snapped thirty-pound test. No trouble. Joe made quick work of snelling the shank of a new hook. He tied on the leader to a three-way swivel and added a bank sinker to complete the rig. Without looking, he reached into the bucket to fish out a new eel - he didn't want to choose, that made it worse. For this was the part of fishing Joe couldn't stomach. No matter how you justified it, rigging live bait was cruel. For eels, you had to push the heavy, sharp hook through the skin at the back of the head just above the fins. The creature must feel pain. To say the least, it must know the difference between having a hook run through its head and not having a hook run through its head... Joe swirled his hand within the icy bucket of water, the slimy things swimming, slithering between his fingers. Finally, he clutched one and pulled it out, surprised to see he'd properly grabbed it at the top, a thumb behind its head. A bigger surprise came, however, when Joe held the eel up for inspection. The head was discolored. While the body was the dull, grey-green he'd expected, the head was a sleek, shiny, jet-black.

"Hey. Bill," Joe said. "You ever see this before?" Joe looked to Bill who wasn't looking at the bait but at the sky ahead.

"No, but I've seen that before," he said, pointing. "We're gonna get clobbered."

Joe looked to the sky. A single dark cloud, fat and low, was moving their way - fast. Small flashes of light came sporadically from within. The wind kicked up. As did the waves slapping against the side of the bobbing boat. From the second deck, one of the mates ordered them into the cabin.

The friends reeled in their lines and secured their rods. Joe went to drop the eel back into the bucket, but the creature thrashed about wildly, angrily, moving in a serpentine manner. Before Joe could release his grip, the eel coiled around his thick wrist twice. He tried to shake it off.

"She must like you," Bill said.

"Need help?" Zoe said.

"I got this. Meet you inside," Joe said.

Pebbles, hard and coarse like gravel, pelted them.

"Ice?" Eli said. "It's a hailstorm!"

"This time of year?" Zoe shouted over the rush of wind. Her sunglasses blew off her face, skittered across the deck and went overboard. She ran to the rail to look over. Eli grabbed Zoe's elbow and pulled her back.

"They're gone," he said. "We gotta get inside."

The two made their way towards the cabin door at the starboard side. Bill hurriedly slipped a tee shirt over his head.

"Let's go, big guy, before we become fish food, ourselves." he said.

The hail, now the size of marbles, pinged off the deck and cabin windows, the machine gun-like cadence deafening. Ice balls bounced off the brim of Joe's cap, struck and raised welts on his bare arms. Joe looked up towards the second deck for the mates, but they were gone, hunkered down someplace.

"Let go," Joe said to the eel, trying to pry its coils from his wrist.

Pain flared within his forearm as the green coils tightened. Joe's teeth clenched, his face contorted into a grimace. He turned his back to the cabin windows so the others wouldn't see his struggle. HIs fingers throbbed. The whole hand went numb. Turned white. A hailstone struck the top of his ear, the pain ferociously intense - Joe wobbled, but did not fall.

"Let go!" he shouted.

The coils tightened more.

Agony. Joe went light-headed, dizzy. He squeezed the eel with all the might he could muster. He concentrated, pressed, tried to crush the serpent's head with a powerful thumb. The ocean churned, the boat thrown, up and down, left and right. The sea spilled over the deck. Icy water rolled over Joe's sandaled feet. He threw himself toward the bow's railing, nearly toppling over, the bar stopping him, punching his stomach. His cap was ripped from his head, stolen by the squall. Joe reclaimed his footing and beat the eel's black head against the metal, bringing it down hard, again and again. Its grip eased and uncoiled. He flung it overboard. Joe massaged his wounded wrist and made way toward the cabin door. Hail, rock-hard golf balls, rained down. Hundreds hit the water sending up spouts. Many struck the deck like hammers and ricocheted. One found Joe's shoulder. Another, the crown of his head, dropping him to one knee. Joe recovered, pushed onward to the cabin door, swung it open, and stepped in. He yanked it shut behind him.

The noise was cut in half. And though the boat was still tossed about and things creaked and groaned, there was a feeling of security inside. The three gaped. Blood ran down Joe's head from his temples in streaks.

His cheekbone was raw, bruised, as was the heel of one foot, a spot he'd not realized had been struck.

"You okay, man?" Bill said.

Joe was surprised by the seriousness of his tone, the ashen complexion of all their faces. They all stood, holding the vertical poles like exotic dancers. Eli wore an orange life preserver cinched around his neck.

"Yeah," Joe said. "Knocked around a bit, but I'm good."

"You're bleeding," Eli said.

"I'll be fine," Joe said.

"Not if this old bucket takes on water," Bill said.

"We'll all die," Zoe added. "There's nobody around to save us."

Joe was taken aback. With the exception of Eli, his friends weren't prone to fear. Why were they scared now?

"Well, I have faith in this old boat. I'm sure it's not the first storm it's been through," Joe said. "And, besides, I trust the captain. He'll see us through it."

"Trust him?" Eli protested. "We've never even seen him."

The silence to follow spoke more loudly than the gusting wind outside. Joe scanned his friend's blank, worried faces, looking for something. What? He didn't know what. All he knew was that it wasn't there.

"Well, I trust him," Joe said finally. "Don't blame the captain for the storm. He promised to take us out and back, and I believe he'll keep that promise.

Look at this whole thing as only a mist we're going through."

"A mist?" Eli said, dumbfounded.

A moment passed.

"Joe B," Zoe said. "Do you know what hail-storms during this time of year mean?"

Joe shook his head no.

"Tornado," Bill answered.

Zoe nodded her head yes.

"Tornado," Eli concurred, his voice a whisper, a raised finger directing attention to the cabin's port side window. He then repeated the single-word warning, shouting this time. "Tornado!"

All turned to see.

5

Joe adjusted the knob and found a local news station. He was alone, driving along the vacant parkway, headed home. The news anchor told of the county executive being investigated regarding campaign financing, the closing of a public performing arts school due to budget cuts, and an upcoming parade honoring Grenada war veterans. The program then gave a teaser - a man yelling look at that, it's coming right at us - in reference to a tornado that touched down on the east side, before cutting to a commercial break.

Joe took the ramp fast and the tires chirped as the Cooper rounded the curve. He wasn't sure what had him unnerved. Maybe witnessing the tornado over the ocean. They'd all viewed it from within the boat's cabin. Bill and Zoe went eerily silent as Eli repeatedly muttered We're gonna die…We're gonna die… Meanwhile, a preternatural calm fell upon Joe. He studied the twister with a surreal sense of detachment. Watching it through the cabin's large window gave it life and motion in the way cranking a mutoscope flips through old

B&W photographs. The gray funnel manifested, rolled itself like a cigar, extending downward from the storm cloud, narrowing to a point three hundred yards in front of the vessel. Fully formed, it moved like a pinball in a machine. At first, it seemed it would stay in place, but a dark force pulled the plunger and the funnel shot upward, only to come back towards the boat, the vessel listing, waves breaking, crashing over its bow. The cabin shook. Wind whistled through every gap. Day turned to night. The whirling column ricocheted off invisible bumpers, propelling it, firing it off at sharp angles... Ultimately, the tornado targeted the boat again, only to be batted away by invisible flippers operated by unseen hands. Effectively deflected, it headed inland, towards the very place where Joe drove recklessly now.

He mentally focused. It would be foolish to survive a tornado only to die in a car wreck. He surveyed the area. No damage to the storefronts on route 24a or to the houses along Piedmont Avenue. This was good. Joe's world was small. The fabric of his life was woven tightly. Most of his friends, family, neighbors, colleagues, and students resided nearby, and he didn't want anything bad to happen to them. With the string of commercials ended, the news broadcast skipped to the sports report and Joe felt cheated. The tornado, he realized, would be included with the weather. If nobody was killed, hurricanes, tornadoes, and floods were merely inclement conditions, an inconvenience to be casually mentioned and forgotten. He turned onto Beech Wood - no damage.

The three had recovered quickly within the cabin, too. After each had drawn a full breath and exhaled slowly, they'd snickered, and then became giddy. Joe watched his friends exchange high-fives like they'd scored the winning goal. Each accused another about being more frightened. Did you see how white his face turned? Me? What about you? You were a glass of milk. All in fun. Nobody talked about how close they'd actually come to meeting their maker. Joe forced a smile though he didn't feel the same release. For him, the threat manifested itself retroactively. As the three joked, his legs trembled, his mouth went dry, and an ominous feeling spun within his gut like a second tornado.

He turned off Beech Wood onto Juniper and then onto Birch. He leaned over the steering wheel as he cruised by the first signs - garbage cans toppled and trash strewn over the street, branches down, a maple tree lying on its side with exposed roots overhanging a huge crater. Then more. Wet leaves carpeting a driveway, shingles stripped from rooftops, sections of cedar fence missing… Joe settled back. Bad, but not devastating. No structural damage to the homes. They'd be okay.

The news switched to a woman newscaster talking about a tornado touching down and how it frightened a bunch of toddlers in a playground.

"Were you scared?" the interviewer asked

"Yeah," a small girl said and laughed nervously.

"It chased us," a boy chimed in. "Like a monster. Raaaaa."

"Oh, my. So what did you do?"

"We told it to go away," the girl said, like the answer was obvious.

Joe turned onto his street. A group stood in a semicircle gawking at a white panel van upside down on a front lawn. At another house, a man was on a ladder hammering plywood over a broken picture window. On the radio, an expert from the community college said tornadoes were rare to the region but could happen anywhere. He recommended sheltering in a basement or a bathtub. The reporter said they'd gotten lucky as there were no casualties and only minor property damage. She went on to give the five-day forecast - Mostly sunny with highs in the low to mid-seventies. A chance of showers Thursday morning...

Gone. Removed with surgical precision.

Stunned, slack-jawed, Joe arrived at his house, or to be more precise, what was left of his house. A police cruiser and a small fire truck were at the curb. Joe pulled in behind the truck. A barrier of yellow caution tape from tree to mailbox to fencepost to tree formed a perimeter around the small lot. A cop walked the cordoned-off area with a German shepherd on a leash. Joe stepped out of the car. The scene was like a hard slap to the face. The fireplace and chimney were all that stood amongst the ruins. The roof had been ripped off and flipped into the backyard, crumpled like a brown paper bag. The remainder of the small cape - sheetrock walls, studs behind the walls, plumbing, electrical wiring - were mostly in a pile, collapsed into the cellar, an open grave. A lone fireman was looking through a handheld gadget at the rubble, measuring heat, Joe presumed.

"You live here, buddy?" he asked.

Joe plodded without purpose like a zombie. Their home... It was hard to take it all in. A mattress was wedged in the upper limbs of the oak tree. The bathtub was outside, nested in the flowerbed, and filled with debris. Luckily, no one had sheltered within it. The hot water heater floated in the neighbor's swimming pool. Everything gone. The family crest his dad had nailed above the front door, a few golf clubs, sports trophies, and a family photo album were at his feet, all caked in mud. Big shoe prints were in the plowed earth, formerly his father's prized lawn. If anything hadn't been destroyed during the storm, it surely had been trampled beneath a dozen shuffling boots. Not that there had been much left. Everything had been yanked from its place by the whirlwind, taken, dropped, thrown, crushed, or shredded like confetti. Furniture reduced to kindling. The wrought-iron bird bath twisted into a piece of modern art. Glass shattered, pulverized into glittering pixie dust. Tufts of pink fiberglass insulation, as though blown from a canon, were caught in the uprooted shrubs. Only the chimney stood, ancient-looking, a monument to a forgotten people, his family's Stonehenge.

Joe ducked under the yellow tape.

"Hey!" the fireman snapped, catching the attention of the cop. "This your house?"

"Used to be."

His grandma's oil painting, of her childhood village that had hung in the dining room for half a century was underfoot, wet and torn. As were the baseball cards from his collection. The living room couch sat on the driveway as if placed there on purpose. Old lady bloomers and bras decorated the branches of the old evergreen like a perverted Christmas tree.

The cop led the dog in a zigzag path, around the debris, across the yard. He addressed Joe. "You sure nobody was home?"

The silver-haired officer was in a navy blue tactical uniform with a million pockets, part of a special unit. The dog studied Joe with unblinking, keen intelligence. Joe explained only his mom and himself lived in the house, and she had left this morning to visit her sister. He left out details regarding the cancer and chemo.

"The fish must be throwing her off, then," the cop said. He patted the dog's side in consolation.

Fish?

Sure enough there were dead, black-eyed fish - silvery, scaly things Joe took to be porgies - pressed into the mud. Scanning more closely, there were more, millions of tinier fish - everywhere. While he'd been away, it had rained mummichogs. Poor dog. The air smelled like the muck in the bay during low tide. Everything saturated. Joe marveled at the amount of seawater the tornado lifted and carried until he realized the firefighters had doused the entire house and yard with water. They'd ruined whatever heirlooms might've survived the storm.

"Guess we lost everything," Joe said, stating the obvious.

"You're alive and your mom's alive" the cop said. "That's what counts. Things can be replaced."

The officer jotted down Joe's name and number and wished him luck. Joe watched the cop take the rescue dog to the police cruiser and open the rear door. The dog jumped in. He'd write a one-paragraph report before going. The firefighter approached. Joe regarded him. The green rubber suit and boots were expected, but the amount of equipment attached to the utility belt - flashlight, pry bars, grappling hook and rope - looked absurd, as did the man, himself. He stood as tall as Joe but presented a larger build. His face with its smooth-skin, round-cheeks, and cherubic appearance didn't match his gargantuan size.

"The power company turned off the electric and we capped the gas lines," he said. "Then we soaked the whole area; you won't have to worry about a flash fire."

"Thank you," Joe said, and he meant it. Emergency responders risked their own safety to protect others. This was no small thing. Yet, did they understand? Could anyone?

Joe was at a loss to explain to Baby Huey what it meant to lose this small, common, exceedingly ordinary home. Joe's mother and father moved into the little cape on their wedding day, September of 1952. This house, supposed to be a starter home, was where the family had eaten leg of lamb on Easter and spareribs during backyard barbeques. It's where they'd peeled wallpaper and painted walls and ceilings and tiled the bathroom and installed sinks and toilets with their own hands. Joe had lived there forever, including his time in community college. Heck, he'd probably been conceived in the upstairs master bedroom. This house, this rubbish heap as far as anyone could tell now, was the special place where his tiny family talked, argued, laughed, and loved. Yet God Almighty had allowed this. Why?

"There doesn't seem to be any asbestos, so we don't need to worry about abatement," the firefighter went on. "But you'll have to arrange for a temporary fence to be put up around the property and no trespassing signs or you'll be responsible if some neighborhood kid gets hurt."

He went on to talk about fines, civil penalties, and possible jail time if the household chemicals and other environmental toxins weren't cleaned up properly. Though he nodded frequently, Joe only half-listened. Soon, the firefighter would pack up his truck and go.

Joe looked about and sat on an untouched patch of grass, a little island of his former life, next to the flagstone walkway. Though he couldn't be certain, he was fairly sure this was where he'd found his dad's body. Joe sprawled out his legs and leaned back on his elbows. Time - a half hour? An hour? - passed without him thinking about much of anything. The devastation was so complete, the loss so overwhelming, it brought on a weird tranquility, a form of mental and physical paralysis. Something caught his eye. Joe picked up a shard of pottery and wiped the dirt from it - a near perfect yellow triangle. In the sixth grade, they'd mixed up his schedule and gave him art instead of wood shop. He'd made his mother a fruit bowl out of clay. He molded it, sculpted a design with an exacto knife, and had Mrs. McKenna bake it in the kiln. Afterward, because he was a dumb kid, Joe painted the bowl with the brightest, glossiest yellow they had. The finished piece was as gauche and misshapen as a kitschy 1970s ashtray, Of course, she'd been thrilled to receive it on Mother's Day as much as he'd delighted in the unveiling. Of all the gifts he'd ever given his mom, she'd truly treasured his ugly bowl... He racked the shard against his bare forearm, making white streaks in the skin. A familiar blue SUV with faded paint rolled up to the curb, stopped. Rebecca stepped out. She took a tentative step towards him and then ran.

"Joe? Joe, what happened?"

He looked up, tossed the piece of pottery aside, but didn't answer.

"Joe, you're hurt. You need a doctor."

With all the emotions involving the house, he had forgotten the lump on his head and the wound on his cheekbone. He must've been a sight - bruised and battered by the hailstones, stoned from up on high.

"They showed your neighborhood on channel twelve from a helicopter. One house was... It looked like yours, but I wasn't sure. Where's your mom?"

"Why are you dolled-up on a Saturday afternoon? You look like you're hosting the daytime Emmy Awards."

Rebecca tugged at the hem of the sparkly dress and touched her hair spiraled up into a fancy doo. "Joe, where's your mom?"

"At her sister's. She's fine. Well, not really. I mean she's dying. What are you doing here? Shouldn't you be in Bermuda with Dr. what's-his-face?"

"The Bahamas. We're going in two weeks. Look, I only came by because I was worried. Who'd think I'd find you sitting on the front lawn looking gnomish?"

"Looking what?"

"You know, like one of those dwarfs with the beards and the creepy grins leaning on a toadstool… Never mind!"

Joe knew he was grinning but had no idea why.

"Well, nice of you to stop by. Can I get you anything? I'm not sure what we have. Egg drop soup? Upside down cake? Butternut squash?"

"Don't be funny."

"What should I do? Cry?"

"You want me to take you to the E.R.?"

"I'm fine," he said.

"You sure? You seem delusional."

"I thought you said gnomish."

"Why you acting like this?"

"Like what?"

"Like a jerk."

"I'm tired, that's all."

Rebecca considered this, twisted the ball of her foot into the dirt. She spoke more tenderly.

"What do you mean your mom's dying? Is she hurt?"

"She has cancer."

"A tornado can't give you cancer," Rebecca said, though she seemed uncertain. "I'm going to call her later."

"Don't worry. Mom's alright. I think she's more afraid of the bees."

Rebecca swiveled on her heels and scanned the air about her head. "Joe, I'm calling an ambulance," she said

"Go home, Rebecca," Joe said. "Everything is good. All I need is a roll of duct tape, a box of wood screws, and a whole lot of spackle."

Rebecca crossed her arms over her chest and tilted her chin upward. "Joseph Bustamante, you're making jokes, really? You're injured. Your mom is sick. A tornado destroyed your home and ripped your hair out at the roots. How can you sit there with a stupid grin, acting stupid, and saying stupid things?"

Joe thought his heart might burst from the amount of love being poured into it. "You've missed me, haven't you?" he said. "If you ask nicely, maybe I'd consider taking you back."

Rebecca stared, mouth open, incredulous. Upon recovering, she huffed. "Well, don't hold your breath 'cause I'm not asking," she said. "You still don't get it, do you? We're not good for each other, Joe. We don't add up right. It's really that simple."

"What's that mean? Sometimes I think you should come with subtitles, like a foreign movie."

"I mean when you add us together, the sum doesn't come out right. It's like playing blackjack at a casino. You, know, the game where the dealer gives you two cards and you're shooting for twenty-one… If the first card he gives is a king or a queen, you're in pretty good shape no matter what the second card is, but what if you get a deuce? What chance have you got? It's already over at the start. And what if you get dealt another deuce? You're certain to lose. Life is like that, Joe."

Her voice became a whisper, she looked away. "I know I'm not a queen. I'm not very smart and I'm not very pretty… I'm a deuce… So, I'd better find a king… Of course every girl wants to marry for love. My mother married for love. And our family paid for that love. Our lives have been a constant struggle. You know, we had an empty mayonnaise jar we used to put our spare change in. We were going to roll the coins and take them to the bank when it got filled. The only thing was, it never got filled 'cause we kept dipping into it. We were never more than one missed day's work away from being evicted. And you know what? My mother's love for my father doesn't seem like love anymore. It seems like obligation. You hardly ever see them in the same room, nowadays. Seems like their love is only toleration, nothing more. I don't want to end up like that. I won't make the same mistake. Joe, we're both deuces. Go find yourself a queen."

She turned her face back to his. "Why are you smiling like a goon?"

Joe didn't answer but continued looking up.

See?" she said. "This is another reason why we can't be together. You don't react like a normal person. I'm going to write you a check. You're going to need money for a hotel room."

"What do you mean normal?" Joe said.

"I have four hundred dollars I saved to bring home souvenirs for people from my trip, but this is more important."

"What do you mean normal?" Joe repeated.

"Darn, I don't have my checkbook. Can I bring it to you? Where will you stay?"

"I don't need or want your money," Joe said, annoyed. "I want to know what you meant. What do you mean when you say I'm not normal?"

Rebecca shifted from foot to foot. She spoke rapidly. "A normal person would be upset - crying and yelling and cursing God and stuff. But not you."

"Why would I be mad at God?" Joe swung an angry arm, motioning over the ruins. "He gave me all this and now he's taken it away. Should I only accept the good but refuse the bad? Is the Lord my genie-in-a-bottle?"

"I don't know. But you must've made him mad. Did you notice yours is the only home that's wrecked? It's like your roof had a bull's-eye painted on it."

"Well, I'm not calling out God on this. Something worse might happen. He might send down fiery brimstone or a swarm of locusts. Who knows? I could get zapped by lightning. Will you bring a date to my funeral?"

Rebecca's eyes welled with tears that she refused to release.

"More jokes? Seriously? You know what you can do, Joe? Curse God and die." she said and strode briskly to her SUV.

"Rebecca!" Joe called out. "I'm only clowning. I'm sorry."

She climbed in the car and slammed the door. Joe stood and yelled. "By the way, when you get dealt two deuces in blackjack, that's when you're supposed to split but then double down! That how you turn a losing hand into a winning hand!"

She threw the vehicle into gear, the tires spitting gravel.

Joe rose and walked the yard. He kicked and overturned the debris looking for something, anything, to smash. There was nothing worth smashing or salvaging. Nothing.

Not knowing what else to do, Joe pulled out his phone and texted Zoe: Storm damaged house. Pretty bad. Nobody hurt. Need help.

He read his message before sending. He hated texting. It seemed a huge step backwards in communication. Like society reverted back to sending telegrams or carrier pigeons. But it was the only way to reach his friends, though they, Zoe, in particular, often didn't respond for hours. When it became clear Zoe wasn't going to answer on this occasion, Joe went to the sofa on the driveway, plopped down and curled into a fetal position. The cushions were sodden and already smelled of mildew. The sun lowered over the horizon. Joe could see it glowing red through shut eyelids. After a quick catnap, he'd feel better. Zoe would call and would give sound, practical advice - she was smart like that. She was a good egg, to borrow an expression Joe's dad had been fond of using before he'd croaked on the front lawn like a frog. Boy, did he wish his dad was here. Maybe Zoe was his one true love, hiding in plain sight all along. He was a good egg, too. Maybe together they could become an omelet. Eli would be crushed, of course. But what was Joe to do? It was too hard to face life alone. Everyone needs somebody. The world could be so very, very… What was the word? Mean, that was the word. And if you didn't find somebody special to be your anti-venom, the world's bite would turn you mean in a very short time.

The answer was clear. Joe's course of action had been decided by fate. He'd spin the tornado in the opposite direction. As soon as Zoe arrived, he'd ask her to marry him. Why hadn't he thought of this sooner? He needed rest first, though. After he caught a few winks, he'd wake up refreshed and write her a poem. He wondered how she'd react. Wondered what she'd say...

6

A hand clamped onto his shoulder, squeezed, shook.

"Hey," the voice said. "Wake up, ya' bum."

Joe opened his eyes to see a figure backlit by a corona of sunlight, a woman, an angel. Joe sat up, squinted, and shielded his eyes with a wrist.

"Zoe? Wait... I meant for you to come tomorrow."

"It is tomorrow," she said, a peculiar, raspy quality to her tone. "You slept here all night? In the driveway?"

"It's Sunday?" Joe said, panicked. He rolled from the sofa onto his feet. "I'm missing church."

Zoe gripped him at the elbows, an anchor to reality.

"God will understand. Your house…" She trailed off and looked about the yard. There was nothing to be said. The destruction said it all.

"Yep," Joe said. "Pretty bad."

"I read your text late last night. I came with plastic garbage bags. I wasn't thinking," she said, and rapped the side of her head with curled knuckles. "I thought we'd be picking up branches and raking leaves."

She laughed in a short burst. Joe stared, lips parted but unable to form words. A hidden door opened into his heart. Zoe hurt for him. Touching but strange. They'd named this mysterious connection empathy though it couldn't be fully explained using human language or logic. Zoe hurt for him, specifically for Joseph Bustamante Jr. This had to be true love. Tongue-tied, weak-kneed, Joe stared into her face. That pretty face. Behind the folds of skin that narrowed her eyes were irises as brown and rich as the finest chocolate. Why hadn't he ever seen her before? The shiny black hair, short in the back, long in the front, locks draped over the sides of a roundish face…the cute, flat nose...the plump lips covering a slight overbite…

Zoe stared back. A lone tear formed at the corner of one eye.

Crying?

One time, after she'd downed a few-too-many vodka and cranberries at a wedding reception, Joe helped her to a discreet place outside and watched her throw-up into a fancy marble fountain. While on the same beach volleyball team, when asked to be the lookout, he peeked and saw her squat and relieve herself in the dunes. After she'd repeatedly pounded upon the hood of her cheating ex-boyfriend's car as he fled, Joe went to her apartment and iced her bruised and swollen hands - they'd ordered Chinese takeout and talked till dawn. But for all the puke, pee, pummeling and pupu platters, despite how intimately they'd known each other, Joe never once saw Zoe cry - until now.

The tears came as series of coughs. Zoe hid her face in her hands. She tucked her elbows into her ribs like a boxer.

"I'm so sorry, Joe," she said, voice cracking. "Your home… It's fu-"

Joe pulled Zoe to his chest in an embrace. Probably because she had such a large, punk-rocker personality, Joe had never before realized how physically small she was. Tiny. He needed to crane his neck downward to rest his chin on her head. She nestled her face and cried warm breaths into his chest. It felt nice.

After she'd calmed, Joe pushed her outward, arms pinned to her sides, his mind gone gaga, not sure if he wanted to plant a kiss or pop the question. The queer moment must've went on too long, for Zoe's face squinched, a suspicious expression falling somewhere between concern and repulsion.

"What?" she said.

Joe would have to phrase this exactly right. Zoe wouldn't go for a mushy proposal.

"Zoe, there's something I need to-"

The orange pickup pulled up to the curb, actually striking, rolling over the curb - Eli's funky ride, his failed attempt to prove he wasn't a stuffed shirt. Joe released Zoe. They watched Eli and Bill step out, approach.

Bill shook his head and whistled a long low note. Eli's lower jaw fell open, and he twirled about as if on ice skates. Nobody said anything. Joe would've welcomed a goofy or insensitive remark from Bill, but was disappointed to be greeted by a funeral face.

"You alright, buddy?" Bill said, and pulled Joe into a tight hug. "We're here for you, man."

Joe stood frozen, speechless, unaccustomed to unbridled displays of male bonding. Bill withdrew, showing misty eyes. Eli gave Joe a quick, awkward squeeze and then slid fingers underneath thick eyeglass frames in order to rub his own reddened sockets. Joe forced a lighthearted laugh.

"C'mon, guys," he said. "Everything's going to work itself out."

The three grim faces that stared back belonged on Easter Island.

"I could understand this happening to me," Bill said. "Considering all the stuff I've done in my life. But you, Joe B? You don't deserve this."

"Yeah," Eli added. "Why you?"

The question hung in the air as a Damocles sword on horsehair.

"Well," Zoe said finally, "guess we should get to work. Try to salvage whatever we can."

"We're going to need pictures before we touch anything," Eli said. "And we need to write down the serial numbers off all the appliances and electronics. The insurance adjuster is going to ask for a list."

"Look, I'll take care of this mess," Joe said. "You're all in good clothes. Zoe, those are your new boots, right?"

The three ignored Joe's concerns. Eli snapped photos while Bill and Zoe overturned planks and pieces of wallboard.

"We'll make two piles: one with things to be saved called lobster and the other for crap to get tossed called liverwurst," Bill said.

"I like liverwurst," Eli protested.

"You would," Bill said.

"Guys, you're gonna get dirty," Joe said.

"Relax, Granny. We're here to help," Zoe said.

They went to work. For the first hour, it was almost fun. They marveled when Eli found a live crab scuttling sideways through a mud puddle. Each stopped to try removing a dinner fork discovered stuck deep in a tree trunk. When none could free it, they'd nicknamed it excalifork and spoke for a while in exaggerated, medieval British accents. Joe's three helpers would occasionally, in turn, hold up a household item for Joe's adjudication.

"Hey, Joey, lobster or liverwurst?" one would say.

"Liverwurst," Joe would invariably answer.

Before long, the liverwurst pile was tall and wide, spilling over onto several adjacent mounds, while the lobster pile remained tiny. What became clear after three hours was that they hadn't accomplished much; there was nothing worth saving and the clean-up would require a professional demolition crew with a backhoe and several large dumpsters. The collective enthusiasm waned as morning turned to afternoon and the four trudged about working quietly. Bill discovered the household refrigerator lying on its back. He worked to pry the door open and rummaged inside. He closed the door and sat on the fridge drinking a beer and gnawing at a large, leftover turkey leg. Zoe scraped her palm on an exposed nail. She cursed, sat in the dirt, and cradled her wounded hand, and cursed some more. When Joe asked to see the injury, Zoe insisted she was OK.

"Why don't we stop? You're getting filthy and ruining your clothes," Joe said.

Zoe looked up, eyes gleaming with defiance. She grabbed a clump of wet earth, held it over her head, and opened her grip. The dirt dropped onto her hair.

"Don't be like that, Zoe," Joe pleaded.

Zoe gave her signature, wry, half-smirk, and repeated the dirt shower. Bill took notice. He smiled with an open hole of a mouth. As a perpetual teenager, he'd never outgrown the fondness for rebellion. He walked to Zoe and handed her the leg. She immediately sunk her teeth into it and pulled off a big piece of meat and chewed. Bill grabbed a handful of dirt and let it cascade onto his own head. Zoe nodded approval.

"He's being a wardrobe Nazi, too," she said, mumbling, drumstick held between clenched teeth. She clutched her tee shirt at the collar and tugged. She pulled hard, grimaced, and at first, it seemed nothing would happen, but then the fabric ripped to the waist exposing smallish breasts behind a flimsy black bra like dual eye patches. Bill's face brightened in delight.

"Is that so?" he said, and grabbed his own shirt and easily tore a sleeve off, and the other, in turn. The result was a muscle shirt he'd likely wear again.

"Get over here, Eli," Bill shouted.

Eli shuffled-stepped over, reluctant.

"Drop some dirt on your head."

"Why?"

"'Cause we did."

Eli bent over and pinched a minute amount of soil, rose halfway, let it fall onto his head and immediately whisked his short, springy ringlets with both hands to remove it.

"That was torture to you, wasn't it?" Bill said with real sympathy. "Like being water-boarded."

"Is there something wrong with being clean?" Eli muttered, feelings hurt.

"Now rip your clothes so Joe B can stop obsessing," Zoe said.

"No way!" Eli said. "It's a new shirt."

Zoe got to her feet. "C'mon, Sexy, show us them moobs."

She grabbed Eli's shirt at the lapels and yanked them apart. Buttons shot off in different directions. The bleached white V-neck undershirt restrained a doughy torso.

"Hey, no fair," Zoe said. "Yours are bigger than mine."

She tickled Eli's chest. At this, they all laughed, even Eli, who, after trying to shield himself, yielded to the moment.

"Joe B, you seeing this? If I did this to her, I'd be in jail," Eli said, squirming.

"You'd be in the morgue," Zoe said.

"Alright. You guys made your point," Joe said, though his three friends continued to carry on and make jokes.

It felt good to laugh. As much as things had changed during the past twenty-four hours, there was still so much to be thankful for. Joe was truly blessed and he would never take that for granted. Not ever.

Soon, they'd bagged the lobster items and called it a day. Zoe took forty dollars from her pocket and forced Joe to accept it. Bill handed him a twenty.

"My wallet must be home," Eli said, patting pockets.

"Damn, Eli. You are tighter than a crab's ass," Bill said, picking up and flinging a dead crab. "And that's watertight."

Zoe asked where Joe would stay tonight and suggested he crash at her apartment. Considering he'd seen walk-in closets bigger than her place, not to mention they'd have to share a futon, he said no. Eli said he'd call his parents and ask if he could stay in the room above the garage, and Joe thanked him but said he wasn't the Fonz. Bill said Joe could stay with him, that is, if he'd allow a day or two for Bill to clear it through his probation officer. Joe assured his friends he'd rent a comfortable room at the Eaton, and this satisfied them.

"Alright. Call you later. Hang in there, clam lips," Bill said, punching Joe's shoulder. "Let's go, Eli. Take me home, bro."

The two meandered towards the pickup. Their conversation became a little one-act play intended to cheer up their host.

"Can we stop at the mall? I need a new shirt and a pair of slacks," Eli said.

"Not happening, dude."

"Why not?"

"Because I have gonads. I don't go clothes shopping with other men," Bill replied. "And don't call them slacks - that's a little pink."

"OK. I need a new pair of trousers, then. These ones are stained."

"Don't call them trousers, either."

"What do you call 'em?"

"Pants! Men wear pants!"

"Pants is derived from the word pantaloons. Now there's a pink word if I ever heard one," Eli said. And then sang, "Pant-a-loooons."

Joe, Zoe, and Bill laughed despite knowing this would only cause Eli to repeat the one-liner. On the rare occasion Eli got a good one rolling, he tended to drive his jokes until they sputtered and ran out of gas.

"I need a new pair of pant-a-loooons," Eli sang again.

Even while the Jeep pulled away, Joe and Zoe could still heard Eli's battle cry through the closed windows, "Pant-a-loooons..."

Joe couldn't stop smiling. He had three of the most wonderfully stupid friends... When he turned to Zoe, he was surprised to find her smiling, too, beaming, actually.

It was go-time.

Joe dropped to one knee and tenderly clasped one of Zoe's hands in both of his.

"Joe...whatcha doin'," she said with suspicion. "Don't!"

"Zoe, I didn't have time to write a poem, but -"

"Stop! You weren't born with a normal embarrassment filter, were you, Joe? You know, the one that keeps you from embarrassing yourself and others."

"Zoe, we've known each other a long time. We already love each other as friends."

Zoe tilted her head up and away, grinding the heel of a boot into the ground. She held her shirt closed. Joe continued.

"We both are teachers who love our jobs. We both love kids and small animals. I could learn to love tacos and Ultimate Fighting."

"Joseph..."

"Zoe, will you be my wife? We can hunt for the ring I was going to give Rebecca or shop for a new one."

Zoe pulled Joe up to his feet. For an agonizing minute, she seemed to debate on how to respond. Though Joe inwardly pleaded for a yes while preparing for a no, not in three lifetimes would he have been able to predict the actual answer to his proposal. Zoe took a deep breath before she spoke.

"I like Bill," she said.

Joe stood dumbstruck, face frozen in an impish grin, rendering him gnomish as Rebecca had said. Zoe's expression went from agony to relief as if revealing her secret was akin to pulling out a splinter. Zoe provided no further explanation, offering only a sheepish shrug of her shoulders while hooking thumbs into pants pockets.

"I see," Joe said, though he really didn't see.

Joe's first thoughts were of Eli and how the little guy would be crushed. Then he considered how there had never been any indication. Or had there? Was all the teasing and back-and-forth banter just the dipping of each other's pigtails into the inkwell?

"Has he ever talked about me?" Zoe asked.

"Who?" Joe said.

"Bill," Zoe said, annoyed.

It really didn't make any sense. Eli was a CPA with a steady job who adored her and would make her life goals his life goals. Bill, on the other hand, would... Well, Bill would bring nothing but frequent headaches and ultimate heartache.

"Why?" Joe said. "I mean, why Bill?"

"I don't know...he's fun."

"Bill? Our Bill?"

"Do you know if he likes Asians?"

This seemed an oddly racist question. Joe didn't know how to answer. He recalled a black girlfriend in high school who ended up breaking Bill's nose but decided it wasn't relevant. Joe raised his hands to indicate he didn't know, wouldn't tell, or maybe he was just surrendering.

"You're some big help," Zoe said.

She frowned and shook her head to indicate she'd expected as much. Suddenly, Joe experienced what people nowadays call a WTF moment when he realized Zoe was seeking help with a hook-up immediately after he'd just proposed marriage in front of his demolished house. The thought depressed him.

"So, you don't love me?" he said, more a statement than a question.

"No. And you don't love me, either. Joe, you're in love with the idea of being in love. You are married to the idea of being married. That's all cool, but you have to be patient. You can't marry somebody just because you're both in love with the idea of being married. There's more to it."

Her words confounded Joe. He never understood why people spoke in riddles. Was Zoe saying she desperately wanted a committed relationship, too? Did she want to marry Bill? And why couldn't you marry somebody just because you both wanted to be married? It seemed you'd have a much better chance of success if that were the case. He would be a loyal and supportive husband to Zoe - didn't she see that? But the big lingering question was what was wrong with Joseph Bustamante? Why did he love everybody more than they loved him?

Despite the uncertainty, or perhaps due to the uncertainty, Joe smiled. He said he was happy for her. This was true, though he left out the part about feeling miserable for himself. Zoe made him promise not to divulge her secret crush. The embrace to follow was a spastic series of starts and stops. The kiss Zoe planted on his cheek was dry and sisterly. They parted and drove away in different directions. Zoe zoomed while Joe went slowly. He wasn't sure where to go or how to get there. Suddenly, he became aware of a sad but undeniable truth: when you don't have a home, there's no direction home. Without doubt, not having a place to kick off your shoes was a terrible thing. Worse, though, was being alone. Joe dreaded the idea of being in a hotel room by himself. Being alone in an unfamiliar place was so...lonely. He clicked on the radio. A cheerful weather girl promised sun, sun, and more sun in the upcoming five-day forecast. He turned it off.

When he arrived at the Eaton, he was disappointed to learn there were no vacancies. Apparently, every room was booked to accommodate the veterans in town for the Granada war memorial. This seemed odd since the parade was a week away and that meant people would be staying and partying longer than the whole invasion had lasted. When Joe tried the Kingsley, the Freemont, and the Motel 27 by the expressway, he found the same thing, indicating more people were attending the festivities than had actually fought in the war. This left only the dingy, little five-story walk-up near the train station over the Flea-Flicker sports bar. They had several open rooms but even if they hadn't, new ones would become available hourly. In fact, the heavyset, unshaven clerk, who came to the barred lobby window in an open bathrobe and boxer shorts, seemed perturbed to have Joe reserve a room for a week in advance. Unsettling for Joe was hearing the clerk refer to the hotel by its well-known but disparaging nickname.

"Enjoy your stay at the Fleabag," he'd said. "Be sure to lock your door."

7

Joe took the key from the clerk but didn't go to his room straightaway - probably a good thing. He might've stormed back to the lobby and flung the key along with a few choice words. Instead, Joe went to Drake's Department Store to forage for essential supplies: soap, toothpaste, deodorant, shaving cream and a razor. Funny that he still didn't need shampoo. The hair sprouting on his scalp didn't even qualify as stubble yet. While there, he also picked up a few pairs of athletic shorts and tee shirts. One benefit of being a gym teacher was the wardrobe requirements weren't demanding. Additionally, he bought socks, underwear, sneakers, shoes, two pairs of jeans and a pair of slacks, as Eli would say, along with a few dress shirts.

The excursion had cost more than expected - four hundred and eighty-two bucks - but Joe withdrew the money out of his debit account. These funds, of course, had been slated for Christmas presents, but there'd be time to replace it. Thankfully, he wouldn't need to touch the Nest Egg. The master plan, the parts of which he'd hastily glued together, would begin by going to work the next day and meeting with the principal. He'd ask Mrs. Shelley for time off at the end of the week in order to tackle the insurance claim paperwork. Once he was further along in the process, he'd drive to his aunt's and deliver the bad news about the tornado to his mom - no point in upsetting her at the beginning of chemo. Let the doctors fix her first, then worry about rebuilding the house. For the moment, there was nothing more to do. By the time Joe got back to the Flea-Flicker Hotel, the Fleabag, that is, it was late and he was tired, so very tired. Too bone-weary to put up a fuss about anything, let alone complain about the accommodations. Besides, his stay was only temporary. A few days, a week at the most.

The metal door opening to the stairs was unmarked and located in the dim, confined lane between the brick walls of the motel and a small factory that made custom kitchen countertops. Oddly, there was no access to the interior of the hotel from the lobby where the fat clerk was stationed. The corridor that used to provide entry had been inexplicably walled-off with two-by-fours and plywood. Spray-painted onto the plywood were the words Keep Out! The clerk hadn't explained and Joe hadn't inquired. He'd use the fire door in the alley.

Three men and two women, each smoking a cigarette, stood in the alleyway, and Joe needed to cut through the circle. They eyed him suspiciously but nobody spoke a word. The door opened with a rusty creak. The inner staircase was so narrow and steep that if it wasn't a violation of state housing codes, the laws needed to be reconsidered. The red EXIT signs offered the only illumination. At the landing for each floor, the stairs reversed direction and Joe trekked upwards, quads straining, to the fourth floor. He pushed open another heavy door. The light from the wall sconces in the corridor were better only by comparison. The hall floor was dark tiled. The wallpaper was ancient and discolored but maintained a discernable pattern - a vine, spiraling and curling down the long stretch of hallway, looping in nooses, camouflaged like snares, to room 402.

Joe unlocked the deadbolt and swung the door inward. A bacterial-laden odor of mildew stung his nostrils. He presumed it came from the plush, wine-colored carpet that was inexplicably damp and mushy beneath his sandals. He flicked the wall switch next to the door. Something hummed but no light came on. Joe made his way blindly to the table lamp near the bed. Despite its missing shade, it worked. The bare bulb, however, was of insufficient wattage and left half the room, the area by the closet, cast in shadows. Joe would've preferred not to view what the lamp did illuminate. The bed had no sheets. It also had no pillowcase, which really wasn't a problem because the room contained no pillow. The remainder of the accommodations provided no redemption. Had the interior decorator intended a minimalist effect, he'd surely succeeded. Within this dark wood-

He regretted not buying pajamas, opting to sleep in a new pair of gym shorts. He kneeled beside the bed and recited the Lord's Prayer by rote before pushing his belongings to the far side of the mattress and rolling up onto it. He turned off the table lamp and lay sprawled on his back. The only light came through the window from the street several stories below and the moon many miles above. Something about the room, maybe the old furnishings or the rotary telephone, made Joe feel he'd been transported back in time. It was easy to imagine himself as a fugitive on the lam. Thinking of this place as a gangster's hideout was better than seeing it as a gym teacher's new home. Without sheets, the mattress felt itchy on his skin, but Joe pushed the sensation out of conscious thought. He also ignored the boisterous voices leaving the bar rising from street level and the rumbling and screeching of steel wheels on the train yard tracks to the south.

After finally succumbing to sleep, Joe woke only twice. The first disruption came via laughter, footfalls, and rattling metal outside his room window. Joe opened eyes to see a flurry of knees and feet happily scampering upward. It took a moment for his sleep-fogged brain to deduce what had happened; an amorous couple going to a room above had opted to use the fire escape rather than the stairs. The second disturbance was more worrisome. At 3am, there was a faint tapping. Joe told himself it came from the corridor, somebody looking to be let in a nearby room. This theory was debunked,

8

The water pulsed against his bare body - ahh. Joe would never again take this simple pleasure for granted. He craned his neck down to wet his head beneath the spray. Clearly, the showers weren't meant for a man his size - not surprising. Everything at the middle school - desks, water fountains, urinals - was scaled down by one-third. No reason to think the boy's locker room would be designed differently. He imagined himself a giant stumbling upon a foreign land and making himself at home. At least this shower, in contrast to the one at the Fleabag, not only worked but had strong pressure. Joe welcomed the sensation. The hot water soothed his muscles and splattered at his feet, hard. The sound echoed, becoming the rush of a waterfall. Soon, steam filled the open space, providing at least a small degree of privacy. This was welcomed, too. The middle school's showers offered no dividers - not a single wall, door, or curtain - to separate each of the six stalls from one another or the locker room. Essentially, he stood exposed within a large, slippery, tiled cube with floor drains. No wonder he couldn't recall any students ever using it. Most of the kids were modest. The shy ones still wore gym shorts underneath their pants like in elementary. Nothing to worry about, though. It wasn't even six-thirty. More than an hour and a half before the first bus arrived. Still, he'd be quick about it. He worked the bar soap into a lather and vigorously massaged his body, working his way up, starting at the toes. The scent was fragrant. He paused and held the bar beneath his nose and sniffed - lilac, a little girly but nice. He resumed washing, rubbing in circles on his belly and chest while humming a tune.

Joe never heard the locker room door swing open from the main gym. Never heard anyone enter. Never expected anyone would enter. Transported by his imagination, he was alone in a rainforest, a hobbit's hovel far removed from his many troubles. He turned his back to the main room and vigorously massaged an armpit, making the funny noises the way fifth-graders do for laughs. He giggled. Though he hadn't heard her walk in, he'd felt a presence; he whipped back around to face someone no more than eight feet away, the aisles of metal lockers behind her. She wasn't laughing.

The woman, a custodian, was probably only forty but looked fifty - squat, disproportionate, most of her heft carried in the buttocks and legs while her top half was small, narrow-shouldered. Joe had seen her once or twice but didn't know her name. Or maybe he'd been told but forgot. He believed she didn't speak English.

She held a mop handle she used to push the big, yellow, rolling bucket from wherever to here without bending. Not that she moved, at all, during the current encounter. She clutched the pole as if clinging onto a window ledge, her expression that of cartoon fright - eyes enormous, mouth open, tongue poking out the space where teeth should be, and short frizzy hair, standing on her scalp.

Reflexively, Joe dropped his hands to cover his privates. The cleaner's eyes tracked his movement, her gaze dropping down, pausing a second, before returning to his face. This horrified, wide-eyed inspection repeated two or three more times, the woman's gawk traveling up and down like a yo-yo.

Joe didn't move. Didn't speak. Didn't have time to apologize, for the woman gasped, stepped back, and slipped on the wet tile. She fell hard to one knee, the mop dropping with a clack. With head bowed, she let out a low, gravely groan.

Without thinking, Joe stepped out of the stall. Forgetting his nakedness, he reached out, intending to help her.

"I got you," he said.

The cleaner looked up, shocked, fearful. She yelped as she threw up her palms. Only then did the scream come. And it did it come – earsplitting, undulating, and banshee shrill, a cross between a shriek and a yodel. As Joe took a second step, the woman dropped onto one side, twisting on the tiles, thrashing, kicking wildly, sending the mop bucket rolling, skittering, water sloshing, across the locker room floor, the bucket crashing into the lockers. Joe tried to grip the wiry woman.

"I got you," he repeated.

"Alejarse!"

"Let me…let me…"

"Nooo!"

"I'm trying to…stop moving so I can…"

With unexpected spryness, she rolled onto her knees and gave a powerful, mule-like kick to his shin.

"Oww!" Joe shouted, and raised his leg and cradled the bruised bone, balancing on one foot like a giant pink flamingo. He drew upon the limited ability acquired from his ninth-grade Spanish class but recalled only the title of the textbook.

"Seamos Amigos!" he pleaded.

The woman huffed with a wide-open mouth, clearly offended. She grabbed the mop handle and got to her feet. She waved its sodden head, side-to-side, tendrils flopping like a dead squid on a stick while yelling something in Spanish—a scolding or a warning maybe. Joe raised his hands over his head as if held at gunpoint. The woman turned, dropped the mop, and briskly limped, almost skipped out through the doorway into the outer room. This time, Joe heard the gym door open and swing back forth before coming to a sudden, hard stop.

Joe returned to the shower and hurriedly rinsed, dried, and dressed. The whole thing had transpired so fast. If it weren't for the abandoned mop and bucket, he would've thought it a dream. He walked the long, empty corridors, popping his head into vacant classrooms, the music room, the art room the nurse's office, looking for the woman. He wanted to apologize. In hindsight, after he entered the school, the uniformed officer mysteriously absent from his post behind the lobby desk, Joe should have sought out the nighttime custodial supervisor and informed her he'd be using the locker room shower. At the time, it hadn't occurred to him that somebody might walk in. It really wasn't his fault. The school appeared abandoned. Regardless, he felt awful. The woman had been scared. From door-to-door he went, but nobody was home. The search took considerable time. The school was huge. During the excursion, Joe realized he'd never been in any of these rooms before. His normal routine involved walking from the staff parking lot to the gym in the morning and back again in the afternoon. Amazing how small his world was now that he thought about it. He made his way to the rear of the building, located the door leading to the custodial office and entered.

It was more of warehouse than an office. He traversed a maze of tall metal shelves housing stacks of industrial-sized tubs of cleansers, toilet paper, and surprisingly, rodent traps and poison. The school was kept immaculately clean and the only rodents Joe ever heard about were the pet gerbils that had once escaped from Sue Miller's classroom. He moved through the narrow aisles of supplies, and the room opened to what looked like a garage with a twenty-foot ceiling with thick girders, corrugated metal walls, and a roll-up bay door. He imagined the cleaning staff must roast in the summer and freeze in the winter. At the center of the open space were a clunky wooden desk and a red couch. A slender, old black man with a scruffy salt-and-pepper beard and matching hair sat on the battered sofa preparing to eat a huge sandwich, the wax paper open on his knees. The delectable aroma of eggs and greasy meat made Joe hungry.

"She gone," the man said, not looking up.

Joe approached. He knew Vern Wallace. He came to the gym with cat litter and a broom whenever anybody puked after the 600-meter run. Joe introduced himself like he hadn't heard.

"Mr. Wallace, I don't know if you remember me. I'm Joseph Bustamante, Joe, that is, from Phys ed."

This, of course, was obvious. Joe was in shorts and a tightly tucked tee shirt and new, white socks pulled high on the calves. For the first time, it felt ridiculous for him, a grown man, to report to work dressed like this. Maybe that's why the elder man stared.

"She gone," Vern repeated. As if to punctuate his statement, he opened a can of cola by the tab. Pchhhtttt. "And I know who you are, Joe B. And I heard what you done. Shameful. You can't go dangling around a school in these times. It's not like the old days."

He slurped from the can without tilting it. A profound feeling of consternation came upon Joe combined with general fatigue. He was made confused and tired by this egg-sandwich-eating oracle. Was there a time nudity was permitted within the school? The thought disturbed him, as did the weird way he drank, holding the can upright and pursing his lips as though performing in a jug band. Why was he drinking cola so early in the morning, anyway?

"Listen, Mr. Wallace, you just came on for the day shift, right? Could you tell me how to find the nighttime supervisor?"

"Delores gone, too. Took Clarabella to the E.R."

"Clarabella? That's her name? Is she hurt? I want to say I'm sorry."

"Might be too late for sorry," Vern said. "Have a seat, son."

The man rewrapped his sandwich, getting down to business. Joe sat noncommittally on the edge of the grease-stained sofa. It looked like it belonged in the lobby of the Fleabag.

"What do you mean, too late?" Joe said.

"Well, Clarabella will surely go out on workman's comp for a couple weeks, maybe even a couple months. She's an old hand at it, believe me. Already called and got a claim number."

"I see," Joe said. "But I really wasn't responsible. And to be honest, the fall wasn't very hard."

"Oh, the fall was hard. More than any of us know," Vern said. "And now you're gonna go through a trial, I imagine."

"You mean like going to court?"

"Not that kind of trial. Though you will be accused."

"But I didn't do anything." Joe sat back, sunk further into the couch, a hole sucking him in. There was a big, black stain of splayed fingers on the arm. Maybe the couch had eaten somebody. If it swallowed Joe, he wouldn't resist. He pressed his palms against the sides of his head.

"I don't understand any of this," he said. "Two days ago, everything was perfect. Now everything has gone to-"

"Perfect? Really?" Vern said, held titled, eyes shining with patience and pity. "Were you happy?"

Joe thought a moment. "I wasn't unhappy,' he said. "So, yes, I guess."

"So being happy is the absence of unhappiness?"

"I'm not sure," Joe said. "Which hospital did they bring Clarabella to?"

Saying the name out loud made Joe think of circus clowns, though he didn't know why. Vernon handed Joe the sandwich.

"Take this back to your office and enjoy. You haven't eaten today, right?"

"I won't take your breakfast," Joe said.

"You didn't eat last night, neither, did you? Take it. It'll make me happy."

Joe accepted the sandwich but eyed it with caution.

"Not poisoned," the man explained, and grinned. "Helping people out brings joy. Lord knows I looked in other places. But I ain't never found happiness at the bottom of a bottle of gin or a can of beer. Never inhaled none at the end of a cigarette or a blunt, neither. And, for sure, ain't no happiness ever squirt out the tip of my-"

"I get it," Joe interrupted, both palms raised.

"That's the way we're wired," Vern continued. "But we keep working against it. We try to rewire ourselves and then wonder why we don't run right. Don't matter what hospital she's in, that's where Clarabella is at. Thinks she's latched onto something that'll make her happy. Should've heard her yapping. She sees this situation as an opportunity. Looking to take. It's a damn shame."

"Take what?"

"Whatever she can."

"But I didn't do anything," Joe said.

"I know it," the old custodian said. "But I also know you're gonna end up on the wrong side of right."

Joe stood up fast, defiant. "I'm sure everything will be fine. I just need to find Clarabella and say how sorry I am," he said. "If she comes back, please tell her I came by. Take care, Mr. Wallace. Thanks for the sandwich."

Vern looked, his expression a flat line. He lifted the can as a toast and took a long, deliberate slurp.

Joe returned to the gym and went to his tiny, windowless office and ate Mr. Wallace's sandwich at the metal desk. The sub was a belly buster packed with a couple of eggs, bacon, ham, sausage, cheese, onions, and red peppers, topped with hot sauce. When done, Joe was full and felt replenished. His brain and body functioned better. He taught the first two periods with energy and enthusiasm. The cacophony of a dozen bouncing basketballs, shouting children, and screeching rubber sneakers on the waxed hardwood brought back a sense of normalcy, revived him. Halfway through third period, however, a teacher's aide handed Joe a note summoning him to the principal's office. It was the same pink slip they used when a kid was in trouble. Scrawled over the blank lines for date and time was a single, large, handwritten word: IMMEDIATE.

Joe folded the ominous note - a pink slip, sheesh - and stuffed it into his short's pocket. After arranging for the teacher's aide to temporarily supervise the class, he made the solemn, silent trek down two long corridors to the main office—a convict's walk to the electric chair.

9

"Are you saying you were indecent when you came into contact with Clarabella Alvarez?" Principal Shelley said. "Disrobed? Completely?"

Her hands were clasped on top of her desk and she spoke with a vague drawl that made Joe wonder if the principal had roots in the South. Though their conversation was relaxed, the principal certainly maintained her well-known steel magnolia quality - things could turn quickly. Barbara Shelley was small, barely more than a midget, with a roundish face, curly blonde tresses, thin, fire-engine-red lips, and deep crow's feet that probably came from squinting in a way that seemed like scrutinizing. She was known to have a velvety, disarming charm draped over a rock-hard fortitude. People said she'd make a good prosecuting attorney. Joe thought with her small stature and sharp wit, she could be a ventriloquist's dummy. Being saddled with inferior staff, the longtime administrator had learned to entertain herself. It wasn't a stretch for Joe to picture her sitting on his lap and making wisecracks at his expense.

"I was in the boy's locker room," he said.

"No swim trunks or anything?"

"Like I mentioned, I had no place to go. My house was destroyed-"

"By a volcano."

"A tornado, actually. It was on the news. Nothing left, really."

"I'm sorry to hear that."

"Thank you. I'm sure we'll work through it."

"It would've been better if you'd worn swim trunks. Less of a spectacle."

The principal seemed poised to say something more but changed her mind and continued reading. Had someone said he'd caused a spectacle? He hadn't paraded across the auditorium stage. Not knowing the allegations made everything worse. Principal Shelley hadn't explained the document laid flat on the desk blotter and Joe hadn't inquired. If it were an official complaint, he'd be told soon enough. The woman kept reading, scowling, and shaking her head.

Principal Shelley's office was smaller than Joe remembered it. It had been nine years since he'd last sat in one of the two leather chairs in front of her desk and answered questions about his ambitions. I'd like to meet the right woman and have ten kids, seven boys and three girls, and lots of animals, he'd responded causing her to lower the resume she'd been perusing and eye him suspiciously over her reading glasses. It only occurred to Joe after the job interview that she'd probably been asking about his career ambitions. Regardless, Barbara Shelley hired him, so, naturally, Joe assumed she'd liked him. Hard to say for sure, however, for they'd had little contact since. When she didn't speak for a long time during this meeting, Joe became antsy. He drummed his fingers on his knees. Soon, against his better judgement, he spoke.

"And the shower in my room at the Fleabag wasn't work-"

"The Fleabag?"

Suddenly, Joe couldn't recall the actual name of his hotel.

"Yeah...the um...down by the train yard. It's one of those hourly romantic getaways above a bar. I'm sure you know it."

"Mr. Bustamante, I've been married thirty-eight years - a few of them happily. I don't frequent that kind of motel."

Joe laughed nervously. He'd always been Joe B until now.

"Oh, I wasn't implying... Anyway, it's noisy by the station. Difficult to sleep. The trains rattle and shake the bed. Forgive me for being a little foggy on the details. "

"So, am I to assume you were nude?"

"No. I don't ever...well, sometimes when I'm home, alone. But only on a very hot night."

"I mean when you had contact with Mrs. Alvarez. You were naked, is that correct?"

Joe squeezed his hands together, confounded. The question was absurd.

"I was showering," he said.

"At school?"

"Yes, ma'am. In the showers. I was showering in the showers."

He sat back in the chair, self-satisfied. Finally, he'd explained his actions in a way even a small child could understand.

"And you had to shower at the school due to the volcano," the principal stated.

"Yes! I mean no. It was a tornado."

"Of course," Principal Shelley paused to jot something down, and continued. "Did you obtain a use of facilities permit in advance?"

Joe didn't answer. He didn't like the unexpected turn the conversation had taken. Principal Shelley continued. "You are aware, Mr. Bustamante, that whenever the building or grounds are used outside of the normal parameters of your assigned responsibilities or outside the scheduled days and hours of occupancy, a use of facilities request must be submitted and a permit issued."

"I...I didn't think a ten-minute shower would qualify as a special use-"

"So, you didn't submit a request or get approval?"

A feeling of such a high degree of incredulity overcame Joe, he wondered if the whole scenario might be a gag thought up by Bill and his friends. Surely he was being punked. He shook his head no.

"I'm just playing the devil's advocate," Principal Shelley said.

Joe never understood why anybody would want to do that. And he certainly didn't understand how this applied to the current situation. He and Clarabella weren't adversaries, were they?

"What way were you facing?" Principal Shelley said.

"Excuse me? I don't understand."

"When you were first exposed to Mrs. Alvarez, were you facing towards her or away?"

Though he didn't grasp the significance of the question, Joe paused and tried to recall.

"Sideways, I think," he said.

The principal removed her reading glasses, shut her eyes, and massaged her forehead with three stubby fingers like he'd just given her a migraine. The hard puff of air she expelled indicated Barbara Shelley considered sideways to be the worst way.

"And then Mrs. Alvarez fell while trying to escape, correct?" she said.

"Actually, I object to the word escape. That implies that Clarabella was in danger, which she wasn't."

"Alright. So you witnessed Mrs. Alvarez fall as she fled."

Joe wasn't thrilled by the word fled, either, but let it go.

"Principal Shelley, to be honest, I think we startled one another. I was just as surprised to see Clarabella as she was to see me. I never intended this to happen, and I'm quite embarrassed and very sorry. But, yes, she did slip and fall, and I'm sorry about that too."

"Is that why you lunged towards her? To apologize?"

"I never moved towards her."

"You never came out of the shower causing her to fall forward and strike her head on the floor?"

Something constricted within Joe's chest.

"She never hit her head," he said. "And I didn't cause her to fall! She slipped on the wet tiles!"

"I'll remind you, Mr. Bustamante, this is only an enquiry not an inquiry. There's no need to get worked up," the principal said.

Joe folded his hands within his lap. Didn't those two words mean the same thing? Or were they different like principal and principle. As a boy, Joe had been given the spelling lesson mnemonic a good principal has principles and is always your pal in the end. Would Principal Shelley be his pal in the end? He could only rest his chin on his chest and wait, in silence. His boss spent the next several minutes in fierce concentration, writing.

Eventually, Joe mustered the courage to ask the silly, childish question he'd mentally formed during the first five minutes of the meeting: Am I in trouble? Only when he molded the idea into an adult sentence, his concern was expressed opaquely, making him appear guilty.

"Principal Shelley, do I need union representation?" he said.

The principal ignored the question. She held up a hand like a traffic cop for what seemed like a long time.

"I think I understand what happened," she said, finally, cheerfully. To emphasize her point, she snapped the pen down onto the desk, a definitive sound, the crack from a firing squad. "Thank you for your time, Joe. We're finished here. You can return to class."

Joe was both dumbfounded and exhilarated. The enquiry was over just like that. He shook the little lady's raccoon-like hand.

"Thank you. Thank you, Principal Shelley. I really was only taking a shower. It was a mistake not to tell anyone - I will never do it again. If only I could talk to Clarabella..."

"Not necessary. I am meeting with her attorney this afternoon and I shall pass along your sentiments."

Though he remained smiling, something soured within Joe's belly. He offered his gratitude and repeated thank-yous between belches. He left the office upon giving a spiritless wave that came across like a Hitler salute. Joe felt depleted, fatigued. His legs were leaden

10

Joe lay on his bed with hands pinned to his chest, a corpse in a casket, on his newly rented sheets. He'd have to buy bedding soon, for the Fleabag rentals did not smell newly laundered. He'd kept his sneakers on as a statement against the hotel's disregard for basic hygiene standards. At least, though, his complaint about the broken shower had been addressed. Somebody, a super or a plumber or whoever, had fixed it while he was at work. Joe could shower now, but wished he'd planned ahead and brought shower shoes. The bathroom floor tiles likely housed mold species as of yet undiscovered by science. He stared at the rumpled and pitted paint on the ceiling above the bed. If somebody would scrape, spackle, prime, and paint, it would be fine. A fresh coat could go a long way - not likely to happen, though. He pushed this thought out of his mind. Pessimism is a poison he did not care to drink at the moment. Instead, he'd focus on the positive. All said, things were improving. As long as you remain a good person, good things will happen. This was the divine order of life. Of course, he now had a situation at work and the giant cockroach was still on the bathroom mirror here in his room, but you can't have everything. Joe considered naming it. Susan… Wally… Sir Thomas Edward Montgomery III…

The doorknob rattled. A small electric shock jolted Joe's heart. He sat up and stared at the room door. Several hard raps came from the other side.

"Who's there?" Joe said, his tone unfamiliar, breathy and light.

The knock grew more demanding.

"Who is it?" Joe said louder, reclaiming his natural baritone.

"Your new neighbor," an unseen man bellowed. "I baked you an apple pie."

Joe rose, walked, unlocked, and pulled opened the door. The man before him was impossibly skinny with thick veins running down his arms and one like a knotted rope in his neck. He'd benefit from a comb and a razor for his wavy, sandy hair was messy and his considerably darker, short, coarse, whiskers were almost a beard. A bar of soap wouldn't hurt, either. The man held up a liquor bottle by the neck.

"OK, so it ain't a pie, but it's close enough."

Joe read the label. It was a cheap bottle of apple brandy. He stared at the stranger.

"Are you going to invite me in? Or leave me outside like a one-eyed mutt with mange."

His tank top was dirty, his pants were dirty, his fingernails were dirty. Joe took his age to be roughly that of his own - only this man's years had hit harder.

Joe wanted to say he was tired. Wanted to tell the man to come back another time, but found himself stepping back, welcoming him with an outstretched arm.

"Not sure if the place is amenable to receiving guests," he said.

"Damn, don't worry. Yours looks like a suite in the Ritz-Carlton compared to mine. I'm in four-o-four... Sorry about last night."

Joe studied the man with features scrunched, waiting for an explanation.

"Last night. Did I wake you? I came back so lit, I went to the wrong room - this room. Surprised you didn't get up and kick my ass. You're a big dude, aren't you? I'm Jerry."

He held out a hand. Joe always found it awkward to shake with his left, but didn't want to offend the stranger. He noticed the crude, black-inked crescent moon tattooed on the back of the man's hand. The moon had a creepy, stoic face drawn in profile. They shook.

"Joe Bustamante," Joe said. "Around three or four o'clock? Yeah I heard you. Wouldn't've minded, except I work early. I'm a teacher."

"Teacher? Cool. Well, sorry. Won't happen again. I'll take my head out of my ass. Let me make it up to you, Joe B. You hungry? I'll order a pizza - on me."

Joe studied the stranger. "How did you know that's what people call me?" he said.

"What? Oh, I don't know. You just look like a Joe B, I guess," he said.

Joe considered this. Maybe it was true. "I'll pick up the pizza," he said. "You brought the dessert."

"That I did," the skinny man said.

They drank the apple brandy out of paper cups while seated at the wobbly little table they'd moved from the far wall to the center of the room. Every gulp tasted a little better, or at least, a little less harsh. After the pizza was delivered, Jerry ate five slices to Joe's two and a half. Joe wondered if the man simply had an overactive metabolism or if it had been a while since he'd last had a meal. The man chattered on even while scarfing down the slices. He'd only been at the Fleabag for a few days and would be moving on soon. He was originally from the West Coast. He'd served four years in the U.S. navy and was honorably discharged but was denied a purple heart. Venereal diseases aren't given proper recognition, he'd quipped. After that, he wandered the country, going as far as Alaska, working as a journeyman acquiring skills as an electrician, carpenter, mason's helper, and general construction worker. I push the wheelbarrow in order to make other people a wheelbarrow full of money he said. He was married, as far as he knew, for he hadn't heard from his wife in six years and had no idea if she'd divorced him in absentia. Jerry admitted to being incarcerated in Atlanta for eighteen months upon conviction for a burglary he described as a case of mistaken identity.

In a weird way, hearing the man's checkered history saddened Joe. Why did everyone he meets seem to have lived a more interesting life than he had? The more they drank, the more they revealed, and the more they laughed. Then the conversation turned serious. Joe talked about losing Rebecca and his mom's diagnosis. He talked about the tornado destroying his home but not his optimism. Jerry offered greater condolences and compassion than Joe's boss, Principal Shelley, had.

At about nine, Jerry abruptly ended the talk. "Well, my friend, I don't want to keep you up on a school night. So, I'll be shuffling off to my luxury accommodations next door."

And that was it. Joe walked him to the door and thanked him for coming by. As they shook hands, this time as righties, Joe glimpsed the tattoo on the back of Jerry's right hand he'd hadn't noticed before. It was an all-black depiction of the sun. The sun had flaming black rays extending from the circle and a face inside. Even a peripheral peek showed the image was certainly not modeled after anything printed on a children's cereal box. The creepy face was expressionless, empty. Joe wanted to ask about the significance of the sun and moon symbols, but decided against it. He and his guest had already been more familiar than made him comfortable.

"So, I suppose I'll be seeing you around," Joe said.

"Yes, sir. For at least another few days. Then I'm off to wherever one of these clunky, old diesel trains we hear all night will take me," Jerry said, and paused a moment before adding, "Wanna tag along?"

Joe chuckled, a stalling tactic, trying to determine if the question was a joke. He concluded the proposition was serious.

"As fun as that sounds," Joe replied, "I have a good job and a lot going on here."

Jerry took on a peculiar, contemplative countenance with pursed lips and narrowed eyes—a look of pity, perhaps.

"That's why I'm asking," he said.

Joe stood motionless, a marble version of himself.

"Sleep on it, Joe B," Jerry said."Night."

Jerry ambled towards his room. Joe shut the door.

The rumble of the trains made sleep impossible. He lay on the bed in the dim room, awake, electrified, peering deep into the darkness, thinking, pondering possibilities, weighing all likely outcomes. Could a man simply run away from his troubles? Maybe he could. Maybe.

☙ 11 ❧

Joe parked his car at the usual stall within staff parking at 7:15am. He walked to the middle school's main entrance. The sun was missing within the battleship grey sky. Though it wasn't raining, a thick mist moistened his skin and semi-smooth scalp. He'd decided to stop shaving his head despite the promise to his ailing mother. Joe now believed his baldness had something to do with Clarabella Alvarez being frightened during the locker room incident. People associate a white man's shaved head with incarceration, neo-Nazism, and mental illness. Clarabella probably thought he was an escaped skinhead lunatic. He ran a hand over the short, prickly sprouts as he walked. The new growth tickled his palm like teddy-bear fur. He strode by Principal Shelley's reserved spot and was surprised to see her Lexus already there. Typically, the administration didn't arrive until after nine. He told himself the uneasy feeling was paranoia. People came to work early for lots of reasons. Maybe she had a school board meeting to prepare for.

As he approached the main lobby door, the two uniformed security guards waiting in the vestibule were harder to dismiss. One - Roy, if Joe recalled his name correctly - opened the glass door like a butler. Before Joe could say thanks or good morning, the second one, a short, pudgy man with slicked-back hair and a pronounced handlebar mustache, spoke.

"Mr. Bustamante? Principal Shelley needs to see you," he said.

"Right now? OK," Joe said. And when it became clear they intended to walk with him, he added, "Oh, I know the way."

"We were told to escort you," Roy said, sounding put-out.

Joe didn't know which was more offensive: being treated like a criminal or being treated like a criminal given so little respect. Neither guard was armed, and Officer Mustache was round with heavy jowls, whereas Roy was in his mid-sixties. He could take both with one arm if he was inclined to do so.

"What's this about?" Joe said. "Because I really didn't do anything."

"Everything will be explained when we get there," Roy said.

That would turn out to be an atrocious lie.

They proceeded towards the main office. It annoyed Joe the newly-formed trio were required to remain in the tiny waiting area outside Principal Shelley's office despite this meeting clearly having been planned in advance. When the secretary admitted them, it irked him to be followed by the officers for what he assumed would be a private session or possibly mediation between him and Clarabella. When the door closed, the guards stood at opposite sides as mismatched bookends. Principal Shelley made a big show of rising and walking around the desk to greet him. She shook Joe's hand and offered a cool, pseudo-smile. This was the little Napoleon people had always warned him about.

"Good morning, Mr. Bustamante," she said, and motioned with an arc of her arm to a chair. "Nice to see you, please have a seat."

When Joe looked over his shoulders at the security officers, Principal Shelley explained their presence, sort of. "I'm sorry but district policy requires certain security protocols under such circumstances. I hope you understand. Please, sit down," she said.

Joe sat while the queen returned to her throne.

"What circumstances are we talking about? I'm not sure I understand what's going on here," he said.

"Joe, due to the seriousness of the allegations levied against you, we are placing you on paid administrative leave while an investigation is conducted."

She held out a sealed envelope. Joe did not reach for it. Fear merged with frustration causing him to speak rapidly, without thought.

"Investigation? Into what? A shower? I already admitted I took a shower. I showered in the showers.

I'm being suspended for what? Did I use contraband soap? Did my shampoo violate someone's constitutional protection against cruel and unusual eye-stinging?"

"Mr. Bustamante, I would suggest you take this matter seriously. A formal complaint has been filed against you. The teacher's collective bargaining agreement allows the school district to put you on paid leave for up to ninety days while we investigate. If during this time, the allegations against you are not substantiated, you will be reinstated. If we determine charges are warranted, you will be placed on unpaid leave until the charges are adjudicated. During the investigative period, you are prohibited from entering school grounds or having any contact with the complainant. Failure to comply with these directives could result in your termination or arrest. Do you have any questions?"

...Arrest?

Nausea, a rising stomach as if on a skyscraper elevator, came upon him. Joe felt weak and wobbly.

"W-what does the complaint allege?"

"I'm not permitted to discuss the specifics of the complaint at this time. A copy of the complaint will be forwarded to you and your union representative within the next ten days."

Joe's conscious mind told him not to beg, yet he found himself doing so.

"Please…please, Principal Shelley. I'll write her a formal letter of apology. I never meant to offend her or scare her. I nev-"

"Please sign here. This is only acknowledging receipt of the suspension order. You are not admitting any wrongdoing."

When Joe's shaky hand finished signing, he could hardly recognize his own signature.

"Alright. Since you have no further questions, I'll ask the officers to accompany you to your car."

"My car? I have to leave work?"

"We'll need to take custody of your school I.D. card and any keys issued to you," the mustached officer said. These words had obviously been rehearsed in his mind. He'd been waiting, yearning to say them. Yet, he was probably married. There was someone for everyone...except for Joe B.

Joe patted his pockets and found what they wanted. Parting with the items hurt. Like a kid's hamster dying. His lower lip quivered. He fought back tears.

The walk back to his car was long and silent except for Roy occasionally telling him not to worry and that everything would work itself out. A week ago, Joe would've believed him for that had been his life philosophy, too. Now, he no longer knew what he believed, if anything, at all. He needed to talk to somebody. But his mother was too sick. And Rebecca had left him for another man. Joe didn't have anybody. He was alone.

12

Pulling open the heavy door and entering Steeples without his friends or plans to meet them raised uncomfortable questions: was drinking solo a seed for addiction? Could a single beer germinate and grow into life-altering dependency? No, Joe decided. One was fine. Alcoholism began with the second drink, not the first. He'd be sure to only have one.

No hostess staffed the station because it was only 3pm - the pub was nearly empty. Later, during the early evening, hordes of rowdy fans would flock together for Monday Night Football. This converted cathedral was still a church, of sorts. For many, sports were a religion. They'd come to worship their idols on a dozen suspended screens, to chant, to sing, and to perform rituals of eating hot wings and potato skins while downing shots and pitchers of beer. Joe proceeded to a stool at the far end of the bar. Normally, he'd sit next to a stranger, for he was a social animal. Today was different, however. Joe didn't want to talk. Making conversation would be a minor form of torture. Putting himself in a position where he'd have to feign interest in the banal - sports, politics, and weather - while he had such serious problems would be like self-inflicting a wedgie.

Joe hadn't actually planned an excursion into the village. The Land of Uz beckoned him simply because he didn't know anything else. Once there, however, he was at a loss. He'd meandered along the city streets with no purpose. He wound up sitting on a bench reading the advertisements on metro busses as they whizzed by and marveling at the dirty box trucks double-parking, their drivers hustling with hand trucks, making deliveries within impossibly small spaces. These men and the ones washing windows, the women behind the counters and waiting tables inside the cafes, the drivers dropping off and picking up out front, and all the rest of the hoi polloi earned their meager paychecks through hard work. Teaching physical education for six hours per day for only one hundred and eighty days per year was a joke. Before recent events, everybody had a harder life than Joe. Maybe he'd been babied—been coddled and didn't think enough about others. Sometimes, when he coached basketball, he'd confront a young hotshot who wouldn't put the team before himself; he might be forced to bench the kid for a game. Now, Joe, himself, had been taken out of his home and job. Was the Big Coach benching him?

He rose from the bench and roamed about. He window-shopped the trendy storefronts and ate a falafel at a pricey coffee shop. He walked some more, eventually coming to Steeples, the familiarity it offered like the song of a siren. The brass door handle felt good in his hand. The old haunt stored good memories inside, or, more truthfully, it offered respite from the bad ones.

Some bad stuff had come to be, recently, and things weren't getting better. Initially, after being suspended by Principal Shelley and escorted off school grounds by security, Joe went back to the Fleabag. The room was hot, so Joe opened the window that led to the fire escape. A strange, noxious smell, an odor of burning tar, came in. Joe sat on the edge of the mattress and used his phone to access Google. With his job on hold for a week or more, he decided to work on the house situation.

He'd called a local demolition company, Homewreckers, and arranged for a construction fence to be erected around his mom's lot and the debris from the flattened domicile to be bulldozed, scooped-up, and carted away – farewell, mementos and memories. The ballpark estimate was a splash of ice water. Likely, it would be even more than quoted, for the company used a complicated formula for man hours, material type, number of dumpsters, and the weight of each load to determine final cost. Matt, the head homewrecker, must've been on a job site, for he needed to shout over the sound of heavy machinery.

"Don't worry about it," he yelled. "The insurance company eats this, not your mom. Screw them bastards! What have they ever done for you besides taking your premiums?"

Joe's next call was to the insurance company. He navigated through a series of automated menus until finally reaching a selection to file a claim. The machine placed him on hold, and Joe listened to an ad for incapacitation and dismemberment insurance and part of Billy Joel's "Just the Way You Are" before a live human, Rhonda, cut in. The agent showed great concern and compassion upon hearing about the tornado and the devastation to his property. She promised to expedite the claim and to send an adjuster. She then asked for a policy number, which Joe didn't have - he provided his home address instead. Again, he was placed on hold. This time for the entire length of "American Pie."

"I'm sorry for the delay," Rhonda said, coming back. "Mr. Bustamante, we don't have a current homeowner's policy on that address. We do show one, however, expiring six years ago."

"That's not possible," Joe said. "My mother would never have let the insurance lapse."

"Well, maybe she switched to another company. You should check. We don't have a current policy on record, and without a policy number, Mutual Liberties cannot proceed with processing a claim. We're very sorry for your loss, but..."

The subsequent call was to his mother, only to discover she wasn't at his aunt's house - she'd been admitted to the hospital. Joe spoke to Aunt Edna as fear coiled within his chest.

"What's wrong?" he said. "The treatments are supposed to be outpatient."

"I wanted to call you, but your mom wouldn't have it. Should've heard her cawing. She's such a stubborn, old crow. Joey, don't be mad. She didn't want you to worry."

"Well, I am worried. Is it the cancer? Did it get worse?"

There was a pause followed by a nervous chuckle. "Oh, no, dear," Aunt Edna said. "She had an allergic reaction. She'll be fine. They admitted her as a precaution and will probably release her today or tomorrow."

"Allergic reaction? To what? The medication?"

Another nervous chuckle. "No, no…nothing like that. Your mother was stung by a bee."

Joe would call his mom tomorrow. During the interim, he'd attend to his job problems. He opened his wallet and located an old, dog-eared business card he'd received when hired. The name on the card read Nicholas Diamond, though Joe knew everybody called him Nicky Diamonds. Joe wasn't thrilled his union rep went by what sounded like a 1940s mobster moniker, but his reputation for getting people off was well-established so he made allowances. The conversation began with formal introductions. The man had a distinct, needle-like voice. And maybe Joe had seen too many gangster movies, for he pictured Nicky Diamonds being small and skinny with a long, rat-like nose. Moreover, because he had never met the man, Joe felt justifiably annoyed by his over-familiarity and predisposition for interrupting over the phone. As Joe was only halfway through a detailed retelling of the shower incident, Nicky Diamonds broke in.

"You didn't ask her to show you her tits, did you?"

"Uh…no, I did not," Joe replied.

"Good. 'Cause that would make things harder. We got this."

"But she's saying I caused her injury, and nothing like that happened. The whole thing is a misunderstanding. I-"

"Misunderstanding? Naah. It's all bullshit. But we have to sit tight until we see the complaint. We don't know what you're being accused of, if anything."

Joe checked over his shoulder as if somebody might be listening in. He spoke in a strained, hushed tone. "What if I get fired? I'd never be able to teach again. My career would be over. I'd lose my pension."

Nicky Diamonds remained unsympathetic, direct. "Look, I've been doing this a long time, and I handle a lot of districts. These are the commandments I tell teachers who want to keep their jobs: Thou shalt not steal, not even a box of paperclips. Thou shalt not touch the students, not even a hug on graduation day. Thou shalt not meet off school grounds, not even to help with homework. Thou shalt not tell anyone what bathroom he or she or it should use. And thou shalt not mention race, even when teaching about the American Civil War. Don't break those and you're usually fine. You can come to class drunk or get busted for possessing cocaine and we'll get you re-hab. You can threaten to kick the superintendent in the teeth and you'll be sent to anger management. Showing your ding-dong to a cleaner? You'll be back after three days of sensitivity training. Heck, I had one health teacher who put his own semen on slides so the kids could see the spermies wiggle under the microscope - and he's back working. I think he went on to win an award for something."

Joe's hand hurt from squeezing the phone.

"But she said if I came to school, I could be arrested!"

"Yeah, so? Don't go there. Why go to school if you're not working? I mean, you got a thing for fine cafeteria cuisine? You can't live without the frozen pizza bagels? You hooked on greasy, day-old curly fries?"

Joe went to hang up the phone but changed his mind. He held the line in silence, waiting. When Nicky Diamonds spoke again, his tone was softer.

"Look, if what you're saying is true, they don't have anything and they know it. But the administration can't bring you back too soon because it'll look like they didn't give the allegations the proper attention they deserved. They're required by law to show due diligence. If they don't, they can be sued. And they're scared of million-dollar lawsuits, not about riling you. That said, Principal Shelley will sit around and scratch her fat ass for a week or two and then dismiss the complaint."

"So, in the meantime, I'm disgraced in front of my family, friends, and colleagues?"

"Yes. Absolutely. And three days after your back working, they'll forget. This may be hard for a guy like you to accept, but everybody has their own lives and interests. They'll be talking about the latest celebrity rumor or the most recent stupid remark by the POTUS or about who's pitching tonight or what's for dinner. Truth is the people you know are only marginally interested in your problems. You can take comfort in the fact that nobody ever really thinks about you to begin with."

The thought drained Joe of the indignation that had been fueling his anger.

"So what do we do now?" he said, defeated.

"They're giving you a ten-day paid vacation. I'd leave town. Go skiing or snorkeling or some mindless shit like that."

Nicky's advice prompted Joe to stride out of the Fleabag, plop into his little red car, and speed towards The Village. He had to get away. He couldn't leave town, though. Not with his house sick and his mom demolished. No. Reverse that. Joe's stress-smothered brain was messing everything up. He needed air. He kept all four windows rolled down as he drove. Wind flapped something tucked under the visor - the parking ticket, he remembered. He drove faster. Faster. A cyclone rushed, swirled inside the car. Taking action felt right. Maybe Jerry, his nomadic, insouciant hotel-mate, was right. If your troubles became insurmountable, maybe it was foolish to try and surmount them. Just run - that was the impulse firing within every nerve cell within his body. Run!

But he'd never run from anything. Whenever things went bad, Joe put his trust in the goodness of the world. If you remained good when things went bad, you never had to wait long before the world righted itself and good things happened.

He signaled for a drink with a raised finger. The short, burly, red-headed barkeep took his time wiping the countertop with a cloth before making his way over.

"Joe B," the bartender said, "what'll it be?"

Joe didn't know the barkeep's name. Didn't know anything about him. He probably should considering how long he'd been coming. But now wasn't the time to kick off a personal relationship.

"A draft, please," Joe said. "Something dark. Anything. Make it the darkest you have to match this dark, dark world."

Joe had intended it as a joke, but a look of profound sadness came over the bartender. He stared a moment with pale, hazel eyes before shuffling down the length of the bar to the taps. A thought came into Joe's head. Something his mom or dad had told him long, long ago. Or maybe it came from a fortune cookie.

When the world is dark, you are called to be the light.

Joe shook the thought out of his head. He watched the bartender tilt and fill a tall pilsner glass while talking to a well-dressed customer on the opposite side of the bar. Funny, but Joe hadn't seen the man standing there when he'd walked in. Though he looked familiar, Joe couldn't place him. The bartender returned with a frothy beer and set it down on a coaster.

"Here ya' go," he said.

Joe smiled and thanked him. He handed over a ten, mumbling keep it.

"You OK?" the bartender asked.

"Yeah, why?"

"You don't seem yourself, that's all."

"I'm fine. I've had some troubles recently, but that's how things go sometimes. I don't blame anybody. Things happen and you just have to push through them."

"On your own?" the bartender said.

"Yeah," Joe replied.

There was a long moment of quiet. The bartender leaned and rested his thick, bare forearms on the bar.

"If ever you want to talk, son, I'm always nearby."

"I appreciate that. I really do. Right now, however, I just need to be alone with my thoughts. I'll figure things out. Thank you, though."

Joe raised his beer as a salute. The bartender nodded and moved slowly away and put the bill in the cash drawer. Joe missed him from the moment he'd left and wished he'd taken the opportunity to talk - pride often begets loneliness. The bartender returned to the customer at the opposite end of the bar. Joe tried to look without looking. The man with the expensive suit and all those rings on his fingers certainly was familiar. Joe had seen that thousand-watt smile before but couldn't recall where.

* * *

"How's your favorite patron getting along, nowadays?"

The tone was singsong. The grin indicated he took pleasure in the misfortunes of others. The barkeep picked up a glass and polished it with a cloth, cleaning the inside first.

"He has troubles but isn't overcome. He blames no one," he said.

The man emitted a short, scornful laugh. "How pathetic. Look at him! Crying into his beer. He's lost faith.'

"No. He clings to the blessed hope of love. If only his faith wasn't misdirected."

"Can't be. No one facing hardship believes in love. Not even that bald-headed simpleton." The customer motioned with a wave of his arm toward the other end of the bar. "It's every man for himself. No one remains faithful."

"You haven't considered Joe B. There's no one like him on this earth."

The man folded his arms and leaned back, his grin slipping into a sneer.

"Well, at least he has his health, right?" he said, and laughed, spittle squirting out of his mouth. "If he were bodily afflicted, he wouldn't be so damn optimistic. Surely, he wouldn't greet you with a kind word and a smile. He'd curse you to your face."

The bartender set the glass back in an overhead rack and stared at the man.

"Very well," he said. "I won't argue. Have it your way."

* * *

Joe scratched his wrist while his mind played hopscotch, jumping from thought to thought like boxes drawn on a sidewalk, stopping, wobbling, turning, and coming back to the beginning. Why was this happening? Why did Rebecca leave him? Why did his mom get sick? Why did a storm destroy his house? Why was he in trouble at work? Why was this happening? When he went back to his room, he'd squash that king roach on the mirror. He didn't want to see it when he saw himself anymore. Joe sipped his beer. The foam was tingly on his lips and the taste of the brew was creamy and earthy. If she were here, Rebecca would've said it tasted like tree bark. Sadly, she wasn't. She'd left him for a doctor. Joe wondered if she was happy. Wondered if she missed him. He looked at his wrist. A little tree of veins was purple, protruding. The area he'd scratched was raw, blood spots forming, yet the itch remained. A bonus of residing in the Flea-Flicker, of course. The hotel was aptly described by its nickname. He pressed a paper napkin on the wound. He could stop at a drugstore and buy lotion. Or maybe he'd go to the pet store and pick up a flea collar.

Joe sat alone, suckling the brew from the glass in small gulps. Suddenly, without thought, he tilted his head back and emptied the glass down his gullet. He considered ordering a second but resisted the temptation. Instead, he stood and walked out of the bar without saying goodbye.

13

"Better? You can almost make out which team is which," Jerry said, while fiddling with the aerial on top of the bulky, box-like receiver. "If you squint…"

"At least you got a TV. In my room, I get to look at the window and watch the pigeons poop on the fire escape," Joe said.

"That's probably more exciting than this league - look! Another time-out. What a surprise. The big, overpaid crybabies complain about every call. You know, I heard that out of a four-hour game, the ball is only in play for about twelve minutes on average."

"Sounds about right. But it's a hard twelve minutes when eleven three-hundred-pound men are trying to knock your head off."

"You kidding me? Don't believe the propaganda. They're all a bunch of pussies - that's why they wear pads. Let 'em take the field with no helmets like they do in Europe. What's the name of that game—the one with the funny white ball?"

"Rugby."

"Yeah, let these sissy Americans play rugby like those crazy Brits. Then I'll show 'em some respect."

Joe smiled. He liked Jerry. Though he didn't have even a rudimentary knowledge of football or sports in general, but that didn't stop him from voicing strong opinions on the subject. Joe was glad he'd accepted the invitation to come over after leaving Steeples pub and returning to the Fleabag. Sitting on the bare floor, eating take-out Chinese food - lo mein, pork-fried rice, beef and broccoli - directly out of white cartons, drinking bottled beer, and watching Monday Night Football through snowy reception felt like camping at a cabin in the woods. In the moment, the loss of modern-day amenities seemed more like a choice than the force of fate.

"Hey, thanks," Joe said.

"For what?"

"You know, letting me watch the game, keeping me company and all."

Jerry put a huge forkful of lo mein into his mouth and spoke while chewing. "Hey. It ain't nothing. You brought the food and the beer. Least I could do."

The stadium audience roared and Joe looked to the screen to catch the quarterback getting pressured. He pulled the ball into his abdomen as a cornerback hit at full speed and plowed him into the turf - hard. The excited broadcasters analyzed the mistakes made by the offensive line that led to the sack by drawing yellow lines and circles over the video replay. Returning to live action, the defensive players celebrated with fist pumps into the air, further firing-up the crowd. The QB was slow in recovering. He stood hunched over, gripping knees, a ref resting a consoling hand on his back. When he rose fully and signaled he was good to continue, the spectators cheered. Apparently, the opposing team fans wanted him clobbered but not permanently injured. Or maybe they simply respected him as a gridiron warrior like a gladiator of yore. Either way, it's weird, when you stop to think about it. The game resumed.

And so did the idle chatter. Joe wanted to talk about his work suspension. Not for advice - career guidance was Nicky Diamonds' department - but for commiseration. He needed someone to confirm the school's actions taken against him were completely unjustified. He, Joseph Bustamante, wanted assurance that he was still a good person. Sadly, he and Jerry did not have a friendship that encouraged delving into such topics. Perhaps someday, but not yet. Better to keep their conversation at arms-length.

"I'm surprised you're still here, in town," Joe said. "Figured you would have moved on by now."

His new friend kept chowing down as Joe marveled at the amount the stick-skinny man could eat. Jerry paused only to tear open the small packets of soy sauce with his teeth in order to dribble additional sodium onto the already too-salty lo mein.

"Soon," he said. "A week, maybe. I found some work - roofing. The boss is too cheap to rent a boom truck. So, this morning, after stripping the old roof, I had to lug bundles of shingles two stories up a ladder, one at a time. At the end of the day, he complained the crew didn't get enough done. The bastard looked right at me as he said it. As soon as I get paid, I'm gone. The ink on the check won't even be dry."

"I envy you," Joe said, and took a swig of beer.

"Envy me? Why?"

"Your free spirit. The bohemian lifestyle. Your don't-take-no-crap-from-nobody attitude… I don't know if I could do it. But I envy you for being able to make it work."

Jerry stopped eating. He seemed to stare into Joe's internal organs like an MRI. "The offer still stands," he said.

Joe shrugged, pretended he didn't know what Jerry was referring to.

"Come with me," Jerry said, undeterred. "Be your own boss. The captain of your own ship. Don't let anyone else decide your destiny."

Joe tried to laugh the suggestion off, but Jerry stayed stone-serious.

"I can't," Joe said. "I just can't… It's not me."

Jerry shook his head in slow acquiescence. He appeared saddened, and something else… Disappointed? Angered, maybe?

They watched the remainder of the broadcast mostly in silence. After it ended, Joe rose. With three hours and three beers behind him, his legs were stiff and his balance unsteady. In a way, he felt like he was back on the deck of All My Glory during the hailstorm. He bent over to gather the mess of empty cartons - a pain like a hot skewer pierced his lower back, extending through to his groin. Joe winced. He wobbled, kicked, and knocked over an empty bottle; it clinked and rolled on the floorboards.

"You OK, man?" Jerry said. "I know you ain't drunk."

"My back," Joe said, through gritted teeth, rubbing the affected area. "I'm fine."

He tried, once again, to bend and reach for the garbage and was afflicted with a second spasm. This one made him place palms to the floor and lower his body down. Tears formed in his eyes, blurring his vision. He lay curled on his side.

"Damn, dude. You need an ambulance?" Jerry said. "Give me your phone."

"No! Just help me up and get me to my room. I gotta lie down. I'll be alright. It'll pass."

"You sure? I think you sh-"

"I'm fine, really."

Jerry shook his head no, but moved towards his guest, regardless. He squatted down, hooked arms under Joe's armpits. As Joe attempted to stand, the force exerted threatened to dislocate Jerry's shoulder.

"You need to work with me, here," Jerry said. "I can't just throw you over my shoulder like a bundle of shingles."

With monumental effort, Joe rolled onto his knees. With Jerry's aid, he rose and stood fully. They walked clumsily, like boys tethered together in a three-legged race, from Jerry's room to the next, down the darkened corridor. Joe handed Jerry the room key. He struggled to open the door while holding up the much larger man. Both nearly dropped as the door swung open and they stumbled into the room. They shuffle-stepped over to the bed. As Jerry let go, Joe collapsed face-first, bouncing onto it. Though the pain in his lower back flared, it felt good to be off his feet. The mattress's vague scent of mildew and piss was like a welcoming spring meadow.

Joe felt Jerry lift and pivot his legs up and over, onto the bed. He then felt his shoes being pulled off. Then came hard breathing.

"Whew... Helping you is going to send me to the ER. What you tip the scale at? Two hundred and fifty pounds?"

"Two-fifteen," Joe said.

"Two-fifteen, my ass," Jerry said. "You probably ain't seen two-fifteen since high school."

Joe let out a short snigger that hurt his side, but it still felt good. This wouldn't last. He'd be OK.

"Don't make me laugh," he said. "It feels like a punch."

"Whaddaya think happened? You pull something?"

"I don't know. It just hit me out of nowhere. Felt like being electrocuted from the inside out."

"That's why I never clean up. Let the roaches carry the trash away. You want me to call a doctor? Or a family member?"

"You mean my next of kin? No, I'm good. I'll stretch out tomorrow morning, and I'll be fine."

"Alright, buddy. You're the expert. Get some sleep. I'll be next door. Holler if you need me."

Joe thanked him and listened to the man walking, leaving the room, and pulling the door shut.

In small, incremental movements, Joe rolled onto his back. Because reaching for the table lamp seemed a colossal feat in his current condition, he lay in the dim ambient light coming through the windows from the street below - thinking, mulling this new development over, and predicting how it would complicate everything else. Someone began yelling and honking a car horn outside but Joe didn't have the strength to lift his head. Soon, he dozed. Or at least, he thought he did. Probably he was adrift in the mysterious inlet between wakefulness and sleep. How much time passed before he was roused to full consciousness, he couldn't say. But when the urge to urinate came upon him, the sensation was so immediate and demanding, he didn't think he'd make it to the toilet. Joe concentrated on not wetting himself as he rose from the bed and waddled to the bathroom, each tiny step a new agony. When finally arriving and properly positioning himself in front of the commode, he discovered he couldn't go. Pain. Acute pain flared down there. Followed by nausea sending acid from his gut to his esophagus like a geyser, burning inside his throat. Then came the perspiration - icy sweat flowed from every pore, chilling his body, soaking his clothes and the short, spiky hairs on his head. As he thought to cry out through the wall for Jerry, a trapdoor seemingly opened beneath his cotton socks. Joe crumpled, dropped...

Blackness.

14

For the next three days, Joe lived like a hermit in a cave. After he'd fainted and woke to find himself on the bathroom floor, he knew he hadn't thrown his back out. Kidney stones were the culprits. The self-diagnosis came from the telltale symptoms - pain in the lower back and groin, difficulty urinating, profuse sweating, and vomiting. Both his dad and grandfather had been similarly afflicted, only they'd been older, less active and less health-conscious. It shamed Joe to suffer through what he considered to be a condition of middle-aged couch potatoes. For reasons of seclusion and self-pity, he closed the heavy drapes.

On the first night, he vomited until there were no more contents within his stomach and then cradled his ribs as he retched in agonizing spasms. He then spent his time alternately sleeping and languishing in pain. Soon, lack of nutrition led to fatigue, and every movement became an effort. Jerry checked in on him the second day and graciously complied with Joe's request to bring a case of bottled water, apple cider vinegar, and lemon juice from the corner store. Of course, Joe knew he should make an appointment with a urologist, but he was determined to treat himself with home remedies. As long as he stayed hydrated, this would pass - literally.

The attacks came in summits and crevices. At regular intervals, usually during the middle of the night, a stone awakened him with the tact of a cattle prod. An hour or so afterward, the pain eased to mere discomfort. He drank copious amounts of water and vinegar during the down times. If he tried while afflicted, the liquid would instantly regurgitate. He realized a strange phenomenon during these ping-pong periods. While experiencing bodily pain, he couldn't think about his work problems, his mom's health issues, or anything else. While relatively comfortable, the unspoken accusations threatening his career brought on incessant worry. Moreover, he was tormented by the thought of telling his mom about the destruction of their home and, worse, the possibility of losing her to cancer. Oddly, it seemed emotional pain is a luxury provided only to those free from physical pain. Either that or he was just plain selfish—it was hard to say.

The hours rolled on without meals as markers. Tuesday and Wednesday might've been a single day from his perspective. After forty-eight hours spent swimming in his own sweat, Joe stank. This, in itself, was psychological torture. He had always been fastidious regarding personal hygiene - cleanliness and grooming defined him. Even while dating Rebecca, he didn't like her calling him her beau because the word reminded him of B.O. But, now, not only was he aware of his body odor, something peculiar tainted the stench. Joe wasn't certain, but he thought he recognized an indistinct nursing home smell. Was he checking out? Did death bring a particular, tangible fragrance? He pushed the idea from his mind.

Though he did receive numerous, increasingly concerned texts from Eli and Zoe, and even a reassuring voicemail from his bee-stung mother, he didn't respond. By Wednesday evening, he didn't have the strength to lift his shoulders from the mattress. Besides, if he were going to die, let it be without whining to his loved ones. That way, everyone could memorialize him as a fighter and not the cry baby he really was.

Joe's personal D-day came at two-thirty a.m., and it made the prior assaults seem small. The pain radiated throughout his pelvis and down one leg. It climbed up his spine and crossed over to his chest, balling at his diaphragm, laboring his breaths. On the deck of the boat, he'd been pummeled with hailstones. Now, he was being stoned from the inside. Helpless, he clutched and hugged the pillow. He asked out-loud for forgiveness of all the sins, even the many he wasn't aware of. He pleaded for mercy. None came. Ultimately, Joe B clamped his teeth on one corner of a blanket and wept. The pain surged further, deeper into his being.

15

When Joe awoke Thursday morning, he was OK. Better than OK, he felt renewed. In cautious, small increments, he rose from bed and performed various stretches and calisthenics. No back pain while bending and touching his toes. No stabs during trunk-twists. No nausea during jumping jacks. He recalled his father talking about kidney stones moving or passing without fanfare, the recovery coming on as sudden and complete as an attack, but this was unreal. Joe didn't trust it. He half-expected the stones to return, almost dared them to with increasingly strenuous movements, yet he remained unaffected - no pain, whatsoever.

The impromptu workout stimulated his appetite, and he had a hankering for ham and eggs. He wondered if there was a diner nearby. The simple acts of showering, shaving, and dressing empowered him. And brushing his teeth proved to be outright exalting. Sickness was a prison, he decided, and becoming well was liberation. Of course, the kidney stones might come back, but he'd been paroled. If he drank sufficient water and exercised, he'd stay free.

Joe collected his money and wallet and searched for his room key. It wasn't on the dresser or the floor. He checked pants pockets and inside drawers. He lifted and shook the bed covers - empty. He dropped to his knees and peered under the bed. He hadn't been out in three days, but he tried to remember where he'd left it. Then he recalled giving the key to Jerry when his friend helped him on the night of the first attack. Jerry was at work, but Joe would drop by later and pick it up. During the interim, he'd borrow a spare. He visited the lobby and spoke to the fat clerk within the little cage. The man rolled his eyes and huffed hard at having to rise and retrieve a spare key from the pegboard behind him. He charged the required twenty-five dollar deposit - cash only. Joe returned to his room and locked the door.

It wasn't hard to locate the diner on Ninth Street. With its shiny, curved, metal facade and abundance of plate glass, it looked like a spaceship landed among the grim, block-like structures of the industrial area. Within, the diner definitely paid homage to its 1950s American heritage with all its chrome, swivel stools, bright red upholstery, and checkerboard floor. Joe asked to be seated at a booth, which, despite the bustling environment of the eatery, offered a comfortable amount of privacy. He ordered the weekday special of two eggs, ham, home fries, toast and unlimited coffee refills at a price so low Joe felt guilty accepting it. He'd be sure to over-tip the server—a cute, friendly girl who had a rather unfortunate old lady's name printed on her nametag: Fanny. While waiting for his food, he texted Zoe and asked if she'd be up for meeting at Steeples that night. She answered u betcha and said she'd pass along the invite to Bill and Eli. Joe had intended to meet with Zoe alone, to solicit advice and a shoulder to cry on, but this was alright. Bill gave heartfelt opinions and Eli had a cushiony shoulder. Besides, when you're down, you're supposed to surround yourself with friends, right? He called his mom. She answered on the third ring.

"About time," Gladys said. "Any longer and you might've had to call me at 1-800-6ftunder.

"Don't talk like that, Ma," Joe said.

"Just teasing, Joseph. Don't be so serious. How you doing, kiddo?"

"Never mind me. How you feeling?"

"Well, the first round of chemo went well - the nurses are sweethearts. Did you know it's really a poison they're shooting into your veins? I responded well. The doctor called me a tough old broad. He's a young wisecracker... Anyway, I'm weak and tired, but it's not as bad as people say - not yet, anyway. Ask me two months from now."

"What about the bee sting?"

"That? Oh, that was just your aunt flying into a panic, as always. I wouldn't have even gone to the hospital if I didn't think she'd have a stroke. She was worried about the swelling. It was a little alarming, I'll admit."

"Where'd you get stung?"

"On the back deck."

"No, I mean, what part of your body?"

The pause told Joe he shouldn't have asked, and that now he'd likely regret it.

"The doctor called it the areola," his mother answered matter-of-factly. It's known to be a highly sensitive area. It's the circle around the-"

"Yes, Mom, thank you."

"The nasty little bugger stung me right through my blouse. I should've known better than to wear a flower print. They like flowers. He must've gotten mad when he found out I wasn't a flower. The sting hurt worse than the chemo."

"Bees inject poison, too."

"Don't I know it…"

Gladys went on to detail the effects of the bee sting and Aunt Edna's attempts to bring down the swelling. Joe let his mind zone-out. He didn't really want to conjure a mental image of his aunt Edna applying an ice cube to her sister in a manner reminiscent of the movies Bill liked to watch. Joe waited for her to come to the end of her story.

"Mom," he said. "We've had some storm damage to the house - pretty bad. But don't worry. I'm on top of it. Did you change insurance companies? I need the policy number."

"What storm? We didn't have anything here. A little rain, that's all. I hope you didn't leave the glass sliders open. When that dining room rug gets wet, it takes a week to dry and smells like wet dog."

"Ma, I need the homeowner's insurance policy," Joe said.

"Insurance? Why? How much damage is there?"

"A lot," Joe said. "We need to file a claim."

A long silence. Joe didn't know if his mother comprehended what he was trying not to state directly or if she was merely trying to recall information about the insurance policy.

"But we don't have any insurance. Not anymore," she said, finally.

Joe's chest tightened. The sudden increase of blood pressure within his brain caused an instant headache.

"Whaddaya mean? The bank makes you keep insurance. It's required."

"Not when the house is paid off. Seven years ago, after I wrote the last check for the mortgage, I let the policy expire."

Joe slapped a palm on the tabletop, rattling the knife and fork settings.

"Why would you do that?" Joe said, almost yelling, gripping the table edge, reminding himself she was old and sick. He looked up and around to see if anyone was watching, and lowered his voice. "You shouldn't have done that... You really shouldn't've...

"Joe, we'd paid those robbers for thirty years and never received one penny back. And they kept raising the premiums and they raised the deductible to a thousand dollars. It seemed foolish to keep paying for nothing. And I needed the extra money for..."

Gladys trailed off, not wanting to say. Joe pushed on.

"For what?"

"Never mind."

"No, really."

"Your thirtieth birthday. That little red car of yours. I thought I'd be able to take the money that used to go towards the mortgage but it wasn't enough... Can you believe a car costs more nowadays than what your father and I spent on our house? Anyway, I needed a little extra so I didn't renew the insurance. It's that simple. Call me a dummy, if you'd like. But I wanted to give you a special present."

"But I didn't need a car! I had a car!"

"That old clunker? It spent more time in the shop than on the road. You needed something reliable. Joe, why are you acting like this? What happened?"

Fanny returned to the table with Joe's order, set the plate before him, and poured a cup of coffee. Though the food smelled amazing, Joe's appetite had waned. He thanked the server while turning his watery eyes away. When he returned to his phone conversation, Joe couldn't find the words. A sense of loss overcame him and he found himself babbling.

"Nothing happened," he said. "Everything's good. You know, things sometimes go wrong, but it'll all work out. You know what I mean - over time. But everything's under control so don't even think about it."

"Joseph, you've never been a good liar. Tell me what happened to the house."

Joe took a full breath. "See, the thing is…the house, Ma…it's gone. I'm sure you heard about the tornado in the news last week. Well, it hit one house: ours. But don't worry. I'm going to have it rebuilt. I'm going to hire an architect and have him draw up plans. Everything is going to be like it was. I'll have the house rebuilt and painted the same colors. It'll be like it never happened. I'm going to take care of it."

An agonizing moment of silence followed. Joe waited for his mother to break down. He'd wanted to wait and tell her in person, but she'd pried it out of him. Now he'd have to comfort her over the phone.

She surprised him by chuckling.

"Well, I always wanted a bigger kitchen," she said. "And the living room was always drafty. And that water stain in the ceiling in the upstairs hallway has kept coming back for thirty years. Used to drive your father crazy. Always on a stepstool with his paintbrush. Guess we finally beat it."

She laughed. Joe did not share in the moment. He wasn't sure his motherly fully understood.

"Mom, everything is gone," he said. "It's nothing to joke about. The whole house is wrecked."

Her tone became soft and serious, patient, as if speaking to a child. "Joe, it's all a mist. The house. You and me. This whole life…it's only a vapor."

"What? I don't think you understand, Ma. We lost everything. That's real. The house is completely destroyed, top to bottom. And now you tell me we don't have insurance? I'm gonna have to crack open the Nest Egg. After all these years. I know we agreed to leave the money alone to grow, but this is an emergency. Don't get mad."

"Mad? Take the Nest Egg and scramble it for all I care. What do I need money for? Having money only makes you want more money. If you need it or want to do some good with it, help yourself. Have a Spanish omelet, Amigo."

Gladys went on to talk about how Joe needed a wife. If you live alone too long, you lose your marbles, she said. Then she told a funny anecdote about her recent stay with Aunt Edna as proof. I'm not kidding. Can you imagine? A sixty-eight-year-old woman doing yoga in the nude! I'm living with an old hippie! After they said their many goodbyes and miss-yous and love-yous, Joe disconnected the call and felt better. He hadn't given his mother credit. She was much stronger than he'd thought, maybe stronger than he was. It seemed as people aged, although their eyesight and hearing faltered, and their short-term memories short-circuited, and their bones became bowed and brittle, they gained in one important regard: perspective.

Joe ate his breakfast with renewed vitality, cleaning his plate, mopping the runny egg yolks up with wheat toast. He considered asking Fanny out on a date. Why not? Maybe she was as lonely as he was.

Fanny flatly turned him down without explanation. Regardless, before leaving, he left a twenty dollar bill under a saucer to show no hard feelings.

∽ 16 ∼

Joe drove to Uz. Beating the odds, he located a parking spot at the curb in front of Love Handles - the people who went here liked to park close. The fitness center was unusual in that, in order to maintain a membership, you had to remain at least fifteen pounds overweight. The gym was open and well-lit but by the looks of all the unused treadmills and stair climbers through the glass storefront, few members were placing themselves in jeopardy of being expelled. Joe put two quarters in the meter and made the five-block trek to the pub with an unfamiliar spring in his step and newfound optimism in his heart. It wouldn't last.

Upon finding his friends in a booth, Zoe's eyes already gleamed - not good. She acknowledged Joe's arrival with a bittersweet smile and an over-enthusiastic salutation - also, not good.

"Hey, big guy!" she said.

The other two looked up. Eli appeared glum and Bill looked like one of his parakeets had died. Apparently, Zoe had told them about the suspension. Though he had never sought to be idolized, Joe knew his friends looked up to him. Sort of viewed him as a role model. How far he'd fallen was hard to say. The booth they'd chosen was off to the side, good for talking. Not that it mattered yet. Except for a few patrons at the bar, Steeples was vacant. It wouldn't get loud until the Thursday night crowd of football fanatics shuffled in. Most, including his friends, wouldn't even follow the game. Football, baseball, weekends, holidays, and presidential debates, anything, at all, were an excuse to drink. Joe slid onto the seat next to Bill. He wondered why Zoe had opted to sit next to Eli considering her secret crush. Who knows why people do the things they do? Most have invisible strings they know nothing about. Bill gripped the back of Joe's neck and squeezed in a manly display of brotherhood and affection.

"Hey, stranger," he said. "Why'd you go AWOL on us?"

"Yeah," Eli said. "You haven't returned my calls."

"Give him a break," Zoe said. "Maybe he's had more on his mind than you two dorks." Zoe leaned over the table and kissed Joe on the cheek. "You OK?" she said.

"No fair. How come I never get a smooch?" Eli said.

"'Cause she doesn't want you to hyperventilate and get an asthma attack," Bill said.

"I'll be OK," Eli said, and held up a blue, plastic device as proof.

"That's a Pez dispenser, dummy," Bill said.

Eli laughed at his own absent-mindedness and pulled his inhaler from another pocket.

"You still don't get a smooch," Zoe said. "Not unless you brought a defibrillator, too."

The three laughed and carried on, trying too hard. When things settled, Bill suddenly became vehement. He jabbed a finger in the air for emphasis. "You're being screwed," he said. "I don't even know what's going on at your job, but I know you, Joe - and you're being screwed."

Clearly, the alcohol had already loosened jaws - the worst sign of all. Joe had hoped for moderation. He didn't like when his friends drank. Their mouths lost their filters, which led to arguments, or worse, mushy expressions of love. What he really needed was to talk or maybe to vent. He wasn't looking for advice or a pity party, necessarily. He simply needed to be reminded that people cared what happened to him. Joe needed this night. He needed his friends. But, ultimately, the kind of get-together this would be determined if each person stuck to draft beer or switched to their respective poison. If Bill broke rank and starting throwing back whiskey, Zoe would soon order shooters and Eli would turn to fruity umbrella drinks. The occasion would then devolve into either a fight or a sloppy, emotional, love-fest.

"So... What are people saying around the teacher's lounge?" Joe asked Zoe, trying to be casual.

Bill poured Joe a glass of beer, emptying a pitcher. Bill wore a mostly red Hawaiian shirt with one short sleeve cuffed high, housing a pack of cigarettes in the 1950s bad-boy, Daddy-O style - a disappointment to know he'd started smoking again. Zoe took time responding, looking up as if the answer was written high on the former church's vaulted ceiling.

"Well," she said, and clicked her tongue. "There are a lot of rumors swirling around. Some of the staff says you got caught canoodling a custodian in the showers. Others say you were arrested for hitting her with a mop. But most say you got suspended for exposing yourself."

Joe spoke fast, more angrily than intended. "Public sex? Assaulting women? Lewd conduct? Arrested? That's what my colleagues think of me? I took a shower. That's all I did, I swear. And it's not a suspension, really. It's called administrative leave. I'm being paid."

The trio stared blankly for a moment. Joe felt stupid. Of course he was suspended. He might as well admit it. Arguing semantics was usually a tactic of the guilty.

"Well, that's a good sign. Right?" Eli said. "If it were serious, they would've put you out without pay."

"I guess," Joe said. "Still seems pretty serious to me."

"Did you tell Principal Shelley about your house? That it was destroyed in the storm?" Zoe asked.

"I did," Joe said. "But I wasn't exactly smothered in sympathy. She said I should've applied for a permit before using the showers."

"That's because Principal Barbara Shelley - Babs - is a cold-bloodied b-," Zoe said, pausing for swig of beer, and finishing, "bureaucrat. You can tell Babs I said so."

Zoe's overuse of Babs was worrying. Possibly the empty pitcher hadn't been the first.

"You need the name of a good lawyer?" Bill said.

"The guy who handled your divorce?"

"No, not that douchebag. He gave away the store. I mean the other one for the other thing. Where you staying, anyway?"

"I got a room at a place by the train yard."

"Not the Flea-Fucker! That place is a dump."

"The what?" Eli said, amidst nervous laughter.

"The Flea-flicker," Zoe corrected.

"How would you know, China Doll?" Bill said. "Good girls don't hang in dives like that."

Zoe turned towards Bill and stuck her tongue out.

Had they always flirted like this? And why were they doing it now, while his life was a tiny, single-seat airplane caught in a death spiral?

"I call it the Fleabag, and, yes, it's a dump. I'll be moving as soon as a room opens in one of the bigger hotels," Joe said.

"Let him stay with you, Eli. C'mon, already," Zoe said.

"Can't...I can't even stay with me," Eli said. "My folks and I have to go to my sister's. We got termites - bad. The pest control guys are going to bomb the whole house. We need to be gone for four days. We're moving out the day after tomorrow."

Eli went on to talk about the infestation and how the structure of the house was being attacked, and how if nothing was done, the place would cave in. Joe drank a beer. Bill held up the glass pitcher as a signal to the server.

Elina came and swapped the empty pitcher for a full one.

"Hey, handsome," I didn't see you sneak in," she said to Joe. "You forget your hair at home?"

Reflexively, Joe ran a hand over his scalp. He thought his hair was growing back nicely. Elina was a curvy, dark-skinned, Dominican woman with her own long, coarse, braided locks hanging like ropes in contrast to Joe's spiky shoots. She was almost pretty if you looked beyond the distinct black hairs on her upper lip and the silver stud pierced through one nostril. She'd worked at Steeples for as long as they'd been coming. Five, six years, maybe.

"Be careful, Elina," Eli said. "Don't compliment him. He might ask you to marry him."

Zoe shot Eli a hard look. Bill grinned.

"You guys could elope," Bill said. "And be married by midnight."

"Not sure my better-half would be too happy to hear about it when he gets back," Elina said. "He's got a bad temper and a big bat. Might mistake Joe B's head for the ball."

The group laughed. Elina's husband played professional baseball in the DR for half the year, and the other half he worked as cook in Uz at a Dominican restaurant. Elina was twenty-three and already married. It seemed there was someone for everyone, except for Joe. She poured Joe a beer before rubbing his head and leaving.

Bill went on to talk about his new job. He'd been hired as a shoe salesman at Shoe Heights in the mall. It didn't pay much but with commissions, he'd do fine. Zoe suggested a round of shooters to congratulate him. Bill told funny stories about how some men came to the store and bought shoes without even trying them on. In contrast, a woman might try on a dozen different pairs only to admit she was just browsing. Before downing the shots, Joe and Eli pledged to only purchase their shoes from their friend at Shoe Heights.

Joe tugged the wide sleeve on Zoe's upper arm.

"What's with the Namath jersey?" he asked. "He's way before our time."

The green jersey with the white trim and big number twelve undoubtedly represented the Hall-of-Fame quarterback Joe Namath.

"It's my dad's," Zoe said. "He loved Broadway Joe. He's still a big fanboy."

"Looks cute on you," Joe said, and meant it. He liked when girls dressed as tomboys.

Joe must have lingered too long, staring, pinching the sleeve.

"Dude," Bill said. "Quit going gaga. You're becoming as lame with the ladies as Eli."

"You are," Eli agreed, happily. "He is!"

Joe's skin flushed; he lowered his head and laughed, busted. He turned to Zoe. "What gives? You told Bill? You weren't supposed to tell him!"

"He wasn't supposed to tell I told!" She landed a playful slap on Bill's arm.

"I never claimed I could keep a secret," he said.

"You know. He used to wear pantyhose," Eli said.

The table fell silent.

"He was known for it," Eli explained. "Joe Namath…to stay warm during the games."

The other three rolled with laughter.

"I thought you meant Joe," Zoe said. "Our Joe."

"Me too," Bill said. "And what unmentionables he wears is a secret I could live without you mentioning."

The next time Elina passed the table, Bill called her back for whiskey on the rocks, a double, and thirty hot wings. Zoe asked Joe if he'd like to do a firefight, and he said yes without knowing what it was. Eli ordered a banana daiquiri. The drinks came quickly. Zoe threw hers down her throat while Joe erred on the side of sipping. The drink lived up to its name. The concoction of spiced rum, cinnamon, and tabasco sauce set fire to his lips. Joe recoiled and guzzled another beer. Zoe sniggered and poked his shoulder.

"You are such a big wuss" she said.

Eating the wings required more beer. Elina obliged with another pitcher. It amazed Joe how effortlessly the brew went down and how quickly the pitchers emptied with Bill being exceedingly conscientious about refilling everyone's glass. If he showed this much attention to selling shoes, he'd be a millionaire. Joe wondered if his friends knew he was wealthy - the millionaire next door, as they say.

Joe didn't realize he was getting buzzed until he stood up and excused himself to go to the men's room. The pub hummed. His head hummed. Not surprisingly, his balance was off, but only by a fraction of a degree. He teetered before finding his center of gravity. People cheered. For a weird moment, Joe thought the crowd was giving him recognition for standing, but quickly realized a big play had happened in the game on TV. He looked about, stunned. Steeples now swarmed with people, many looking at the numerous hanging monitors, all showing the same game, the same Hunter green playing field, white uniforms, and blue and gold uniforms, all in crisp colors. When had the crowd arrived? How did they assemble unnoticed? Joe sidestepped, cutting a path through the throng to the restrooms. Excuse me...coming through…he repeated to people who either didn't realize or didn't care to realize he wanted to pass.

The men's room was empty, antiseptic, and strikingly bright compared to the darkened pub. Joe chose a urinal at the end and proceeded to relieve himself.

"Interesting game. Wouldn't you say?" the man said.

Joe didn't look up. And though he hadn't heard the man enter the men's room, he felt the presence of someone standing at the adjacent urinal. Joe hated this. Not only because the man had chosen the nearest one out of several, but Joe didn't like conversing while urinating, not even with friends, let alone a stranger. He wondered if women struck up conversations through the stall walls while peeing.

"Yep," Joe said, looking to end the dialogue without being openly rude.

"You do realize you're going to lose," the man said.

Joe regarded the man with a quick, peripheral glance. He recognized the blinding smile and expensive suit. He'd been talking to the bartender on Monday, on the day Joe had been suspended, before he went back to the Fleabag and had a kidney stone attack.

"I'm not rooting for either team," Joe replied. "Got no investment in the outcome."

The man threw his head back and let out an unbridled, scornful laugh. Joe looked at him curiously.

"Oh, you've chosen a side, the wrong side," he said. "And you're invested more than you know. Come find me when you grow weary of losing. I'll teach you how to be a winner."

Joe made eye contact. In the strong illumination of the bathroom, the man's eyeballs contained no irises; the entire circle glistened black. Joe wondered if he was on drugs to have pupils dilated in such bright light.

"Let me know when you're ready to say uncle," the man added. He winked before turning and walking out the door.

Joe was left puzzled and more than a little grossed-out. Despite the fancy suit and the flashy jewelry, the man had left without washing his hands. Joe felt unclean merely by speaking to him. He pushed up his sleeves as if scrubbing for surgery and washed from fingertips to elbows with foamy soap.

Joe made his way back through the crowd. The room seemed darker. Earrings and necklaces glinted in sporadic flashes. The crowd murmured loudly. Music blared. In addition to the TVs blasting the game, a thumping, old, George Thorogood song – "Bad to the Bone" - resounded against the ancient stone blocks of the church. Had music been playing before? Had more people come? People leaned into and shouted into one another's ears, but Joe couldn't catch a word. Tomorrow was Friday. How many of these drunks would call in sick in the morning in order to recover so they could party more during the weekend?

When Joe returned to the table, he realized he was near-drunk. So were his friends. He could tell by how they were all talking at once, flush-faced, each animated with grand hand gestures that dropped into laps as he slid into the booth.

"What did I miss?" Joe said. "C'mon, you were talking about me. You all have those canary-that-ate-the-cat expressions."

Eli laughed, unable to catch his breath. Uncontrollable, girlish titters was the telltale sign he'd over-indulged.

"You said that back-asswards. Canaries can't eat cats," he said, and laughed again.

"Take it easy, Eli," Bill said. "You're going to wet your panties."

Eli's laugh became a snort, and he took a few deep, labored breaths in order to regain composure. Bill asked if he needed a Pez, which made Eli go into a fit again.

"You caught us," Zoe said to Joe. "We were planning for your birthday. It's in a couple months, right? We were thinking maybe we could take you out or go away or something?"

"Why?" Joe said. "I've had lots of birthdays. We've never done anything special before."

"Well, you know. You've been going through some stuff."

Joe didn't know if it was the sentiment of his friends reaching out to him, or a delayed reaction to losing his home or his mom getting sick or perhaps it was simply the booze, but liquid emotion started flowing through his body like blood. Against his will, he started talking, not knowing what he was saying, not certain if he even agreed with it.

"Thanks, anyway, but I don't really want to celebrate this year or any year," he said.

The three friends smiled cautiously, waiting for a punchline that wasn't coming. Joe wanted to stop, but something pushed him onward.

"I wish the day of my birth never happened. I wish my conception never happened. My father would've done us all a favor if he'd never done the deed…"

Mouths fell open. Joe tried to settle down, but he'd become a rushing locomotive, unable to brake. He spoke loudly, forcefully. He would be heard, no matter what anybody thought. He rose halfway within the booth to an uncomfortable crouch, palms flat on the tabletop.

"It's too bad my birth date can't drop out of the calendar. That day should be a void where the sun doesn't rise. I should celebrate? Are you joking? On that morning, I hope a dark cloud shrouds the entire sky and blackness overwhelms us all. And on that night, I want the stars to fall from the sky and the moon to refuse to shine. Have a party? Take a trip? What's the point of it all? Why didn't I just die at birth? I wish the doctor had shown mercy and cupped a hand over my face before my first breath. Why'd my mother give me soft, warm breasts to suckle from when the rest of the world is so hard and cold? Why bring me into this forsaken place where all I would ever know is pain? Why is all this happening to me? I have no peace, no quietness, no rest... All I have is turmoil."

All stared, blank expressions suggesting varying degrees of shock. Zoe was first to recover.

"Well, bah-humbug," she said. "If you don't want a party, that's fine. But you don't have to be all doom and gloom about it."

Joe sank into his seat and turned his chin to his chest, ashamed. It took a moment before he could speak.

"Sorry. You are the best friends ever," he said. His tongue went thick, a clunky piece of wood within his mouth, and his words came out rounded. And worse, his cognition became jerky and quirky and he wanted to shut-up but couldn't. Instead, he pointed affectionately at each friend, in turn, coining pet names on the fly. "Bill-Daddy-O of Shoe Heights, Zoe-fer the Namath-ite, and Eli-Pez the termite-nator… I don't deserve you guys. I really don't. I just don't understand what's going on. Why are so many bad things happening to me?"

Bill went to speak but Eli held up a hand. "Hold on! I have something to say," he said.

This indicated the gears of Eli's brain had been generously lubed with rum - he never got tough with Bill. Caught off guard, Bill slumped back, silent, dejected. Eli spoke directly to Joe.

"If I tell you what I think, will you at least hear me out? Will you, for once? Will everyone just let me speak?"

Eli must've expected a disruption that nobody intended to make. Joe nodded hesitantly, not happy about where this was heading. Eli adjusted his eyeglasses and ran fingers though his tight curls, seemingly losing mental focus but quickly finding his place.

"Good," he said. "Joseph Bustamante, we don't want to hear you cursing the day you were born. That's not our Joe. You're the most mature and stable and reliable part of our group. You're the training wheels on the bicycle... The bouillon cube for the soup...The donut in the trunk… Our man in the yellow hat… The…"

"Can I interrupt with one question?" Bill said. "How old are we at the end of this story?"

"Let me speak!" Eli demanded. "I will not be silenced!"

"Go ahead, Eli," Zoe said, and waved a few fingers. "You have the conch."

"Alright then… Joe, think of all the times you've helped us out. Whether it was Bill with his legal problems, or Zoe with her relationship issues, or me with my…with my..."

He trailed off, thinking.

"With your phobias?" Zoe offered.

"Your OCD?" Joe said.

"Your insecurities and paranoia?" Bill added.

"Your car repairs?"

"Your hypochondria?"

"Your oedipal complex?"

"Yes!" Eli said, annoyed. "All those things. Joe, you've been our strength and support. But now trouble comes along and you fall apart? You! You're discouraged and disheartened? Shouldn't the way you teach others be your way? What I mean is, shouldn't you rely on living a good life in order to set things straight? That's what you preach to us - and you're right. Consider this: Who, being innocent, has ever perished?"

A moment of reverent silence followed.

"What the fuck does that mean, Eli? You're talking out your ass," Bill said, finally. He drank his whiskey as a single shot, setting the glass onto the tabletop with a sharp clack.

Eli continued, undeterred. "It means we reap what we sow. Right? God is good and, ultimately, the world is just."

"So what are you saying?" Joe said, neck muscles tensing, a small amount of anger burbling in his belly along with the hot sauce.

"I've been thinking about this since your house was wrecked. I mean, of all those thousands of houses, why yours and nobody else's? Hey, I'm just going by what I've seen my whole life. People can skate for a while - sometimes for a very long time - but thin ice always breaks. Think of all the men who cheat on their wives - every single one of them gets caught, eventually. Every one! Think of the celebrities who go around partying all the time and doing drugs - you can't even count the number of ones who've overdosed and died. Everyone cries about how sudden and sad it is, when we really should've seen it coming. What goes around comes around, right? All I'm saying is that maybe, just maybe—and I'm not faulting you for this, we're all human. But maybe you haven't been living the noble life you think you have."

"Get out of town, Eli," Zoe said, and huffed, incredulous. "Joe B is the best man I know."

Eli leaned forward and his tone became hushed, preparing to tell a secret. "Listen," he said. "This is serious. I had a dream last night. At least I think it was a dream. It was like I was awake and there was someone in my room. Every hair on my body stood on end. The room was dark and I couldn't make out who it was - I only saw a form. When he spoke, I heard clearly. The man said can a mere mortal be greater than God? Can even the best man be more pure than his Maker? And then I woke up. Don't you get it? God is perfect and His standard is perfection. We all fall short! What I'm saying is Joe needs to reexamine his life. Hardships don't spring up from the soil! They don't sprout from the ground like weeds!"

"Quit jerking us around, Eli," Joe said. "Say what's on your mind."

"I'm saying you're being punished, Joe. I'm saying you're cursed because of something you've done. This is Sodom and Gomorrah and Noah's flood all in one. What's happening to you is God's correction. Don't despise the discipline. The Almighty wounds but He also heals. Anyway, that's why all this bad stuff is happening to you. You brought it on yourself. It's not just a streak of bad luck. It's bigger than that. Change your life and you'll change your luck, you'll see."

Eli sat back and folded his hands on his belly, content, finished. Joe turned and looked for his two real friends to come to his defense. But what he saw was Zoe with a fingertip to her lips and Bill scratching at his unshaven chin, thinking, replaying Eli's diatribe over in their minds, nodding in agreement.

Then Joe B replied, "So, you've placed my many sins on one side of a set of scales, and the Lord is balancing them by placing His punishments on the other side. God has to do this in order to satisfy His perfect sense of justice, right? Am I hearing you correctly? Well, there's a problem with your theory. If my misery could be set on scales, it would outweigh the sands of the sea. And for what did I earn this anguish? Did I add too many deductions on my income taxes? Did I return a library book late? Did I forget to put the toilet seat down? If I have all these horrible transgressions stacked up, then name them. Go ahead! Haven't I always helped you guys? Haven't I always been generous with my time and money and compassion? Show me where I wronged anyone and I'll shut up. You can't name one time you caught me in a lie, yet you question my integrity. You say I angered God Almighty? Then why doesn't He pardon my offenses and forgive my sins? Isn't He supposed to be merciful and forgiving? What about that?

Bill poured himself a beer. "Hate to admit it," he said. "But Eli might be on to something - we are punished for wrongdoings. I don't think Joe B did it to himself, though. Seems to me, bad fortune runs in families."

In anticipation of objections, Bill held up both palms. "No, no, hear me out. My dad was a drinker, so I'm a drinker. He had...let's say... questionable morals when it came to taking things that didn't belong to him, and today, my sister steals anything she can get her hot little hands on. My dad walked out on my mom and us without even turning his head. And now, I'm scared to have kids because I'll probably do the same."

Zoe looked down, saddened. When she looked back up, she eyed Bill with sympathy and something else. It made Joe think she was seeking much more than a little fling. Bill went on.

"You see, we are nothing more than the sins of our fathers. We're all born into a hole. And because that's all we can see and it's all we ever know, the hole just seems normal. People don't realize they're supposed to climb out of the hole. That's what I'm trying to do. Not having much success, but I'm trying. Think about it, Joe. You need to look back through the years. Maybe the things you think are normal and good are only what you've been taught. Maybe we're supposed to be...more…I don't know what the word is - holy, I guess. It's sad, but I think you're paying for the crimes of the generations that came before because God knows we all just keep repeating the patterns we've learned - and He wants us to break 'em. But it's hard, man. Anyway, that's why I think you're getting screwed now."

Bill sipped his beer and finished the thought. "If you made a chart, it would lead straight back to Adam. He's the one who dug the hole. He's the dude who screwed us all for a friggin' apple."

Then Joe B replied, "Well, thanks for the poetry, Bill, but I have to call B.S. on that. Under your rules, who can be considered innocent? Nobody can. But I'm telling you, I haven't done anything to deserve what's happening to me. I'm completely innocent. For God to hold me accountable for whatever wrongs my great-grand pappy committed isn't justice - it's madness. Is that the God you worship, some mad king? Not me. My

God doesn't arbitrarily dish out punishment to both the blameless and the wicked. So why am I being pronounced guilty? I haven't done anything wrong. There's been a mistake. A clerical error or something. I think…"

Zoe held her hands up to form a letter T, the universal time-out symbol. Her words were slow and slurred. "Whoa, Trigger," she said. "Hold on, there. I must've missed a memo - do you speak for God now? How do you know you did nothing wrong? How can you say you are blameless and flawless in his sight? Are we working off our own definitions of right and wrong and good and evil? I want to hear it straight from Him; let's cut out the middle man…"

They sat a moment, waiting.

Zoe continued, "OK. I guess we're supposed to figure this out on our own. You guys remember my ex-boyfriend, Chad?"

"The cheating, no-good, lying, egotistical pig?" Eli said, by rote. "Yes, I believe we do."

"Yeah," Bill said. "I ran into him at the pier. He was with a real hottie, Tonya - remember her? The swimsuit model? Chad told me he got promoted to V.P. at his company so he bought a new truck to pull his speedboat."

"That's great, Bill. Thanks for that," Zoe said. "It doesn't bother me. Really. Though the evil he's done is sweet in his mouth now - like the powder inside a pixie straw - and it tastes good. He's able to swirl it beneath his tongue so it can linger and he can savor it and make him think he's king of Candyland… "

Zoe had veered from the main lane of rationality, but then she pulled back. "But that pixie dust will someday sour in his stomach. It'll become like the venom of a viper and he'll spit up all the candy he's stolen. God will make him vomit it up. Understand? He will not be allowed to profit from his evil deeds - he won't! The clock is tocking, I mean ticking. Like the proverbial dung beetle that greedily eats too much dung, Chad is sure to drown in the watery poop of his own making."

"I don't think I'm familiar with that proverb," Joe interrupted.

Zoe raised a palm and motioned as if to slap Joe's face, but changed her mind. "Don't get me wrong, Joe," Zoe said. "I'm not blaming you. I'm just saying…"

She didn't need to complete the thought for the song now pounding in the pub finished for her. They all settled, listened, and bopped heads to the steady beat, great guitar riffs, and unequivocal lyrics of Carlos Santana's "You've Got to Change Your Evil Ways."

Then Joe B replied, "Alright. You three had your say. So, hear me now and then go back to hurling insults. Go ahead, mock on!"

The three protested, denied attacking their friend, and offered conciliatory remarks. The commotion attracted the attention of Elina, the server. She stood watching, listening. Joe didn't notice her.

"Look, I've told you repeatedly, I haven't done anything to deserve what's happening to me, yet you still question my integrity. Do I have to stand on top of the table and scream it? Nothing! I've done nothing! And I'm not working off my own definitions of right and wrong, like you say. I'm not! I fear the Lord the way I'm supposed to. But you are correct about one thing. I am declaring myself a good person, righteous in the eyes of God, because I live my life the way he wants me to. So, you might be surprised to hear - I don't going around stealing and cheating and cursing and bullying and lying and getting laid like most people do. I shun evil because I understand my place in this universe. But now my mother is dying and my house was destroyed and I lost my girl and it looks like I'm gonna lose my job - what the heck is going on? I don't deserve this. It doesn't make any sense! What kind of God is out there, anyway?"

The three fell quiet; the bar noise seemed to grow louder.

"Maybe we should ask Ellie," Zoe said.

"Ellie-who?" Joe asked, confused.

Elina stepped closer, pressed her apron between thick thighs and the table's edge. Joe turned and regarded the server with a half-hearted smile.

"Listen to me," Elina said. "I am younger than you but I know more. Joe B, you justify yourself before God? Without even asking him? And you three? If you are truly Joe's friends, why do you charge and convict him without any evidence? Maybe Joe isn't guilty. It could be that his hardships aren't a punishment at all. Perhaps they're just God's way to build his character or to test his faith. Who knows? After going through these troubles, he might be a better man for it. God uses suffering to soften us, to mold us like clay. Our Father uses fire to refine our goodness - even the purest gold must go into the furnace. After all, though God is mighty and just, He doesn't hate anybody. Not even you, Mr. B. He's not out to get you."

There were nods of agreement. Elina left to attend to patrons at a nearby table and then disappeared into the crowd.

Joe remained silent, stupefied, wide-eyed and aghast. How dare they think the matter was settled. Nothing had changed. He had no greater insight. No deeper understanding. And he was still plagued with troubles! That certainly hadn't changed. He'd thought they were his friends. Didn't they care? Bill sucked the ice from his empty glass into his mouth, spit it back in and swirled it.

"Whaddaya say?" he said. "One more round and we'll call it a night?"

Joe rose from the table, slowly, with purpose. He stood fully and spoke boldly. "My eyes have been opened tonight and my ears have heard and understood. I've seen sides of you guys I have never seen before. You three possess qualities I never even imagined."

Eli smiled. "Well, Joe, we're only happy to have help-"

"You didn't help! None of you did!' Joe snapped back. "If I added your three brains together, they wouldn't equal one moron."

"Hey!" Zoe said.

"That's not fair, buddy," Bill protested.

"You accuse me and smear me with lies? Seriously? Look at your own lives? Do you really believe I deserve worse pain than any of you? You want to help me? Heal thyselves, first! You're all a bunch of worthless physicians. All of you! I'm getting out of here. The sinners are demanding confessions."

"Where you going?" Eli cried out, concerned.

"Take it easy, Jo-Jo," Bill said. "You can't drive."

"We'll all share a cab," Zoe said.

"You take a cab. I'm gone."

"Sit down, kid. We're sorry. Let's talk it out," Bill said.

Joe waved a powerful arm. "I'm through listening to the peanut brains of the peanut gallery. I'm taking it up with the Almighty, Himself."

"What are you talking about?" Zoe said, near tears.

Joe pointed to the ceiling. "I'm going to argue my case before Him. I want to know why bad things are happening to me. And He'd better have a better explanation than you three stooges."

A voice came from behind. "Is there a problem here, Joe B?"

Joe spun around to see the stocky, bulbous-nosed, red-headed bartender. This was the first time he'd seen him on this side of the bar, and he seemed shorter. Joe was ready to brawl, but something about the barkeeper's kind, pale eyes disarmed him.

"There's no problem. I'm outta here," Joe said.

"Sure, son? You want to go someplace and talk?"

"I have nothing to say to you," Joe said, and he brushed by the bartender and pushed his way through the crowd, through the heavy wooden door, and into the brisk, wet mist of night air.

He walked the five city blocks to where he had parked his car, or at least to where he thought he had parked the car, but the spot along the curb in front of the Love Handles Fitness Center was empty. A cold drizzle started. He'd spend the next thirty minutes getting wet, getting sober, checking side streets, retracing his steps back to Steeples and back to the gym. Stolen. The Mini Cooper, the birthday gift from his dying mother, had been stolen. The gym was closed, its interior darkened. The only witnesses were the many treadmills and elliptical machines lined up like soldiers. Joe sat on the curb where the car should've been. The drizzle became a downpour. He slouched with head bowed and hands in jacket pockets, feet placed lazily in the gutter, rainwater washing over his new shoes.

∽ 17 ∼

"Impounded? What do you mean impounded? For what? Are you joking? Unpaid parking tickets! I only got one in my entire life and payment isn't even due yet… Yes, it is your fault. I put a quarter in the meter, I swear! Could you run my plate on your computer, again? You guys took the wrong car. My mom gave it to me as a birthday present. This has to be a..."

Joe stood on cement steps within the recessed doorway. Rain splattered loudly on the sidewalks and pavement all around him, making it difficult to hear and necessary to shout. Though already drenched and cold, at least now, by the grace of God, he was shielded within the cramped, brick alcove as he spoke to the police village dispatcher over his cell. When he'd first called the county P.D. to report his car stolen, they surprised Joe by transferring the call to the local village P.D. It was then he'd learned enforcement agents towed the car to a municipal lot.

"Call back? Normal business hours? You're the police - all hours should be normal! How am I supposed to get home? You people stole my car! What? You didn't give me time to pay the ticket! And I didn't deserve it, anyway! I put a dang quarter in, I swear!"

Joe's next call was to Sunshine Taxi. He had the driver stop at the bank. Joe planned to withdraw five thousand dollars. He suspected the Homewreckers demolition guy would want at least that much as a cash down payment once he discovered the residence wasn't covered by homeowner's insurance. The bank, naturally, was closed at this late hour and the ATM only let him withdraw five hundred. The rain had stopped by the time they arrived in front of the Fleabag. He gave the driver forty dollars to cover the twenty-eight-dollar fare and the old man scowled, slighted by what Joe considered a generous tip.

Though the Thursday night football broadcast was long over, the Flea-Flicker sports bar still had customers inside and just as many milling around outside. Strange to see. Steeples was more upscale and the place always emptied after the game ended. This joint always had seedy characters hanging about, a second home to some he supposed. Zoe, Bill, and Eli were each probably home now, sleeping. They had work in morning. He didn't. Joe checked his phone - nothing. He wished they'd called or texted. He felt they owed him an apology. He walked around the building's corner to the motel's alley entranceway. A few thugs hung out, staring without speaking. Joe thought about the four hundred and sixty dollars in his wallet and almost hoped someone would try to rob him. It would give reason for him to crack open a big, frosty can of whoop-ass. Did people say that anymore? Probably not. Joe was always a few steps behind the current trends. He wasn't even sure what the word meme meant, nor did he know of any. The thugs gave him the hard-eye as he passed but no one moved on him.

That proved to be a good thing. The trek up the staircases gave enough of a fight. Joe paused at the top to rest his hand on his knees. He proceeded down the two dim corridors; sadly, the dump was starting to feel like home. He considered knocking on Jerry's door to see if he wanted to watch a late-night TV movie, or, at least to retrieve the room key in order to have his twenty-five-dollar deposit returned by the fat hotel clerk. But Jerry's door was closed and the light was off. Joe knew his friend's construction job started early, so he thought it best not to wake him.

Instead, Joe went to his own room. When he turned on the light, he saw the roaches had taken over. Normally, they confined themselves to the bathroom, but now a dozen dispersed themselves on the walls, ceiling, nightstand, lampshade, window, and, of course, bed. None moved as he entered. What were they waiting for? Were they planning to eat him alive while he slept? He removed his wet clothes and used a sodden sock to swat two shiny, flat ones off the pillow prior to turning out the light. He collapsed onto the bed.

A moment of inner quiet came upon him. It didn't last.

The urge to itch blew over his skin all at once like a bay breeze. Joe told himself it was his imagination triggered by seeing the roaches. He knew the room was filled with bugs, large and small, seen and unseen. It was only natural he'd feel itchy. It was a mental thing. All he had to do was not think about it. Yes, mind over matter…just don't think about it…

He bounded to a seated position and turned on the lamp. He'd thought the red, open wound on his wrist was healing, but now he wasn't sure. Yes, it had scabbed over, but now the itch was unendurable. He removed the bandage and vigorously scratched off the thick crust to uncover a dark patch beneath - the wrist flared with pain. The itch fired in assault rifle-succession at various parts of his body. His elbow…inner thigh…breastbone… Joe tried to resist but found himself scratching hard and fast, fingers curled, back and forth, as if sanding wood. His mind magnified the torment. He imagined his naked body coated with honey and left on an anthill. He needed the heel of a shoe to reach the spot between the shoulder blades that was causing mental anguish as well as physical pain. The more he scratched, however, the more intense it became. No sooner than he'd satisfied one affected area, the itch flared within another. His shoulder...ankle bone...butt cheek…

Joe stripped and got in the shower. Hot water, even tepid water, hit like pin pricks, inflaming his skin, turning it raw and red, sensitive to the slightest touch. Cold water, on the other hand, provided relief. He turned the knob high, full force, the pipe vibrating, protesting behind the walls. The water intermittently slapped the floor, the tub filling faster than the drain could empty. He stood, leaned into the spray, hands flat on the tiles, elbows shaking, legs tightening, groin retracting, and lips turning purple. When he could no longer stand, he kneeled into the shallow pool at his feet, curled elbows to knees, and tucked chin to chest becoming a ball on the floor. The icy torrent landed on his back and ran down his spine and cascaded as duel waterfalls off the sides of his neck. He remained in this position for the next two hours. Not sleeping, exactly, but finding something close to sleep, a numbness of body and mind that mimicked rest.

Rising and turning off the water proved to be a monumental task. His kneecaps were bruised and his neck stiffened. He stood hunched. He lifted heavy arms, fingers like metal rods, their knobby pads swollen and deeply creased, his large hands rendered nearly useless. With mental exertion, Joe commanded his squishy, gumdrop fingertips to turn the cold water off. The silence was alien, eerie. When he stepped out of the shower, he noticed them. Everywhere.

Most were the size of a thumbprint, but one on his inner thigh was the size of a man's hand. The open sores looked like they'd been finger-painted by a child who had only one jar of paint - fire-engine red. The itch had gone completely; Joe felt no pain - none. Yet the crimson blotches peppering his body were grotesque and frightening. They'd manifested on his chest and arm. Belly and back. Scalp and feet. Joe looked into the bathroom mirror. The one on his cheek was particularly worrisome. This sore was a deeper, darker crimson and tender to the touch - his hand jerked away at contact. He told himself the sores were merely hives, an acute reaction to stress. He'd certainly had his share recently. But what if they weren't? Other, more serious illnesses came to mind - scarlet fever...lupus....AIDS... It seemed unlikely these diseases would come on so suddenly. Maybe it was simply a rash or a food allergy.

He went into the main room and grabbed his phone. As he made an internet search for a nearby dermatologist, the phone rang in his hand, startling him. He answered without checking the calling number, expecting it to be Zoe calling to apologize. It wasn't.

"Yeah."

"Joe B, we've got problems. We gotta talk," the voice said.

"Who is this?" Joe said, aggravated.

The man spoke fast, his words hard for an early morning mind to grasp.

"It's me. Things have gone south. I'm at the school - your school. Did ya' read the complaint? We got fucking torpedoed! Wanna meet for breakfast? I'm friggin' starved. I could eat my own dick fried-up with a couple eggs."

It took Joe a moment to make the mental connection. Of course, Nicky Diamonds; the teacher's union delegate said he'd get back to him. Joe hadn't thought it would be this soon.

"What complaint? Torpedoed? What are talking about, Nicky?"

"They sent a copy by certified mail to your house. Didn't you read it?"

"I don't have a house! My house was torpedoed... I mean tornadoed... I mean... I don't know what I mean, but it's not there anymore. And neither am I. I'm at a dumpy hotel by the trains tracks."

"Ahh...so you don't know? No wonder you ain't going bananas."

"Know what? Look, this whole thing has given me a rash or something. I don't think I can-"

"You got to! It's vital! We have to respond before this thing snowballs. We can't sit around with both thumbs up our-"

"Alright! I'll come."

"Do you know the diner on 9th? Meet me there in half an hour."

The call disconnected.

"But they took my car!" Joe shouted into a dead phone.

Joe hurriedly continued his Google search for a doctor. Nicky Diamonds had to be over-reacting. Had to be! He hadn't done anything wrong. That would come out in the end. He found a dermatologist who accepted his health insurance.

"Dr. Shapiro is at a medical conference in Europe for the next two weeks," the receptionist said. "I have something available on the third of next month. Is ten-thirty OK?"

"What? No...really? A two-week conference? No, this can't wait. You don't understand. I have bloody blotches from the top of my head to the soles of my feet. I look like I've been beat-up with a ball-peen hammer!"

"OK, then. Dr. Shapiro's partner, Dr. Spiera, is taking new patients. I can fit you in next week…no, wait. We had a cancellation. How about four o'clock today?"

Joe's next call was to Sunshine Taxi. He'd meet Nicky Diamonds and find out what triggered the panic attack. Then he'd work on getting his car back from the cops. After that, he'd deliver some money to the Homewreckers before the crew walked off the job. Then it's off to the doctor to deal with this pesky rash. It felt good to have a plan. Maybe that's what was missing in his life - order.

He dressed quickly. His wallet was fat with the wad of twenties the ATM had dispensed the night before. Prior to shoving it in his pocket, he removed three hundred dollars and hid the crisp, new bills in a gym sock within a dresser drawer. Now he was thinking ahead. If the thugs in the alleyway did rob him, at least they wouldn't get it all. This left him one-forty in the billfold. Plenty to carry around. Strange, but this simple action made him feel in control. Maybe that was the problem. He'd been leaving his fate to random chance instead of taking action. Maybe one could plot his own course. Be the captain of his own ship, so to speak.

When Joe walked down the flights of stairs and went through the alley to the front of the building, he heard the taxi before seeing it. The driver in the yellow cab at the curb was honking the horn, impatient, annoyed - the same old crab-ass from the night before. He scowled as Joe approached. Joe ignored the lack of civility, opened the rear door, and slid in.

18

The hostess nibbled her bottom lip, pensive. Seemed she didn't want to allow Joe to enter the diner but didn't know how to turn him away. She swayed foot-to-foot holding a large, laminated menu between them as a shield. Reluctantly, she led Joe to Nicky's table where he was already chowing down on sausage links.

"Hey, Joe B. Good to put a face to a-" He set down his fork and held out a hand, but yanked it back. "Zikes! Whatcha got? Ebola or something? Don't mind if we don't shake. I got a thing about germs."

Joe sat across from him. He wished they'd met in a side booth rather than at the center of a busy restaurant - he wondered if Nicky pre-planned this to keep the meeting civil. The union rep might have some bad experiences with people going off. Regardless, Joe didn't like it. He observed, literally felt, the stares of diners at nearby tables and heard the murmurs of conversation, people guessing what malady afflicted him.

"I understand," Joe said. I wouldn't want to touch me either. Don't worry, I'm not contagious. It's only hives."

This, of course, might be a lie and might not. He wouldn't know until after his doctor's appointment later in the afternoon. In either case, the explanation worked. Nicky Diamonds relaxed, eased into his chair and began cutting into the stack of pancakes. Weird how he sliced the pancakes into little triangles all at once, the way a kid does. He looked pretty much the same as Joe had pictured - thin, with angular features and a long, slender nose. Only he was older than he'd imagined, most of his pushed-back hair turned gray.

"No worries," the union rep replied. "The body rebels when under stress. One time when I was getting audited, I was glued to the toilet for two straight weeks."

"On the phone, you said something about a complaint," Joe said.

"Yeah, we got a complaint alright. I'm going to need it back. It's my only copy."

Nicky opened a briefcase on the seat next to him. He removed a folder and shuffled through the papers within. He handed a single sheet over the table. Joe started reading. The language of the text was formal, written in legalese, and Joe had never been much of a student. *Complainant alleges... gender bias... discrimination... harassment... hostile work environment...*

"Fears for her safety!" Joe read out loud. "What does that mean? Why?"

"What can I get y-" the waitress said, her words cutting off as Joe looked up.

It was the same skinny, pretty girl from the other day - Fanny. Her mouth hung open, mid-phoneme, in horror.

"Nothing," Joe said. "I'm not hungry."

"Have something," Nicky Diamonds said. "The Great Wall of pancakes is amazing."

"Just coffee," Joe said, and continued reading.

"Bring him a blueberry muffin," Nicky said. "And wrap one for me to go."

The server nodded without removing her gaze from Joe. Did he look that bad? Like a car wreck? Nicky Diamonds watched her walk away.

"You know her name's Fanny, as she has a really cute one, a little cantaloupe…You'd have to look at her mom's to know if it will last, though. Could grow to be a watermelon."

"What does this mean?" Joe said, shaking the sheet of paper. "How could she say this? It's all lies!"

"Well, the first thing it tells us is she didn't write it herself. She's got some shyster lawyer coaching her. Hey, why not? They know the school district has deep pockets and an aversion to bad press. So, your little cleaner friend has been convinced she's going to roll away with a mop bucket full of money."

"But none of it is true!" Joe said. "What are they saying? That I attacked her?"

Nicky Diamonds put on a pair of reading glasses and took the sheet back.

"OK, if you ignore the to-wits and other legal mumbo jumbo, she's saying when she went to the locker room to clean, you were waiting."

"Waiting? I was showering."

"Well, she says you either knew or should have known she'd be coming because she's cleaned the boy's locker room the same time every morning for the past six years. She's calling it stalking."

Joe went to interrupt but Nicky Diamonds held up a finger. "She goes on to allege you grabbed your privates. You then stepped out of the shower towards her and said, 'Let me, let me...' She fell trying to get away. You tried grab her and pin her to the floor while shouting, 'I'm trying to... I want to...' She implies you wanted to do her on the floor. Did you really proposition her by saying *Seamos amigos*? Apparently it means *let's be friends*. Hey, has that ever worked for you? I might try it. Anyway, she needed to kick you in order to get away. The attack - her word not mine - caused injuries to her knee, neck, back, and head, leaving her in constant, intense pain. She is accusing you of intentionally creating a situation that led to soft tissue damage, frequent headaches, emotional distress, and night terrors - oh, that's good, not only nightmares but night terrors - as a result of the abuse. The victim - I'm sorry, I shouldn't use that word. The complainant states you have displayed a pattern of sexual harassment and that the school either knew about it or should have known about it by frequently leering at her whenever she bends over to wipe something or to fasten her sandals. She's claiming gender discrimination, racial discrimination, sexual harassment, and physical intimidation. She fears for her safety and cannot return to work due to blah, blah, blah.... And she's seeking your termination along with compensatory and punitive damages from the school lest civil litigation be pursued."

"This...she... This can't be happening. This complaint is bull-"

Fanny returned with the muffins and poured Joe a cup of coffee, diverting her gaze from Joe's pock-marked face. Nicky Diamonds waited for her to leave.

"Of course it's bullcrap," he said. "We know it. The cleaner knows it. Her lawyer knows it. And even that nasty munchkin principal of yours knows it. But it's been written down in a sworn document, so we'll have to respond. Our guy will draft a rebuttal."

Joe hung his head, shamed by the accusations. The attack on his character was worse than kidney stones.

"So, what happens now?" he said.

Once again, Nicky Diamonds pulled out the folder from the briefcase. He removed a sealed envelope and held it out.

"After they faxed the complaint, I hauled butt to see Shelley before she did anything rash. It was too late. The superintendent is on her. The school board is on him. They've suspended you, Joe - without pay. The district is having their attorney write up the charges as we speak."

Charges?

The room spun. The checkered floor, the shiny chrome, the chattering, indifferent patrons, their tables, coffee cups, orange juice, plates, and clinking silverware, all revolved in a tornado of manufactured fakeness. Someday, this diner would no longer be here. Neither would the people. Did anything last? Was anything actually real? As blood pulsed within Joe's temples, the room slowed and stopped. He became wet with sweat.

Nicky set the envelope aside. "Charges don't mean guilt, ' he said. "We can fight this or..."

Joe's mind drifted. He replayed the scene in his head while rambling out loud. "I did put my hands down there, but that was only to cover myself. I never said Ven whatever. I don't even know Spanish, except hola and adios and I don't remember saying those. I don't think I said anything. I've never leered at any woman. Not in my life. Once I saw a girl's top fall off at the ocean, but that was an accident. I'm not sure I ever met Clarabella before that morning. I didn't step out of the shower stall. I don't know why she'd say I tried to pin her to the floor…"

"It makes their case stronger," Nicky Diamonds said softly, a weighty look of sympathy pulling his face downward.

"So, what happens now?" Joe said, though he suspected what came next.

"They want you gone, Joe," Nicky said. "And it's not Principal Shelley; it's the district administration. There's no official offer yet, but I think they're looking to force you out. She wants you to resign - came close to saying so. It would be the usual settlement: charges dropped, accrued vacation and sick leave paid in a lump sum, a neutral reference..."

Nicky Diamonds trailed off and waited. Joe drummed his fingers on the tabletop. "I guess that would be a pretty sweet deal," he said. "For a guilty man."

Nicky Diamonds held up two palms and moved them up and down as a set of scales.

"Guilt and innocence...do they really exist? And if they do exist, do they really matter? In this post-Cosby, post-Weinstein work environment, do you want to get involved with a he-said, she-said disciplinary hearing? What makes you think your testimony would be believed over the poor, traumatized cleaner's testimony? The woman is a single mom who works two jobs to feed five kids. You'd be going before an arbitrator and the decision would be binding. Who knows how he or she would see it? Bottom line is, you were undressed at work without asking or telling anyone - you admit this. She says you came onto her - aggressively. If they believe her story, you're fired. Then, try finding another job as a teacher!"

Joe looked up to the ceiling, took a full breath, and mulled this thought over for a moment. "Tell you what, Mr. Diamond," he said. The chair scraped the floor as Joe pushed backwards. He rose from the seat and continued, "When the administration does make the offer, please do me a favor. Tell 'em to shove it. Yes, guilt and innocence are real and they do matter. And I'm innocent! I didn't do anything wrong. I won't give up my job. I won't be railroaded."

Nicky Diamonds motioned with a hand towards the chair. "Joe, please, we're on the same team," he said, lowering his voice as a signal for Joe to do the same. It didn't work.

"Are you sure about that? I didn't do anything! Nada! Did I say that right? I did nothing! Don't call me until you believe me," he said.

Before Nicky Diamonds could object, Joe strode away from the table.

"Hey, you forgot your muffin!" Nicky shouted from behind.

Joe brushed by a busboy, sliced a path around Fanny, and passed the frightened hostess. He threw open the glass door and exited the diner, stumbled but caught himself, bounding down the steps. He waved an arm in the air.

19

What the...? Joe stood in the doorway. He checked the room number - 402. Of course this was his room, his key had opened it. Yet it was different. Empty. What he viewed was difficult to comprehend. The bed was still there and the dresser and other furnishings were, too, but his things, all his belongings, were missing. The towel draped over the chair, the sweatshirt, the shoes under the bed, the toiletries on top of the dresser, even the sheets were gone. Joe pulled out the dresser drawers. Pants and underwear - gone. Shirts - gone. Socks - gone. The three hundred dollars stashed in the sock - gone. Stolen? During the morning hours? Not a chance. He'd only been away an hour. He looked about. Maybe a maid had come and tidied up, though this seemed unlikely. Joe hadn't seen a maid since he'd checked in. Had the management moved him to a different room? Maybe. But why? He'd ask Jerry if he saw anyone messing with his stuff.

His neighbor didn't answer the knock on his door. Probably at work. Joe trotted down the four flights to the tiny lobby. The fat clerk behind the barred window fiddled with a portable AM/FM radio balanced on his beanbag belly, trying to pull in a station.

"Excuse me," Joe said.

The clerk set the tuner to a religious broadcast with clear reception but then continued moving the dial to select a shock-jock program, mostly static. He swiveled the old radio's antenna in various directions with no improvement.

"Excuse me!" Joe repeated.

"Piece of junk doesn't work for shit," the clerk said. "Hourly or nightly?"

"I'm already staying here. You know me. Did somebody go into my room?"

At first, the clerk looked confused. Then a half-smile of recognition crept across his face.

"I know you. You're the key guy. Your buddy returned the spare - skinny dude, long hair, creepy tats."

"Jerry? He returned my key?

"Yeah. Get your twenty-five bucks from him."

"You gave him my deposit?"

"Don't look at me. If you didn't trust him, you shouldn't have given him your key."

Frustrated, uncertain, Joe looked around the lobby. A lone potted rubber tree decorated the small space. It looked surprisingly healthy and shiny. Joe couldn't tell if it were real or fake. He turned back to the clerk.

"So, you didn't move my things to another room?"

"Whaddya talking about? We don't touch people's stuff unless you leave it after checking out."

"Then who did?"

As comprehension dropped upon him, Joe slapped a hand on the paneled wall startling the clerk. He fumbled the radio but caught it. The device lost all reception and hissed.

"Did Jerry check out? The guy with the hair and tattoos? Is he gone?" Joe said, impatient.

"Yeah. Left about a half-hour ago. Returned your key at the same time."

"Did he have a lot of things with him? Bags of clothes and stuff?"

"I don't know. People come, people go. I just work here."

"That bastard stole my stuff! You got to call the police. Hurry!"

"Hold on, bro. If your friend took your shit, that's between you and him. We don't get involved. If you want to call, go ahead, knock yourself out. The cops may come, but they won't care."

Joe grew indignant. "Not even if he took three hundred dollars cash?"

"Not really. Not here. You should see what happens when someone offs himself in a bathtub or O.D.s or something. I've seen 'em drag the body down the stairs by the ankles, bouncing the skull off every step. Used to bother me."

"It should still bother you!" Joe shouted. "Right and wrong should matter!" Without conscious thought, he turned and barreled out the main door and into the street.

He looked around, considered calling a cab, but decided it would take too long. On impulse, he bolted across the boulevard, cutting in front of a white commercial van. The driver swerved, leaned onto the horn, and cursed out his side window. Joe covered the two blocks with a brisk, determined stride. His blood pumped. His adrenaline spiked. He darted around parked cars at the train station lot and bounded up the fifty cement steps leading to the platform. He clenched his teeth and fists, growling like a junkyard dog. Would he accuse first or strike first? Strike first. He pictured what he'd do. He'd lay Jerry out with a sudden, wild haymaker. If the no-good, two-faced thief pulled a knife, Joe would hoist one of these metal trash cans and… He didn't know what, but he wouldn't get away with this. Con man! Crook! He'd stomp his head. He'd step on his throat. He'd beat him until…

Empty. Just like his motel room. The platform was vacant. No Jerry. No one else, either. A ghost station. Joe looked up, read the electronic display. The morning commuter trains had already departed with none scheduled to arrive. He'd missed him. He'd gotten away.

Joe melted onto a bench. He stared over the concrete platform, beyond its yellow warning stripe, to the sets of rails far below. Instantaneously winded and physically spent, he breathed hard, a deep sadness displacing the anger inside his heart. He'd trusted him. And Jerry had used that trust to betray him. How could anyone be so dishonest? So mean? The dirty pigeons squabbling over a blackened banana peel had no answers. Or maybe they were the answer… Where did he go? Where did these tracks lead? They led to anywhere and they led to nowhere. It seemed unlikely they would ever take Jerry to happiness. But was Joe any better off? What was his direction? Was there any place in this lonely, too-big world where Joe B might find joy?

A weight compressed his chest and a fear of suffocation came over him. There wasn't enough air on the platform. No wind. Not the slightest breeze. Nothing to oxygenate his body or spirit. Fatigue, a forlorn weariness, settled into his bones. Joe wanted to lie down. He resisted a vague urge to jump off the platform and nap on the tracks. Instead, he plodded down the long flight of stairs and along the busy streets, between cars and in front of box trucks, passing the liquor emporium, the vape shop, the Cash for Gold outlet. Slowly, with monumental effort, with every thought a lament, every step a chore, he returned to the Fleabag. To the four flights of stairs. To the dank corridors. To his empty room. To desolation.

20

"Please fill out this. And this. And sign here. And complete this. And initial here. And I'm going to need to photocopy your insurance card," she said. "And let me know if you have any questions."

The receptionist handed the clipboard to Joe from behind the sliding glass. Seemed he was the last scheduled appointment of the day, yet the receptionist remained pleasant, not in a rush. She smiled when Joe asked for a pen, not revolted by his appearance as he'd expected. Somehow, the young woman with the stringy hair and the overbite was prettier for her compassion. Joe glanced at the package of sheets. He wondered if his suspension from work affected his health insurance coverage but decided not to ask. He'd been lucky to set up an appointment on short notice. Mentioning the problems at his job would be like, as Bill was fond of saying, shaving his testicles with a hatchet - nothing might go wrong, but why take the risk?

He took a seat in the large, posh, waiting area and busied himself filling out the required insurance forms and medical history questionnaire. He looked up, trying to recall when he'd first noticed the sore on his wrist. This place was upscale. Certainly, no walk-in doc-in-the-box as Joe was accustomed to. The floor tiles weren't hospital white but brown terracotta. Moreover, artwork, lovely, blurry paintings of flowers and waterways hung here and there. Built into a far wall, a long, narrow marine aquarium was a living, hypnotic work of art. He gazed at the display of craggy, coral-covered rocks where tiny, brightly colored fish darted about and anemones like thin, jellied fingers swayed peacefully in the current. Joe pulled his mind out of the trance and returned his attention to the forms.

He was alone in the room except for a well-dressed woman on the adjacent loveseat. She flipped through an architectural magazine, viewing stately houses and manicured landscapes that regular folks would otherwise never know.

"I'm sorry," Joe said. "Do you know today's date?"

Of course it was a stupid question. Only unemployed bums don't know the date. The woman looked up from the magazine and answered. She then closed it and gave her full attention as though offering assistance. The woman was a looker in a quiet, dignified manner. Her cheeks were chiseled, her entire bone structure, actually, was pronounced without sacrificing femininity. Her lightly tanned skin contrasted nicely with the darkness of her eyebrows, and her hair was neatly pulled-back, entwined in a thick braid. Had Joe's mother been here, she would've described her longish face as being handsome. And though the term has been lost to modern society, Joe would have agreed. The lady was an anachronism. He could relate. Joe often felt vaguely out of place and time, himself. She seemed more so, however. Considering her manner of dress and comportment, the woman might've been a starlet of the silver screen, the Mexican cinema, perhaps, of long ago. She crossed her legs and rested her elbows on knees familiar and comfortable with wearing a skirt. When she oriented her body towards him, Joe noticed a silver necklace at the open collar of her blouse. Probably, she wasn't Hispanic. The chain displayed a tiny Star of David.

"They ask a lot of you, don't they?" she said, sweet, patient like a good school teacher.

"I don't go to the doctor's often," Joe said, clumsily.

"I'm here too often, "she said, and offered a sad little smile.

Joe wondered what afflicted her. Probably something cosmetic. Skin tag removals or whatever.

"I don't normally look like this," Joe said, needing to explain. He made a circle in the air around his face with the pen. "This came on overnight. I think it's hives."

If his condition repulsed the pretty lady, she did an excellent job hiding it.

"I'm sure you'll be very happy with Dr. Spiera. He's well-recommended. My husband and I have been coming frequently. He has melanoma."

"Oh," Joe said because he didn't know what else to say. Why did people get cancer? Nobody deserved it. Joe wanted to bring up his mom's cancer, but decided against it. Sharing his pain would do nothing to help relieve hers. He mentally tried to patch something supportive and optimistic together by adding, "Well, the treatments for that are very advanced, nowadays. Right?"

There was that little sad smile again. "We're receiving good care," she said. She held out a hand. "I'm Ruth,"

"I'm Joe. But we'd better not. I could be contagious. And you don't want what I got."

Her hand remained out, even as a nurse opened a door and called for him.

"Joseph?"

"Well, so long," Joe said to his new acquaintance. "Nice meeting you."

"It's going to be okay, Joe," she said. "Everything works towards our good. We must put our trust in that and not rely on our own strength."

Joe nodded in agreement, though he wasn't sure he agreed. He wasn't even sure he comprehended what the lady's cryptic comments referred to. His skin condition? Her husband's cancer? Who knew?

The examination office looked the same as any other he'd been in - cramped. A counter with a tiny sink and boxes and jars with swabs and other supplies. A colored chart. A rolling metal stool. A light on a moveable arm. A high bench seat covered by a roll of white paper. The paper crinkled as he sat on it. The nurse left saying the doctor would be in shortly. Joe waited. And waited... He wondered if he had to wait, why he hadn't been left in the waiting room. There, he could talk to the friendly woman, at least. His skin itched, but he suspected that was only because his mind was focused on the sores. They looked worse but felt better. He saw this as an improvement.

The door swung open and the doctor entered.

"Mr. Bustamante, I'm Dr. Spiera. Goodness. Let's see what we have going on here."

He sat on the stool and perused the pages on the clipboard. He set it aside and pulled a blue pair of rubber gloves from the breast pocket of his thin, white jacket.

"When did this come on? Last night, you say?"

Joe told the story of the sore on the wrist and about staying at the seedy hotel and the itch attack he'd suffered through. The doctor turned on the light and maneuvered it into position. He put on a thick pair of eyeglasses of which one of the lenses had a little scope attached. To Joe, he looked like a jeweler evaluating a diamond. But, of course, he wasn't. The doctor was searching for parasitic organisms, the microscopic bugs that can eat you alive. At first, he used a gloved finger to press the open raw sores on the hands and forearms, and Joe felt discomfort. Then, he opted for what looked like a metal pencil to poke and prod the purplish one on the cheek. This hurt like…

Joe jerked back.

"Hmpff…" the doctor uttered, and continued the examination.

After a few moments of silence, Dr. Spiera rose and pulled a fat medical journal off a shelf. He flipped to the index and scanned, running a finger down the page. He turned to the middle section of the book and read in silence, intense concentration furrowing his brow.

Joe watched him read. To say the doctor was a good-looking man would be an understatement. Dr. Richard Spiera was tall, tanned, physically fit, and strong-jawed, with a healthy mane of dirty blonde hair, combed back except for a rogue lock falling over his squarish face. Joe's feelings were mixed. Though, so far, the quality of medical care was fine, Joe felt ambivalent towards his soap opera doctor. Likely, this was due to experiencing an unfamiliar twinge of envy. The guy was his own boss. He ran a successful, upscale practice in an exclusive medical building in the best part of town. He probably drove a luxury car and parked inside the three-car garage of a sprawling house on a lake with walls of windows and open-air decks overlooking the private dock where he kept his sailboat. Dr. Spiera looked nice, smelled nice, and probably had a nice, gorgeous investment banker for a wife. And what did Joe have? Nothing. Nobody. A skin disease so rare, a full-time dermatologist had to look it up in a book.

"Have you been out of the country, recently?" Dr. Spiera said.

"No."

"Had a mud bath in an unlicensed facility?"

"No."

"Gone more than ten days without washing?"

"No."

"Come in contact with any dead animals?"

"No."

"Ingested any fecal matter?"

"What? No!"

"Well, this is peculiar. I've never come upon this before, but…" He went back to poking with the shiny, metal stylus.

"But what? What is it, doctor?"

"Looks like invasive dromedary camel worms. They're a parasite, a bigger, badder cousin to hook worms, which we see from time-to-time. They're ancestors to the common ringworms we find in domestic cats."

"I knew it! I've been staying at a seedy place by the train yard. I sprayed the mattress but I guess it wasn't good enough. It's infested, right?"

"Oh, I don't think you picked up camel worms in a motel room. And I'm fairly certain those nasty buggers are the culprits." The doctor handed Joe a magnifying glass and used the stylus to direct his attention to a sore on his arm. "Take note of the red tracks. If you look closely, you can see the wounds are connected by tiny, hair-like tunnels. The parasite that causes this pattern of markings is found only in the intestines of certain large mammals. The type that come almost exclusively from animal feces, primarily camel dung, hence their name. These open sores are called cutaneous larva migrans, and they come from the parasites burrowing into the skin and laying eggs."

"Lovely," Joe said. "What can we do to get rid of 'em?"

"I'll apply a strong, topical antiparasitic cream here. And I'll give you a prescription for a stronger one and a special soap along with an oral antibiotic, just in case any of the sores become infected."

"That's all? That's not too bad? Right?"

"No. It's not too bad," Dr. Spiera said, unsure.

"What's wrong, Doc?"

"Well, eradicating the parasites doesn't necessarily solve the riddle of how you acquired them to begin with. First off, they're not from this part of the world. They're mostly seen in the Middle East. And, secondly, when it comes to parasites, they're a great, great granddaddy."

"What do you mean?"

"I mean, camel worms were common during ancient times, but they are rarely, if ever, seen today."

"Lucky me. I guess I won the prize," Joe said.

This caused the doctor to pause, look over his eyeglasses, and smile. "We can get rid of them," he said. "But we also want to make sure they don't come back. If you did get them from your hotel room, it's time to move."

The treatment took considerable time. When it was over, Joe had thick white blotches of white war paint all over his body and face. The markings were even more noticeable than the original open sores. He thanked the doctor and was directed to see the receptionist to schedule a follow-up visit. The doc told Joe he'd be on vacation the next week but would like to see him after that. Joe returned to the lobby area and was disappointed to see the lady he'd met, Ruth, was gone. The waiting room seemed larger, desolate by her absence. The pleasant, stringy-haired receptionist was also gone for the day. At the desk behind the sliding glass sat a different woman—a good-looking gal with dark hair, a nice yellow skirt, a matching blazer and a familiar face.

"Rebecca!" he said.

"Joe!" she said.

They stared, trying to make sense of this encounter.

"W-what are you doing here?" she said.

"Seeing the doctor. What are you... You work here?" Joe said. "What about the beauty shop?"

"No. I don't work here. Vicky had to pick up her son from aftercare. I was...covering.... What happened to your face? You saw Dick?"

She tilted her head and squinted, confused. Joe nodded yes though he hadn't understood the question.

"Who?" he said.

"Dr. Spiera. You had an appointment with Richard Spiera, my boyfriend?"

"Dr. Dick...I mean, Dr. Spiera is your boyfriend?" Joe said, utterly perplexed. He pointed with a thumb beyond Rebecca's workstation, towards the examination rooms. "Are we talking about the same Dick?"

Rebecca peeked over her shoulder and spoke in a lower, deeper tone. "Joseph Bustamante, did you do this on purpose? To spy on me?

"What? I didn't know he-"

"O-M-G... You are so friggin' immature! How could you?"

"What? No? Are you crazy? You think I gave myself parasites? Dick was the only one who'd see me today."

She looked over her shoulder once again. They continued in restrained, harsh whispers.

"Stop calling him that!"

"You called him that!"

"I'm allowed to call him that! Just get out of here. And take your bedbugs with you!" Rebecca said, and waved a dismissive hand.

"They're worms! Camel worms, to be precise. And they're very rare," Joe responded with no small amount of pride.

"Just go already! You're gonna mess everything up."

"Whaddaya mean? Mess what up?"

"Do you know how hard it is to meet a doctor? You need to have class. I told Richard I was on the rebound from a serious relationship with a sophisticated, handsome, well-to-do college professor - not an immature, baldy-bean gym teacher with camel slugs."

"Worms!"

She lowered her face towards the desk and looked side-to-side. "Whatever. Just go!"

"You're embarrassed of me? Your EX-boyfriend? That's insane!"

"Go!"

"I can't."

Rebecca's dark-painted lips contorted. Lines formed in her forehead as she tightened her long, bony fingers into fists and shook them. "Why not?" she whined.

"Because you have to make me an appointment first."

"You can't come back here! Not to this office! Find a new doctor!"

'"But I like him," Joe said, without thinking. "I'm happy for you."

Neither spoke for a moment until Rebecca softened. "Really?"

Joe didn't respond. After emitting a huff of air, Rebecca sat, adjusted the chair into position, and clacked at the computer keyboard while studying the monitor. "OK. But don't tell him we know one another. Let's see…next week is no good."

"Because he's taking you to the Bahamas, right? And you're going even though you hardly know him."

Rebecca moved the mouse and clicked. Her painted nails looked nice.

"Don't start, Joe, please." She tapped at the keyboard some more. "How's you mom?"

She'd always asked about her. If Joe didn't know better, he'd suspect Rebecca loved his mother.

"I think she knows she's dying but is afraid to tell me."

Saying this out-loud gave it weight, made it real. Of course, he'd known her fate, his fate, all along, but wouldn't allow the thought into consciousness. But now that it had breached the barrier, there was no denying it. His mom was dying… His mom was dying…

"I'm sorry," Rebecca said, not disputing the statement as he'd hoped. She knew, too. Everybody knew. To his surprise, she added, "If you need to talk to somebody, give me a call."

Taken aback, weakened, Joe said nothing. He wished they'd go to a waiting room sofa and hold hands and talk right now, but things don't work like that. Rebecca wouldn't do that. And Dr. Spiera certainly wouldn't understand. Human kindness only goes so far. And it's not far enough.

"Thank you," Joe said.

"OK," Rebecca said. "How's Friday in two weeks? Same time? That way you won't have to take off work. I remember how you feel about doing that."

She smiled. It was a nice face. When she was happy, Rebecca had a face you wouldn't mind looking at forever. Joe didn't want to ruin the moment by telling her he'd been suspended - that she needn't worry about his work schedule, that any time was good, nowadays.

"That would be perfect," he said. "Hey, you have a great trip. Bring your sunscreen. Don't let yourself get burnt."

Rebecca looked up; trying to read him, but Joe showed no outer expression of his inner pain. He turned and walked towards the lobby exit door.

"Joe..." Rebecca called out.

But Joe opened the door, stepped into the carpeted corridor, and closed the door behind him.

21

Joe couldn't fault her for being suspicious. With his spiky hair and yellowed bruises from the hailstone storm and the white blotches from the anti-parasitic medication, he must've been a sight. Besides, fifteen-thousand dollars was a lot of money. After repeatedly looking, matching his driver's ID photo against his face and checking and re-checking his account balance on the computer monitor, the teller behind the high counter excused herself to consult the branch manager. The manager came to the workstation and repeated the process. Ultimately, albeit reluctantly, she signed and stamped the withdrawal slip as a signal for the teller to proceed.

"How would you like it?" she said.

"Three hundred in twenties, the rest in hundreds," he said.

Of course, this would deplete Joe's savings down to near-nothing, but what choice did he have? The suspension at work meant he'd no longer be drawing a biweekly paycheck. He needed money to survive. To eat. To replace the clothes and other belongings Jerry stole. To move to a better hotel, preferably one that didn't come with complementary worms. He also still needed to pay the demolition company for the work they'd started on his former house, though now, he didn't care if the crew walked-off the job. With his mother dying, rebuilding no longer was a priority. The teller asked if he wanted the money put in an envelope. Joe said yes.

He went back to the cab - the driver had waited like she'd promised. The money bulged within his front pants pocket. He patted it several times to make sure it hadn't vanished. He wondered what his two million dollars in Pillbox Pharmaceutical shares would look like if he cashed out all at once. Would it fill a suitcase like in a movie? Two suitcases? He might have to crack-open the Nest Egg soon. Unload a few hundred shares, at least. The fifteen grand was a fat wad in the pant leg at the moment, but it wouldn't last. The taxi fares, alone, were costing a mint. Rent, even more so - he'd have to find a cheap apartment soon. Selling-off would be a shame, however. His grandpa's baby, the biotech stock he'd invested in sixty-five years ago, would presumably double over the next few months. Robber Barons Monthly rumored that Pillbox was going to be swallowed-up by Brighter Tomorrow, the largest drug manufacturer in Hong Kong. If the acquisition was approved by the SEC, Joe needn't worry about his suspension. Heck, he wouldn't have to work at all - not ever.

His next stop was the Village PD station where he thanked the cabby and doled out thirty dollars over the fare. There, the uniformed desk officer acknowledged the Mini Cooper had been impounded by mistake - his plate number being one digit off from that of a repeat parking offender the cop referred to as some low-life scofflaw. Apparently, the enforcement agent had typed in the wrong number setting off a chain of events, the last link being the towing of Joe's car. For procedural reasons not made clear, the officer required Joe to pay three hundred and twenty-five dollars, cash only, to obtain the car's release. Muttering only a token protest, Joe paid the fine and surcharges under the assurance he'd be reimbursed in four to six weeks. As a gesture of goodwill, the desk cop arranged for a different cop to drive Joe to the impound lot in a marked SUV.

The holding lot turned out to be located in an enormous junkyard at the outskirts of town. This designated area was nothing more than open space of dirt and mud puddles with a single posted sign prohibiting trespassing. When Joe found his little red car packed tightly among two dozen other vehicles, including a large RV and a stretch limo, he immediately noticed a gouge in the paint. The thick, undulating, scratch ran the length of the driver's side, front quarter panel to rear quarter panel. When Joe pointed out the damage to the officer, the cop appeared disinterested.

"Maybe it was there all along and you never noticed it," he said.

Joe insisted he'd been meticulous, almost obsessive, regarding the care of his car. "It was a thirtieth birthday present from my mom," he offered as definitive proof.

"Don't look too deep. Three dollars' worth of compound ought to take it out," the cop replied.

When Joe inquired about having it repaired properly at a body shop and receiving compensation, the cop said the police department wasn't responsible and that he'd have to take it up with the towing company. Joe said he'd definitely do that with both of them knowing he never would. After about twenty precise maneuvers - reverse, drive, cut-the-wheel, forward, cut-the-wheel, reverse - Joe freed the car from its confinement. It wasn't until he turned out of the weedy, bouncy, dirt ruts of the junkyard and onto the smooth, paved, open roadway did he feel better. Being in his car brought a sense of liberation. For the first time in a week, he had a feeling of control. He was in the driver's seat now. Joe lowered the windows and let the cool air rush in.

He drove to Drake's Department Store and repurchased the clothes and supplies Jerry had lifted. Joe even replaced the shoes; though it seemed weird his neighbor had stolen them as it was unlikely they wore the same size. Thieves steal, he supposed. They take anything for the same reason coyotes howl at the moon. It's in their nature, part of their DNA. He removed money from the envelope discreetly, not wanting to draw attention to the huge sum he carried. He left the checkout with four large bags. The plan was to check-in at an upscale hotel, drop off his things, and then return to the Fleabag and say goodbye to the hole-in-the-wall hotel and its fat, uncaring clerk forever. The plan was naive.

"I'm sorry. We are not going to be able to accommodate you," the manager said. "If you like, I can direct you to nearby hotels or emergency housing services."

Joe stood holding bags in a huge, open-spaced, glass wall and ceiling atrium that were the lobby of the Eaton. The manager on the opposite side of the reservation desk was short, round-faced, and nearly bald but neatly groomed. He looked spiffy in a red jacket, shirt collar buttoned without a necktie, black pants, and shiny leather shoes. He stood shoulder-to-shoulder with the young Asian male hospitality attendant who'd called him over upon Joe's arrival. Even from five feet away, Joe took note of the manager's aftershave. He smelled good.

"I don't understand. Why not? Why can't you accommodate me?" Joe said, standing, holding his four bags containing everything he owned. "Isn't the Grenada convention over? You must have vacancies."

"I'm sorry, but we believe it's in the best interest of our guests to deny you a room. And, perhaps, you'd be more comfortable staying someplace else. Am I right? I'd be happy to provide a car and driver to take you to a place more suitable. There's an economically-priced hotel with convenient access to the commuter railroad called the Flea-Flicker."

"What? Wait. I know what you're implying. I'm no bum. I have money. Cash!"

"I'll ask you to lower your voice."

"I only need a few days. I promise I'll move on. I'll pay in advance."

"Mr. Bustamante, you are being denied a room. Now I'm asking you, as a gentleman, to leave or I'll be obliged to have you removed."

Joe swiveled his head left and right. Two large men, one on each side, wearing identical gray business suits, stood nearby, watching patiently, relaxed with clasped hands - hotel security, he assumed.

"This is discrimination!" he said. "This is not the end of this!"

One of the goons smirked while the skinny Asian kid looked on with a pouty-lipped expression of pity. The manager, conversely, remained stoic.

"Goodbye, Mr. Bustamante," he said.

Joe started walking away, but stopped, turned.

"Hey! How do you know my name?""

"Goodbye, sir," the manager said.

Joe continued walking towards the huge, revolving glass door. The two big men trailed him as an informal escort.

"Hey, how does he know my name?" Joe asked one. "I never said my name."

No reply came.

Joe received similar welcomes at the next two hotels he tried. It didn't make sense. He packed fifteen thousand bucks in his hip pocket. Sure, he looked a little beat-up and his clothes looked slept in. But his sores would eventually heal and he'd bought new clothes - still had the tags on 'em. After a shower and a shave, they wouldn't recognize him. Tomorrow morning, following a good night's rest, he wouldn't recognize himself. Oh, what a feeling it would be to sleep on a queen-size bed with clean sheets, but it wasn't meant to be. Nobody would have him. Not at any price.

Defeated, rejected, he drove past the manufacturing plants, the abandoned factories, the barred storefronts, the topless bar, and the gun shop, navigating the bleak, narrow avenues back to the Fleabag.

The nearest street parking he found was four blocks away - it seemed a hike. How quickly he'd been spoiled by the cabs dropping him off out front. Joe hoofed down the darkened sidewalks, occasionally patting the stack within his pocket. He'd planned to leave the money in the room safe of his new hotel before coming back to check-out from this one, but that plan had been sunk by an unseen iceberg. Here, he found himself alone, dog-paddling in the frigid, black deep. Now, every stranger in every doorway was a threat. Every guy hanging out on every corner, every vagrant pushing a shopping cart, every strung-out dude leaning on a lamp post was a criminal poised to pull a knife. All no longer human to him. Each a big, furry spider lurking, watching, waiting for an opportunity to strike, to show their fangs. Joe rounded the corner to the alleyway.

Five stood in a circle. The red metal door leading to the stairs was just beyond. Three had long beards, all had tattoos. Some wore leather, others denim. Two had wallet chains. A biker gang? Joe thought to turn and change direction, but didn't.

"Hey, speak of the devil," one said. "Told ya' I'd seen him around."

This attracted the attention of the leader, the barrel-chested, big-gutted, bulging-armed, elder who turned around to reveal a graying beard and squinty eyes.

"So it is," he said.

"You got me confused with someone else," Joe said, attempting to cut a path around the group.

The leader, the silverback gorilla, stepped in front, and confronted Joe squarely.

"I don't think we do," he said.

"Yeah. That's the filthy son-of-a-bitch, alright," another said.

"Whaddaya know," yet another said. "It is him."

"Get out of my way," Joe demanded.

"Look who's giving orders," the leader said, and shoved Joe's chest with both hands, the force sending Joe reeling backwards. "Why don't you try taking on a full-grown man, tough guy? Or do you only like little boys?"

Joe's heart thumped. If high school wrestling matches didn't count, he'd never been in a fight. He neither wanted to hurt anyone or get hurt. No point in arguing with drunks. He'd sleep in his car. He turned with the plan to walk briskly out of the alley. Two stepped in front of his path. Another tried to grab his arm, but Joe yanked it away. Someone shoved him from behind.

Out of anger, or perhaps out of fear, Joe turned and stepped forward while throwing a perfect, powerful, overhand right catching the ringleader beneath the eye, opening a cut, blood spurting. The man, stumbling backward, dropped onto his ass. Three were on Joe in a flash of movement, attacking as a pack of jackals. Get him. Fuck. Take him down. One grabbed Joe's shoulders, tussling, trying to judo-throw him to the pavement. Another gave a rapid series of short rabbit punches to Joe's ears, the side of his head, attempting to jab a thumb into an eyeball. Fuck… Bastard… The third clutched, pulled Joes' shirt - the fabric ripped. Joe tossed the first off. Gave a short uppercut to the second's ribs hitting with a meaty thud- ufffff. The man cried out, dropping to his knees, cradling his abdomen. Joe swung a left at the guy who'd been punching, but his knuckles only grazed the man's jaw. Still, the attacker wobbled on his heels. Joe retracted his elbow, lined-up for a second shot. From behind, a beer bottle, held by the neck, struck the back of Joe's head, popped and shattered. A second of blackness, followed by light returning, bringing disorientation and double-vision. Joe remained standing.

The attackers moved in blurs, regrouped, and circled, clockwise, counterclockwise. His legs! His legs! Take him down! Joe raised both large hands into enormous fists. He swung wildly while enduring kicks to the thighs and parrying jabs at his face. He never saw the board. Someone had grabbed hold of a thick piece of lumber from among the alleyway garbage and swung with the perfect form of a major-leaguer. The impact across the shoulder blades, the spine, sent him forward, face-first to the asphalt, fast, hard, no time to get hands out. A reflexive turn of the neck spared his nose but not his teeth. On impact, pain exploded through his jaw and skull.

Several stomps landed on his back. Unable to rise or fight back, Joe shielded his head with his elbows. Lying prone, he looked up to see the leader returned to his feet. Joe saw the demon behind the bearded face, the hate. The leader drew a leg back. The steel toe of the boot struck the top of Joe's head. After a few seconds, it came again, harder. Joe went blind. Though his vision failed, he heard the taunts, strong, emphatic. Look at you now, ya' twisted piece-of-crap. Got what was coming, you sick bastard. Joe heard shuffling feet. Scuffling. Curse words. Grunts. No, Leo, you'll kill him... He's not worth it... Forget this scumbag... Let's get out of here...

Then silence.

At first, Joe didn't believe they'd left. His body tightened into a ball, expecting the gang to come back, preparing for the assault to resume. When it became evident they were gone, Joe's consciousness floated in suspended animation, a pool where neither time nor place mattered. Soon, he drifted further into the deep end, and sunk slowly into a formless, dreamless slumber.

༄ 22 ༄

Joe lifted the side of his face from the oily pavement, brain humming, not knowing where he was. Remembering the fight, his muscles contracted, fists clenched, and his gaze darted about the alleyway - empty. They'd gone. Had ten minutes or ten hours passed? It couldn't have been long. Somebody would've seen him. Even in this neighborhood, people didn't step over bloodied, unconscious men, did they? Joe stood up in stages like an old dog. Clearly, he was hurt. At the least, he had a concussion. Possibly internal bleeding. Yet, he wouldn't call an ambulance. Taking a beat-down from a band of thugs was bad enough. Getting treated at the E.R. would hand them an even greater victory. He would call the cops, however. They needed to be held accountable. The guy who kicked him in the head, especially, belonged in jail.

He wobbled but found equilibrium - sort of. He planned to walk quickly to the front of the building, to the main door, into the lobby, and have the clerk call the police, but his limbs stiffened with use. Each unsteady step required work as an invisible force seemingly pulled him backwards at the shoulders. Determined, he plodded onward, holding his arms straight-out before him as counterweight. When he rounded the corner, Joe encountered two young women coming out of the sports bar. The pardon me he'd intended came out as a growl. One gasped. The other shrieked. Both ducked beneath his outstretched arms and scurried away like he was the Frankenstein monster. Joe entered the lobby.

"Call nine-one-one!" he said, through the barred window, his own voice unfamiliar, slurred and heavy like he'd come from a root canal.

"What for?" the fat clerk said, disinterested, occupied by two metal S-shaped links, a type of puzzle he was attempting to detach from one another.

The question dumbfounded Joe.

"Look at me. Notice anything? A gang attacked me in the alley."

He stretched his torn shirt, dyed with blood, outward for inspection. The clerk paused and looked up.

"You nuts? Going into the alley at night?" he said.

"That's where the entrance to the upper floors is!"

"You staying here?" the clerk asked.

Joe shut his eyes and massaged the back of his neck in disgust. He touched his face. His lips had swollen and were tender. His entire face ached. He wondered if there was a working ice machine in the entire building. Before he could ask, the clerk became animated.

"Wait! I know you! I saw you on the news," he said, delighted.

"No. I live here. You've seen me be-"

"Yeah. I saw you. Today. I knew the picture looked familiar."

"What picture?"

"The one on the TV."

"TV? Me? You sure?"

"Yeah! You're that teacher."

The only benefit of Jerry stealing Joe's stuff and disappearing was the vacancy. Jerry's old room had a television. Joe asked to switch. The clerk swapped the keys without complaint.

"They're all the same, you know," he said. "The grass ain't any greener. But, hey, no skin off my fat ass."

Joe shelved the idea of calling the cops. Watching the news was more important - vitally important. He made the journey out of the lobby door, onto the street, around the corner to the alleyway - fear constricted his chest like a heart attack. No, everything was OK. The alley was empty - the reaction a false alarm or PTSD or something. Joe quickly made way to the red metal door, blood pulsing, ears ringing. He was halfway up the four flights before the adrenaline surge waned.

The next two flights were hard. As were the two corridors. It vexed Joe when his key didn't work, but then he realized he'd switched rooms and had gone to the wrong door. Jerry's room was the same as he'd remembered, except somebody had cleaned the Chinese food cartons off the floor. Seeing the bare mattress made Joe recall the new blanket and sheets he'd bought at Drake's Department store. Luckily, he'd forgotten the bags of supplies and clothes in the car trunk before he'd been mugged.

Mugged?

Robbed!

Panicked, Joe patted his pocket - empty! The money! Gone! No, wait...wrong pocket. The wad, the whole envelope, was still there. He pulled out the envelope, removed the bills and fanned them, hands trembling. One hundred and forty greenbacks, give or take - mostly hundreds. All those unsmiling Ben Franklins sporting an epic mullet and glaring in unison unnerved Joe. Money was the root of all evil. No, that wasn't right. The love of money was... People would literally kill for the stack he carried. But if the bikers weren't robbing him, then why? Why attack and leave him for dead?

Joe pulled the power knob and the TV came on. A wide, black band bordered the picture, at first, but the image went full screen as the set warmed-up. The tube-filled relic had a rotary dial that thunked as Joe turned from channel to channel. Several were pure snow. Some had interference but decent audio. Others had fine pictures but crackling sound. When Joe located Channel 12, he spread and moved the rabbit ears on top of the set. The picture came in fairly well until he let go of the antennae and it went unwatchable - visual static and hiss. Joe tried again and pulled in a good picture, but letting go, the screen became a great ant race. The process repeated itself until he grew frustrated. He dragged a chair from the small table and sat in front of the set, thinking. The picture became sharp, clear. When he stood, however, it turned to static and hissed, once again. In an a-ha moment, Joe realized he himself was causing the interference. As long as he remained seated and still, the image on the screen was viewable. So, in lieu of adjusting the aerial, he adjusted his body. To get the best result, Joe sat as a statue, leaning forward; one wrist draped on a knee, the other curled beneath his chin, evoking the image of Rodin's Thinker, that is to say, Dante at the gates of Hell.

Channel 12 broadcast local news mostly. Though it had only four live broadcasts per day, the station ran twenty-four hours, replaying the day's big stories in a continuous loop. If Joe waited long enough, he would see the identical story the fat clerk had viewed hours earlier. The bit currently airing talked about illegal dumping and the harm to local wildlife. Apparently, a rare type of loon was mistaking plastic grocery bags for jellyfish and eating them. Many were dying, but one, nicknamed McMurphy, was saved recently after an emergency tracheotomy. The bird wore a bandage as a collar. The veterinarian interviewed assured viewers that McMurphy would survive but might never again make a tremolo call, that is, the raucous, crazy laugh loons are known for. A dozen animal rights activists, seeking tougher environmental protection laws, petitioned on the steps of Town hall by carrying placards and yodeling at passersby. Joe wondered why nobody ever yodeled on behalf of the poor families, prostitutes, drug addicts, and various loons who lived year-round in the Fleabag. Nobody cared what they ate. The story ended and a teaser came on promising interesting pieces about a local man training to cross the country on a pogo stick and a high school senior receiving acceptance letters to all eight Ivy League schools. Tied to that story was this: *Teacher accused of lewd conduct.* The station reminded viewers to stay tuned as it cut to a long string of commercials.

Time shifted into low gear. The walls closed in. The chair became a rock. With muscles tensed and mind numbed, Joe sat, waited, and watched - advertisements for breath mints, a personal injury law firm, dishwashing liquid, a Caribbean cruise line, a luxury sedan, vitamin water, and a repeat of the same breath mint ad they'd begun with. Finally, the news program returned. The male and female co-anchors were thrilled to report the preparation of the founder of *Pogo for Peace* in his bid to bring a divided nation together through pogoing. The male anchor made all the obligatory puns. *He expects to arrive by spring... If he sticks to the plan, he'll be hopping in by Easter...*The woman anchor responded, in turn, with all the scripted, good-natured groans and eye rolls. More stories followed. The county legislature was considering a property tax hike to cover the cost overruns of a sewage treatment plant currently under construction. Unknown vandals toppled cemetery headstones. A violinist was reunited with a violin he'd lost more than forty years earlier... The wait for the teacher story - his story - became increasingly unbearable, but Joe couldn't move, couldn't fully breathe, without knocking out the TV reception. Next up - the cheerful student scholar who'd earned a place at all eight Ivy League schools was turning each one down in order to pursue her dream of owning a pizzeria. I'm sure, someday, she'll make a lot of dough, the male anchor said, making Joe want to put his foot through the screen. Still, he didn't move. Finally, it came on. The female anchor took the lead on this more serious piece. She provided a clumsy segue.

And in other, less inspiring news from the classroom, a physical education teacher at James K. Polk Middle School has been suspended from his duties. In quick succession, the video showed the interior of the school, a close-shot of its name engraved on a large stone, and then cut to the playground with children playing on the swings. *Following an accusation of having exposed himself within the gymnasium's boy's locker room, school administration says thirty-six-year-old Joseph Bustamante violated numerous school district policies and was placed on unpaid leave subsequent to an administrative hearing.* An image of Joe's face filled the whole screen. The picture was taken from the awful school ID photo. It showed him with a full head of dark hair and a self-important, smug smirk, looking like the whole accusation was a joke. The scene then cut to Principal Shelley being interviewed in her office. *It's our duty to protect our students, staff, and faculty and to ensure an environment that is conducive to learning.* The field reporter nodded in agreement. The principal continued. *Safety is paramount, and we here at the middle school have adopted a zero tolerance policy towards any reported misconduct.* The view cut to boys playing soccer on the field. Then the on-site video ended. The woman anchor closed the story by saying, *the school has handed its investigation over to the county police to determine if criminal charges should be filed against Mr. Bustamante.*

"I only took a shower," Joe said to an empty room.

For two silent, solemn seconds, both news anchors looked down and shook their heads. A scrolling teaser at the bottom of the screen read, *still to come: Goldilocks-picker? Homeowner finds a would-be burglar sleeping in his bed.* The station broke away to more commercials, the first being an ad for the state lottery. *Now over two hundred and fifty million dollars…*

Joe rose and shut off the television. He sat back down on the chair and stared at the illuminated dot at the center of the darkened screen until it disappeared.

It took time to mull over the implications of the telecast. They'd shown his face and accused him of sexual misconduct in a school. Within a boys locker room, no less. No wonder the bikers beat him up. Maybe the attendants and managers at the Eaton and the other hotels caught the news, as well. Or, maybe, the daily paper published an article with his picture. Who knew? Whatever the case, his reputation was ruined. He felt nauseous, dizzy. People thought he was a pervert or worse. What would his family and friends…

His mom!

Joe sprang from the chair. Without a plan, without thought, with no physical pain, he found himself bolting out from the room and bounding, almost falling, down the flights of stairs. He covered the four blocks to the car as effortlessly as a Sunday stroll. Getting the key into the car's ignition proved harder, however. Finally, starting the engine, throwing the car into gear, he peeled away from the curb only to immediately get stuck at a red light. No matter. Soon he'd be on the highway where he could floor the pedal. He had to get to his aunt's house and talk to his mother before she saw the news or read the paper or heard from somebody else. Joe couldn't have his dying mother thinking her only son was a… The label was so offensive he couldn't bring it to conscious thought. She'd believe him, though. If he could tell her what actually happened before all the liars grabbed her ear, she'd understand. But he needed to reach her in time.

The traffic signal turned green. The front tires chirped and the rear end shimmied as he accelerated fast only to stop hard at the very next red light.

23

"You sure?" his aunt said. "Fresh blueberries are hard to come by and the cream is homemade."

"Wish I could, but I can't," he said. "The vegetable lasagna was more than enough. I may not eat for a week."

He and his aunt sat on opposite ends of the old sofa dressed up by colorful afghan, chatting about nothing, waiting. Both pretended not to hear Joe's mother vomiting and moaning in the nearby bathroom. And other than asking if he needed ice, she hadn't inquired about his facial injuries after he said he'd run into some trouble. Edna never pressed, she was good like that. Her entire bungalow smelled aromatic from the essential oil - frankincense, a mood-enhancer he'd been told - misting from a diffuser on an end table.

Joe had arrived at Edna's tiny house an hour and a half earlier and had yet to see his mom. Apparently, Gladys hadn't been truthful about how well she'd been tolerating the chemo treatments. She'd slept through dinner and scurried into the bathroom upon awakening. There'd been retching noises since. When Aunt Edna inquired through the door, Gladys insisted she was fine. In Joe's estimation, showing up unannounced proved to be a bonehead move. He provided no benefit by being there. The two women were in no position to entertain a visitor. And he didn't necessarily want to know how bad things were. Yet, there he was.

"They're very good for the skin," Edna said.

"What is?" Joe said, distracted, worried, hands gripping kneecaps.

"Blueberries. They're a superfood."

"No, really, I'm fine," Joe said, suddenly conscious of his skin sores.

His aunt tended to advocate health food in the dogged way a drug dealer might push crack. Edna was two years younger than her sister, but despite being thinner, she looked two years older, wrinkled and leathery. She'd never married yet maintained a quiet contentment Joe found odd. To him, wanting a life-partner and children was akin to respiration, an essential part of existing. Strange to see someone who didn't need to breathe. Still, she'd always been a generous and doting aunt and Joe considered himself lucky to have her in the family. Especially now. She'd opened her very modest domicile up to a very sick woman, and that's no small thing. It humbled Joe to think about. Made him feel petty for missing the meat in her meat-less lasagna.

The bathroom door finally opened. Gladys came out and approached in jerky baby-steps wearing a pink robe and slippers. She pulled the robe shut. Old. Shockingly old. A fossil of her former self. With her hair turned thinner, whiter, her skin had taken on an ashen, ghostly hue.

"There you are, pretty lady," Joe said. "I thought you were avoiding me."

He stood and greeted her with a cautious hug. Somebody had replaced his mom's skeleton with bird bones. She smiled, sort of. Her eyes were fogged-over, distant, probably due to the meds. Her face was gaunt and her nose huge. Joe wished he'd brought flowers. She deserved 'em.

"What happened to you? You look like a bad cantaloupe."

Joe had changed his bloody shirt in the car and washed up in Aunt Edna's kitchen sink, yet remained swollen, split-lipped, and bruised, obviously pummeled. No point of lying.

"Some thugs picked a fight outside a bar. Just a little stupid scuffle," he said, not wanting to get into it.

"But you're not a brawler, Joseph. And a little too old and smart to start now."

He nodded in agreement, embarrassed.

"Did ya' win?"

"You should see the other guys," Joe said, and forced a grin and a wink.

"That means no," Gladys said. "You never could lie, could you? Never learned properly from your father. That man was a first-class bullshit artist."

"Gladys!" Aunt Edna said.

"It's true!" Gladys said. "He was a smoothie. He would've conned your thugs into lending him money."

The three laughed. It was a nice moment but one that seemed to take his mom's strength. Joe helped her to the couch.

"You need a doctor? You're banged up pretty bad," she said.

"Do you?" Joe said. "You look worse."

And she did, too, with her frail body and yellowed eyes.

"I have too many doctors already," she said. "Including this one." Gladys swept a lazy hand towards her sister.

Aunt Edna smiled warmly. "I'm going to take care of the dishes. And then I'll make you a cup of tea."

"I want real tea with lots of milk and five sugars - light and sweet like me." And then she added, looking at Joe, "That's if the tea-Nazi will let me have what I want."

"You'll have green tea with honey. Your sugar addiction hasn't worked," Aunt Edna said, and added directly to Joe, "There's nothing sweet about this old sourpuss."

This brought a genuine smile to his mom's face. Despite being opposites in personalities, lifestyles, interests, and nearly everything else, the two sisters were truly fond of one another. Edna went to the kitchen. Joe paced the small sitting area and made small talk about the hotel, the camel worms, and about seeing Rebecca at the doctor's office. His mother told about the cancer treatments and how sick she felt - how the cure was worse than the disease. Joe continued pacing, even as they ran out of things to discuss.

"What's on your mind, kiddo," Gladys said. "You got ants in your pants."

Joe sat on the edge of the couch cushion and clasped his mother's hands. "Mom," he said. There's something you need to know. Something bad. Did you see the news?"

Gladys closed her eyes and opened them. A profound serenity came over her. "Yeah, I saw the news, alright. No point in crying about it. We're broke."

The remark threw Joe. He tried to read her face, waited for more.

"I knew we should've sold off a year ago, while riding high. Guess we got too greedy. Now look what happened."

"Ma, what are you talking about?"

"Pillbox! Those crooks."

Joe shook his head, confused. Gladys continued. "You didn't hear? The class-action lawsuit? They filed it in court today. Apparently, all these thousands of women who wanted Cleopatra lashes got them alright. Beautiful, long, thick eyelashes like the Queen of the Nile. But, it seems the cute little pink starfish pill has some side effects that aren't so cute. You haven't heard?"

Joe opened his mouth but didn't speak, puzzled, dumbstruck. Gladys went on.

"Seems the women got more than they bargained for. The hair under their arms and other places continued to grow...and grow...and grow. This for months, even after they stopped taking the pill! It screwed up their hormones. The endocrinologists say it may never go away. You should've seen these poor ladies - and a few men, too! Some have fur down to their knees. And as soon as they trim it, it comes right back within a few days. They can't go to the beach. One lady can no longer ride a bicycle. Another has to comb herself with a dog brush. Rapunzel Pubes is what they're calling it. It's ruining their lives."

"Ma, what happened to our stock?"

"Wait till the late-night talk shows get ahold of this. Who's that black guy with the British accent? He's going to have a party."

"Ma, the shares? What are they worth?"

"Not worth the paper they're written on. The FDA has pulled Starfish from the market. Stephanie LaPlace has gone into hiding. Why'd we ever trust a company with a CEO named Stephanie, anyway? What kind of name is that for a man? That rat knew about the side effects all along. He had the results of the clinical studies altered in order to get approval. They're talking about indicting him. I hope he goes to jail. I never liked seeing him on TV with his cocky attitude and ridiculous eyelashes."

"How much do we have left?" Joe said, straining, taking care not to crush his mother's delicate hands.

"You know, now that I think about it, it is like a starfish. You know, the way you can cut off one of their arms and it grows back. Isn't that a strange coincidence?"

"Ma! The money! The Nest Egg!" Joe said as a controlled shout.

"Pillbox Pharmaceuticals closed at four dollars and forty-two cents today," Gladys answered matter-of-factly.

Joe needed to replay what his mom just said within his head. He couldn't have heard right.

"From four hundred and forty-three to four! It can't be!" Joe did the mental math. "Are you telling me our three million dollars is now only…what? Twenty-five thousand?"

"Don't upset me, Joe. I don't want to think about it."

"Mom! We needed that money. Our house is gone - demolished! And the little we have left won't rebuild it. Not even close. No bank is going to give us a mortgage. We'll have to sell the property and-"

"Joseph, stop it! It doesn't matter. Take what's ever left and do whatever you want. I won't be here to spend it anyway. I'm demolished!"

Her words hung and swung like a noose. During the silence, Joe became aware of the ticking clock mounted high on the wall. He spoke in a whisper. "What do you mean by that?" he said.

Gladys retrieved an envelope from on top of the end table and handed it to Joe. "I almost forgot. Take this. Rebecca brought it by."

"Rebecca? My Rebecca? Here?"

Joe rotated the enveloped within his hands, confused. He opened its flap and pulled out four one hundred dollar bills.

"What this?"

"It's the money she owes you," Gladys said. "Such a good girl. She brought soup – homemade pasta e Faggioli. You should've come sooner; we had it for lunch – delicious. A young, pretty girl who knows how to cook in this day and age? You should marry that one. What a kind heart."

Joe squinted and jutted out his chin while jabbing a finger towards the floor.

"Rebecca? Here? With soup?" Joe said, incredulous.

"Which part is giving you trouble, dear?" Gladys said.

"Ma! First, Rebecca has never borrowed money from me, not a dime. And second, why is my ex-girlfriend coming to visit my mother to pay back money she doesn't owe?

"Joe, she heard I was sick. We have a relationship. She wanted to see me and I wanted to see her.

What? Just because you broke up with her means I have to break up with her?"

"She broke up with me! And she called me a deuce."

Gladys considered this. "Well, if she called you a douche, you probably gave her good reason. Lord knows I called your father worse when he made me-"

Joe waved a dismissive palm.

"Ma, what did you mean just now when you said you were demolished? What did the doctor say?"

"Nothing," she said.

"Don't lie. You've never been good at it, either."

"I don't want to talk about it."

"Well, I do. What did he say?"

She inhaled and expelled a full breath before explaining what was already known to both of them. "Joseph, they did a biopsy. The cancer is the aggressive kind," she said, and emitted a mournful chuckle. "I didn't know there were different kinds. I thought cancer was cancer... Anyway, the chemo is only buying time - and not much at that. If I were a stock, you certainly wouldn't want to invest in me. You'd lose your shirt."

"Mom, please. No jokes," Joe said, tears coming. "What do we have to do to make you better?"

"Joe, it has spread everywhere. They said I have four to six months at most. I wasn't going to tell you. You'd only worry."

"So, what happens now? They'll try some type of experimental treatment, right?" Joe's hands shook.

His entire body quaked. He didn't want to hear what was coming.

"I'm taking myself off the chemo," she said, and then added, surprisingly stern, "Don't try to talk me out of it. I've already made my decision. If I only have a small amount of time left, I don't want to squander it with doctors, hospitals, and throwing up in the toilet."

"You say that now. But you'll regret not trying to-"

"No, Joe. I won't. I'll have no regrets. I had a good run. More importantly, I had a very special son. What more could I want?"

"Grandkids," Joe snapped back, and instantly wished he hadn't for he watched his mom's face turn down and her gaze drift off to a faraway place. Regardless, he pressed on, "My kids…my children will be cheated."

"Joe, don't. This is hard enough already."

Her eyes watered, pleaded for mercy. Still, Joe couldn't stop himself. He stood up fast. His words came without thought, angry and hard. "You know, I never thought I'd say this, but I will now. You're putting your suffering ahead of our suffering. That makes you a coward. And selfish. If you fought, you could beat this thing. Instead, you're willing to roll over down and die without caring about the ones you leave behind - your friends, your sister…me."

"Joe," Aunt Edna said, now in the doorway balancing a teacup on a saucer, "it's going to be alright."

"You're on board with this?" Joe said. Tears streamed from…what? Fear? Rage? No. Betrayal. "You're giving her green tea like it means anything. My mom is dying! And you're just gonna watch it happen?"

"Joseph," Gladys said. "This is my choice, not hers, not yours. Try to understand."

Joe's body jerked like he'd been stomped and kicked again. "I don't want to understand. And I'm not gonna watch it happen," he said.

Joe swung open the front door, committing himself to leaving, surprised that both stared blankly, neither his aunt nor his mother trying to stop him.

"I'm not going to be a part of this. It's...a...a…slow suicide, that's what it is. I may not be able to prevent you, but I won't be forced to watch it. I can't…

Joe was out the door and in his car driving away from the neighborhood before being fully aware he'd left. When he did, he realized he'd forgotten the reason he'd visited - to tell his side of the work suspension and the awful allegations and the fake news that made him a monster and a pariah. But there was no going back. Not to his aunt's house. Not to the Fleabag. Not to the middle school. Not to Steeples to meet his friends. Not to his own home that wasn't there anymore. There was no place for him. His life had been hijacked. There wasn't anything for him. There was nothing left.

So, Joe knew where he needed to go, but had to be sure, first. He pressed a foot on the accelerator, rounded the ramp, and entered the parkway at breakneck speed.

24

"You tell me you don't love me and I'll go! You'll never see my face again! Not ever, I promise!"

"Go home, Joe."

"I don't have a home."

"Well, just go then."

"No! Not unless you can tell me you don't love me… I'll wait down here until tomorrow morning if I have to. I've blocked your car in. You'll have to see me sometime."

"I can call the police."

"Fine. Maybe they'll shoot me."

"I'm coming down. Stop talking so loudly. You'll piss people off and one of them will call the cops."

The call ended. Joe returned the phone to his pocket and sat on the hood of the red coupe. He had effectively blocked her in. The front bumper of his car nearly kissed the rear bumper of hers. He was in one of several small parking lots within a complex of brick two-story garden apartments. The grounds were grassy and well-maintained with lots of benches and flower-beds. The lots were newly paved with the lines and numbered spaces freshly painted, but the illumination from the low, old-fashioned wooden light poles was insufficient. Joe had often worried about her parking and traversing the lot alone at night, but she assured him the complex was safe. Seeing how quiet the lot and adjacent buildings were, he suspected the area, unlike the Fleabag, was not accustomed to crime. If the police were called on this night, the novelty of the event would draw many curious residents outside to see what was going on.

Rebecca took so much time in arriving, Joe worried she'd changed her mind.

"You know what you're doing is illegal," she said, walking into a yellowish ellipse of light. She was without make-up and was dressed in an old gray sweat suit with frizzy hair falling down onto her shoulders – a far cry from the way she'd been dolled up the last two times he'd seen her. She looked more beautiful than ever.

"It's my car. I'm allowed to sit on it," he said.

"I'm talking about blocking my car. You're falsely imprisoning it or something."

Joe slid off the hood and stood. "Sorry," he said. "I was desperate."

Rebecca became nervous, tried to slide hands into pants pockets prior to realizing the sweatpants had no pockets. She settled for crossing arms over her chest and shaking her head. "Desperate? About what?" she said.

"I realized something," Joe said. "You broke up with me and told me you had a new boyfriend but you never actually said you don't love me."

"Joseph Bustamante, you know that's implied. Don't make me say it. What's the point of that?"

"Well, I need to hear it come from your mouth."

"Joe, don't do this."

"If you don't love me, it should be easy for you. But you can't because you do love me. That's why you visited my mom. And that's why you gave me four hundred dollars that you can't afford to give."

Joe struggled to remove the envelope from his pocket. He tried to return her money, but she refused to raise a hand to accept it. Joe flung the envelope at her feet. Rebecca stepped back as if it were on fire.

"Joe, I'm leaving for the Bahamas tomorrow with Dick," she said.

Her words were a punch to the stomach. Joe winced but recovered and held his head high. He took a step towards her and outstretched his arms.

"That's still not saying you don't love me. You can't say it because you do still love me. I still love you and always will. We could have an amazing life together."

"Joe…"

"We could care for one another and support each other. We could grow a family."

"Joe..."

"We could grow old together. We could have the kind of relationship that most people don't even know is-"

"Joe! I don't love you."

A line of tears came from one of her eyes. Joe arms fell to his sides and he shook his head.

"I don't love you, okay? I never wanted to hurt you. But I don't love you," she said, voice hoarse. "Now go!"

Joe wobbled on his heels. His vision blurred. His head spun. He turned, averting his eyes from her, opening the car door and sliding in. He started the engine and backed out without looking. He wasn't sure if she remained standing beneath the streetlight or not as he pulled away. He wouldn't look. Couldn't look. Pain flared within his chest. His breaths were short, labored. Low moans came involuntarily from his throat. He thought to pull over but didn't. His vision blurred. His mind became addled. He drove as if drunk, leisurely, the car steering itself, in the only direction left to go: towards the water.

25

The last man on earth. That's what it felt like walking the deserted seaport town. Like being in one of those old, spooky TV episodes where the hero wakes up and inexplicably finds himself alone. The cobbled square was vacant. So were the planked walkways running in front of the shops, as were the shops themselves. And there were lots of them. So many places to spend your dough in July and August. Each more inviting than the next. An old-fashioned town freshly painted. Sadly, all closed. Joe hiked up the rucksack on his back and continued on.

The word quaint is what came to mind - and not in a patronizing way. The locale was pleasant and he liked it. Always had. He'd been here several times, and it held fond memories. During the tourist season, the numerous storefronts were filled with happy people in long shorts and tied-dyed shirts and tube tops and even bikinis milling about - a sea of flip-flops and big-brimmed hats and sunglasses. Families went to ice cream parlors or salt-water taffy shops or brownie bakeries. Women browsed the souvenir shops where they sold kites and beach towels and artsy things made from driftwood while the men hung out in small pubs with open fronts drinking craft beers. There'd been well-to-do people dining in white-tablecloth restaurants overlooking the pier and younger people atop tall stools in fried clam eateries or crammed into open-air bars with live reggae bands performing, steel drums resounding, the whole place made vibrant, festive.

Of course, the party was over now. The summer residents had returned to their permanent homes. The throngs of carefree day-trippers had left, too. The umbrellas removed from the round tables, the tables covered with green tarps. The vendors missing. The caricature artists not to be found. The shops shut. Many with cutesy signs hung in the windows - Closed for the Freezin' or That's Fall, Folks. Yes, sad to see the whole island shuttered, though it was what he'd hoped for.

Joe walked the decking, stopped at a posted map behind glass. He traced from the orange YOU ARE HERE balloon to where he wanted to go - not too far.

The night before now seemed ages ago. He'd driven to the docks from Aunt Edna's only to find no boats for hire at that late hour. So, he'd gone and bought supplies, beginning with the large, green rucksack from a surprised but shrewd guy waiting for a bus - he wanted two hundred bucks. Joe filled the bag with the clothes he'd purchased from Drake's along with dozens of canned foods - raviolis, soups, stews, veggies, refried beans - he'd bought at a 24-hour supermarket. When finished, the sack felt like it contained bricks and its strap dug into his clavicle. Joe drove back to the docks and slept, cramped in the car. The first fishermen began arriving right before sunrise. A good part of the morning would pass before one took the bait.

"I need to get across to Barrier Island right away," Joe said.

The man was older, slim, ruddy-faced, and scruffy, chin dotted with spiky whiskers.

He fiddled with the inboard engine through the open compartment and went to the front and turned the key. The engine cranked and huffed and spewed black smoke before settling into a steady rumble.

"No water taxis running. Seasons done," the man said, not looking up. "Come back in a few months."

"What about you?"

"Really can't. Already lost some time. Drop the lines early, you'll bring home Moby Dick. Drop 'em late, you won't get dick."

Joe withdrew the envelope from his pocket and counted off fifteen unamused Franklins.

"I can pay in advance. Say, three hundred?" he said. "I really need to get away."

The water churned against the hull and Joe bounced in his seat as the boat cut through the green bay water. Cool air rushed across his face, sea spray ice on the skin. Though the fisherman steered from his seat only a few feet away, the rush of wind stole most of their words. They conversed as best they could in economical bursts, often needing to repeat. At one point, Joe's cell rang. He removed the device from his pocket and without determining the caller, cocked back his elbow and chucked it far into the sea.

The fisherman studied Joe a moment, but concluded he wasn't a threat.

"You ain't kidding about wanting to get away," he barked through the wind. "I understand. Believe me. Ever since my wife caught the Rapunzel Pussy, she's been a terror. Maybe I'll come with you."

When the fisherman docked the boat, Joe stepped off knowing there was no going back. He looked to the opposite shore. Although the mainland was only a mile and a quarter away, it would challenge even a strong long-distance swimmer to cross - the currents were killers as were the man-o-wars and the sharks. He'd have no chance. Despite being a Phys Ed instructor and generally athletic, Joe wasn't a swimmer; he was a sinker.

"Good luck to you, friend," the fisherman said, giving a two-finger salute. "Hope you find whatever it is you need to find."

Joe thanked the fisherman and lifted a hand, though he wasn't looking to find anything - he was attempting to get lost. And, apparently, he'd come to the right deserted island. All the slips were empty. The docks, the entire pier unoccupied. The island, itself, was a relatively small, thin strip of land, only one-half mile wide and seven miles long that separated the mainland from the ocean. They called it Barrier Island having labeled it with the same limited imagination of whoever had named the moon. A rocky beach lay on the bay side and a wide, sandy shore greeted the ocean on the other. Except for the one town, the remainder was mostly wooded, hidden amongst the trees. The island consisted of numerous small bungalows, a campground, and an exclusive community of higher-priced houses on the bluffs overlooking the ocean. Everything, including the pricey homes, was scaled down in size, though. Even the so-called hotels were mere ten-room pink or saffron-colored stucco structures with lots of arches and big leafy plantings within gigantic stone urns. But none of this is what Barrier Island was known for. Oddly, the island's renown came not from what it had, but from what it didn't.

There were no roads. No official streets, at all. That's because there were no cars, no motor vehicles of any kind permitted on the island. Visitors and residents had to find alternate means of transportation. Bicycling was the norm and the narrow paved lanes and dirt paths were never wider than three persons, most opting to ride single-file. These bicycle paths came with funny names like Egret Avenue or Cottontail Turnpike, and with the tall pines and dense copse bordering them, a feeling of complete seclusion was fostered while traveling. Most people enjoyed the serenity. To some, the isolation produced claustrophobic anxiety, especially during the winter months. Though Joe suspected he might find a few stubborn holdouts that had stayed, there wouldn't be many. No bridges connected the island to civilization. No way on to this strip and no way off. No going back to the Land of Uz. To Joe, that was its main appeal.

The seclusion would be welcomed soon enough. For now, he roamed the island's only merchant district, surprised to realize it, too, had completely cleared out. He came to the office, a rustic cabin nestled between the miniature Town Hall and Visitors Center. The sign read Last Resort Realty. Another read Come on in! Joe obliged by opening the door. A buzzer sounded.

Two chubby, older women looked up from behind the counter, one seated behind a desk. The nearer one, the lady with the round spectacles, spoke.

"Morning. Checking out?" she said.

"No. Hopefully, checking in," he said.

The ladies exchanged glances. The one at the counter spoke. "Today's our last day, actually. We're only open to accommodate the stragglers who haven't left."

"I know," Joe said, conscious of his right eye swollen shut, aware of their suspicion, and, therefore, careful in choosing his words. "But I'm looking to lease a small place for the off-season, the entire period."

"Well, I don't think we have any owners interested in-"

She trailed-off as Joe produced the envelope and fanned out the bills, counting with a thumb. "I can give you twelve thousand dollars for the next four months. I'll pay up front. Cash. Right now."

This caused the one behind the desk to raise her gaze from her paperwork. The one at the counter studied Joe, perhaps weighing the offer, or maybe, evaluating his mental health and assessing the imminent risk he posed. She grew nervous. Her voice quavered as she turned him down with caution.

"I'm sorry. We're really just collecting keys, returning security deposits and whatnot. Not open for any new rentals. Sorry, I-"

The other one, the boss, Joe realized, graciously overruled her.

"Joan, I think we can accommodate this gentleman. He can have one of mine."

"You sure?"

"It will be fine. He seems like a respectable young man."

Joe smiled. They were sweet ladies, he decided. Polite. Plump and nurturing, like mother hens.

"OK, then… Kay, here, actually owns two units, herself. If you'd like to see some pictures, I can pull them up on the computer."

"Either will be fine," Joe said and smiled. "I trust your opinion, Joan. Let me have the one you'd take, yourself."

"Well, alright, I guess. I'll need your driver's license and you'll have to sign the standard rental agreement."

"Of course," Joe said.

Joe provided the license. The realtor looked it over and addressed him tentatively. "Mister...Bustamante? You do understand the ferry won't be running until spring. They'll be no way for you to go back to shore unless you call someone."

"I understand."

"And there's no landline phone in the cottage and cell phone reception on the island can be kinda spotty…"

"I'm looking forward to the seclusion," he said.

"And no police or emergency services. I mean, the bay constables patrol the waters and the docks, of course, but they shut down the station here in town."

The other woman pulled a single sheet from a filing cabinet and approached. "Here's the agreement, Mr. Bustamante," she said. "After you read and sign, I'll notarize it. If you have any questions, just ask. That's what we're here for."

"Is there someplace I can rent fishing equipment?"

"You'll find several rods and tackle and nets in the storage closet at the cottage. You'll have to catch your own bait, of course. But I don't know how much fishing you'll want to do when the weather turns - it gets brutal cold by the water."

"Well, since the market and the restaurants are all closed, I'd better not be too picky about the weather or I'll starve to death."

The three shared an uncomfortable laugh.

"Mr. Bustamante," the lady with glasses said, "are you a writer or some type of artist? 'Cause that's usually the only people who stay through winter."

Joe needed to think. "I'm a guy," he said, "who needs solitude in order to remember why I don't want to be alone. So, don't worry. I'm not hiding out. You won't find my face on the Most Wanted signs at the post office."

This seemed to ease the first woman's concerns, and she smiled for the first time since his arrival.

"We'll be gone and this office will be closed, but I'll give you a contact number for Kay if anything goes wrong in the unit - heat or plumbing or what have you. But like I said, don't expect anyone to reach you quickly in an emergency. Don't ever be in a hurry around here."

Joe laughed at this. "Sounds perfect," he said. "I'll get a break from the hustle-bustle."

After the paperwork was complete and the rules explained, Kay offered to lead him to the unit and give a tour but Joe declined. Making the chubby old gal climb atop a bicycle and pedal the paths to the cottage on her last day would not be gentlemanly. He opted for a paper map where she drew a line and circled his destination. Joe thanked them both and said goodbye. It made him nervous to hear them wish him Happy Holidays so far in advance.

The thick canopy of the trees shaded the trails. Most of the houses were completely hidden from view while walking, mailboxes atop of white posts along the trails being the only indication they existed at all. The distance was further than it appeared on the printed map, the rucksack bruising his shoulder. At one point, he thought he saw a fellow traveler approaching from the other direction but soon realized it was a female deer. The animal lumbered along, coming up to him without fear or the slightest hesitation.

"Hey, girl," Joe said. "You're a brave one."

The deer was more interested in lolling her clunky head and pressing her nose against the sack than greeting. Joe knew the homeowners hated the deer, regarded them as nothing more than big raccoons for all the damage they caused. The locals frequently called for a cull while the tourists adored them, gorging them with churros and French fries. Naturally, no hunting was permitted. Joe considered patting the doe's head when he noticed patches of missing fur and a chunk of flesh gone from an ear. Better to be standoffish than risk contracting any additional exotic skin conditions. Joe continued down the path. The animal followed for a while before growing bored and turning into the woods.

He finally came to the crushed bluestone path leading to the cottage. He swung the low, broad, green gate open and stepped upon the property. The colorful cottage was tucked into a clearing, surrounded by heavy forest, without view of the sea or neighbors. It had red plank sides with yellow trim around the windows and a slate roof and stone chimney. There was a front porch with two blue Adirondack chairs. To the left of the cottage was a small pond with lily pads showing bright white flowers.

The inside was equally attractive. Dark plank floors without a speck of dust. The whole place clean. Spotless, actually, and a utility closet packed with cleansers, mops, and brooms to keep it that way. A stone fireplace. A living room with minimal furnishings. A country kitchen with white cabinets having little glass panes in their doors. A pantry fully stocked with canned goods and coffee, boxes of pasta and jars of sauce. A linen closet - also stocked. A laundry room with washer and dryer. A small deck off the back with a gas barbeque grill. A rope hammock strung between trees. One bedroom with bunk beds. A larger one with a four-post bed and lots of pillows.

Joe pulled off his shoes and sprawled out on the bed. The soft, thick duvet smelled like fresh-cut flowers. He shut his eyes and inhaled. The quiet of the house presented a new experience. Never before had he witnessed such a near perfect absence of sound. Had there been a spider on the ceiling - which there wasn't - he would've heard it breathing. Sleep came immediately. Joe slumbered the next eighteen hours, waking refreshed and renewed.

It took two days to fully relax, though. The emotional steam built-up needed to be released, allowed to hiss out slowly as if from the fancy pressure cooker in his new kitchen. The days after that were joyful. The cream Dr. Spiera prescribed worked wonders, the worms dying, the lesions healing. The clean sheets and firm mattress induced proper rest. Ice and time brought the swelling in his face down. The hot showers reinvigorated his body. The island air rejuvenated his lungs.

Joe took two mesh waste paper baskets and wove the openings together to form a cylinder. At each end, he cut a hole and bent the wires inward to make cones. He tied a cord to the center. The result was a pretty good bait trap. He took a bucket, a rod, a net, and the trap to the bay. Quickly, he learned the best spot to trap live killifish. He carried the killies in the bucket across to the ocean side of the island. He used them to fish for porgies. With the surf cold on his lower legs, he cast the line. It felt good to be doing something, anything. That day, he caught four. The next day, eight. He brought them back to the cottage and filleted, wrapped, and saved them in the freezer. If he could squirrel away enough, he'd have enough food for the winter.

A day later, he needed to comb his hair back before leaving at sunrise. Soon, he'd have to figure out how to cut it - a good problem to have. On the bay side of the island, he became proficient at digging clams with his toes, sometimes blue claw crabs digging his toes. Both were delicious when sautéed in olive oil and garlic and served over spaghetti. He saved some of the raw clam for bait and hooked five bluefish in one morning off the pier. After some trial and error with various spices from the rack, he learned to grill them to where they didn't taste quite so gamey.

There was something exciting about living off the land, or rather, the sea. Though he could see boats in the bay and passing through the inlet, within his mind, he was a castaway. A stranded man left to his own devices, not only surviving but thriving. Who needed work? Who needed friends and family? They only brought pain and suffering. Joe's evolving plan was to find a job on the island in the early spring before the tourists returned. Of course, he'd have to leave the cottage, but maybe a handyman job at a hotel, or a dock worker position might come with a room. He'd sell snow cones or sweep floors if he had to. He wasn't going back.

One late afternoon, upon nuking popcorn in the microwave, he heard scratching at the backyard deck. Joe opened the glass slider to greet the deer from the first day, the one missing a piece of ear.

"How'd you know, girl? You have a bionic nose?"

Joe needed to block the doorway with his body to keep the animal from entering the house. He closed the slider until returning with the bowl. The deer ate the popcorn from his hand, licking his palm with a thick, rubbery tongue, nibbling his fingers long after finishing. Joe set the bowl down on the deck and watched the deer turn its head completely sideways and chow down.

"You are aware, my friend, that popcorn was supposed to be for me," Joe said. The deer toppled the bowl with a hoof, seemingly to spill its contents on purpose. "Hey! Be careful! That's not mine... Well, if I'm gonna yell at you, I guess you need a name. How about Van Gogh? You OK with that?"

The deer stopped, looked up, and resumed eating.

"I guess that means yes."

From that day on, Joe and the doe were near constant companions. At daybreak, Van Gogh would often be waiting by the rear door where Joe could serve frozen waffles.

When Joe went fishing, Van Gogh followed to the beach and waited, either lounging in the sand on the ocean side or munching on the vegetation that grew between the sharp black rocks near the bay. One time, she ran straight into the bay. It amazed Joe to see the big animal tread water, only its long neck showing. Then only its head.

"About time you took a bath," he shouted.

She swam better than she walked. Joe's dad would've called Van Gogh a slacker. This deer fit his definition - never in a hurry, always ten paces behind.

Joe often called back over his shoulder, "You coming? I should've named you Slow Poke."

In the early evenings, Van Gogh might show up at the cottage's rear doors. Joe would talk to her through the glass.

"I'd invite you in if it were my place… Ahh, don't look at me with those big doe-eyes…"

Joe imagined on the coldest nights of winter, he'd build his friend a fire in the fire pit.

On mornings Van Gogh didn't show up, Joe missed her. If a whole day went by, he grew concerned.

"There you are, pretty lady," he might say when she finally showed up. "I was worried someone had turned you into venison."

Joe left out bowls of water and oatmeal. When not fishing, he explored the island, sometimes with Van Gogh, sometimes not, walking the numerous paths and footbridges. He went west and watched the colorful sailboats, and further out, the huge, gray cargo ships resembling the battleships in the board game he'd played as a kid. On the east side, he sat on giant, slimy boulders, the surf exploding around him, showered by spray and white foam. He loved exploring his new home. To see all the cool stuff... Woodpeckers and bats and fox dens and frogs as big as his hand. A futuristic house that looked like three enormous glass globes… Often, he found hidden treasures like a hand water pump that still worked! A bush that smelled like black pepper. A tree split by lightning yet thriving, tall and leafy green. An overgrown, old family graveyard with headstones, found to be dated in the 1800s when he wiped the dirt away… All these remarkable things hidden behind creaky wrought iron fences and ancient stone walls covered with vines.

On the eighteenth day, Joe woke feeling good. He flexed his pecs and biceps in the bedroom full-length mirror. The muscle aches were gone. The swelling to his face reduced. The skin sores healed. He'd lost weight yet felt stronger. When he sucked in his gut, he had the beginnings of six-pack abs. Well, maybe a two-pack, but it was a start. Yes, it was undeniable. Escaping to the island had been a great idea, a turning point. He went outside to the rear deck to collect his pole and tackle box and other gear, happy to see the killies alive, swimming in the bottom of the bucket. Without needing to trap bait, he'd get an early start. He'd go to the pier. Though the weather remained temperate, the ocean had not. Over the past week, the water had gotten so cold it hurt his feet though sneakers. Sitting on the a bench on the pier in the sunshine seemed far more appealing.

Joe rounded the corner of the cottage to see Van Gogh, head down, lapping-up water from the pond. He wished he'd kept his phone. The scene would make a great photo. One he could look at from time-to-time when he was down.

"Coming, Van Slow?" Joe said. "No? I'll be down at the pier if you get lonely."

Joe didn't know if animals got lonely, though he supposed they did. Humans do. He sure missed his mom. He'd have to figure a way to contact her and Zoe soon. He hoped they'd understand why he needed time away.

He walked the bluestone path to the dirt trail and left the gate open in case Van Gogh decided to follow, which she did. Joe first saw it off to the side in a muddy part of the trail. He walked over to it. Measured the length of the impression with his foot - twice the size of his sneaker. And he wore a size 13! Not possible. There were no bears on the island. Yet there it was. Clear. Unmistakable. A humongous paw print.

He stepped into the print. His foot went deep, the mud making a slurping sound. He remembered hearing an animal's weight can be estimated by measuring the depth of its footprint. If that were true, this beast weighed more than his car. Joe crouched and studied the track as if he were a hunter who knew what he was doing - which he didn't. The impression showed a deep broad palm with another smaller pad print beneath. Above the palm was a series of toes - splayed wide - and above each one, a deep, circular pencil hole in the earth…caused by the claws, Joe decided…six. He counted again but came up with the same number - six. Didn't bears have five toes? And would the paw print really be this huge? He stuck a finger in one claw hole and it didn't touch bottom.

"You know anything about this, Van Gogh?" Joe yelled.

The deer was twenty yards behind. She stood with a rubbery nose to the air, nostrils twitching, back arched, fur bunched and bristly.

"Nothing to worry about," Joe said. "C'mon, girl."

Without warning, the deer turned, sprang, kicking back divots of dirt, bounding in the opposite direction, cutting hard right, disappearing into the woods. Joe rose and stood watching, waiting to see if she'd come back. When she didn't, he felt a loss.

Of course she'd panicked for nothing. No bears lived on the island. These weren't real woods. They were suburban woods. Even staying in the campground wasn't real camping. The campsite provided hot showers and a cell phone charging station. Campers had pizzas delivered to their tents. There was no danger. Visitors were warned about ticks, not ferocious wildlife... Joe walked in the direction of the pier. He wasn't worried. The track was a hoax or a prank. Far too big for a black bear or even a grizzly. Somebody had tried to be funny and used a homemade set of Sasquatch snowshoes. Nope. Couldn't be real. When he saw another track further down the path, he didn't stop. He refused to give the pranksters the satisfaction.

On the pier, fishing from the bench, overlooking the glinting, turquoise bay, Joe couldn't shake the image of the paw print in the mud. If there were bears on the island, it wasn't safe to walk around. The way his luck was running lately, the odds of being mauled didn't seem as low as they should. Bears were shy, though, weren't they? He recalled seeing an online video of a crazy Russian man, a shirtless hairy bear himself, chasing a meek one away from garbage cans with a broom. On the other hand, he'd read newspaper articles of hikers being killed, or worse, surviving the attack. That would make the beating the bikers gave him seem like a bunch of love taps. Obsessing over the possibility wouldn't help, however. And there was no one to ask to put his mind at ease. In two weeks, he hadn't seen a single person on the island. Not even a mail carrier. Not a cop. Nobody.

He looked across the bay. With the sun directly overhead and the air without its usual haze, Joe could almost see to the other side. He could make out a flag pole and a few boats. When he squinted, he could see people as little dots of colors on the rocky shore - a red shirt, a white pair of pants, a green windbreaker. He wondered if he'd make it. That is, if he had to… Not that he would ever be in that position. Yet, would it be possible? No, he decided. He'd surely drown.

After six hours, Joe packed-up, readying to return to the cottage. He poured the three inches of smelly water and the remaining bait into the bay to lighten the load. Not that he had much to carry. This was the first excursion where'd he go home without a single fish. Maybe that was a good thing. Who knew? Perhaps the bear smelled the catch in the same way the deer smelled popcorn. He returned home while scanning for fresh tracks but didn't find any.

He ate a bowl of beef barley soup for dinner. Van Gogh returned, scratching at the back deck. Joe poured an entire box of corn flakes he'd found in the pantry into a large mixing bowl and brought it outside.

"Sorry, I don't have any milk," he said.

Van Gogh didn't seem to mind. With the animal occupied, Joe went to the front of the property and shut the green gate. Though there were many ways in and out of the yard where the fence was either broken or missing, the gate provide a token sense of security, regardless. He went back inside the cottage to watch the game shows he'd become hooked on. Oddly, the cottage had satellite TV, an amenity unheard of at the Fleabag. He lay on the sofa in a semi-comatose stupor mumbling answers in the form of questions. What is an aperture? Who is Dr. Jonas Salk? What are four and twenty blackbirds baked in a pie? Joe started to doze, drifting into a wonderful place of non-thought. The snarl jolted him to full alertness and he sprang to a seated position. The noise came from outside, distant yet distinct. Van Gogh! He went over to the glass sliders. His friend was gone, the cereal toppled, golden flakes scattered.

Joe moved to the front windows and peered through the blinds. The sun was down, the only illumination being a dwindling purple twilight. He couldn't see the gate. He stood, waited, not breathing. He turned an ear towards the glass – nothing. No sound from outside. Only the soft, steady schooomm of his own circulating blood like he'd cupped a seashell over an ear. He took a breath, relaxed. Nothing to be scared of. Nothing, at all. He turned away from the window, feeling silly. He'd been alone too long. His mind was pl...

A crash, earsplitting, bone-rattling. Joe dove onto his belly. Face down onto the hardwood, hands clasped behind his head. Noise from outside - grunts, growls. Porch chairs thrown, splintered. Drumming, pounding on the decking, a buffalo stampede - walls shaking, framed pictures falling. The front door struck, rattling within its jamb but holding. Window glass shattering inward, spraying fragments on his back, his head. A moment of nothing. Followed by a thunderous boom - the house's structure shifting on its foundation. Strident scratching, clawing, stripping the exterior planks. Walls shaking. Soot dropping down the chimney, black powder rolling out from the hearth and expanding as a cloud. Another boom, the kitchen light fixture swinging, its lights, all power going out. Sudden darkness. Things cracking. The cottage tipping, ceramic dishes sliding out of the cupboards, crashing onto the floor.

Joe heard it, felt it move around back. He jumped to his feet and made for the front door and swung it inward. The glass sliders exploded behind him. He hopscotched over the porch's missing boards. He crossed the yard and through the opening, the gate gone, a split piece hanging on a bent hinge. He chanced a look over his shoulder. The animal remained behind the cottage yet Joe saw its muzzle pointing upward over the rooftop, its huge teeth exposed. Joe stood awed as its enormous claws stripped the slate shingles from the roof as if peeling a banana. He sprinted the bluestone path and turned on to the dirt trail. Within a dozen yards, he saw it. His heart seized. The lump in a shallow gully at the side of the road. The two rear hooves crossed at the ankles. The two slashes across its abdomen, its innards spilling out slimy pink onto the dirt. Joe knelt beside the deer, lifted, and turned her head - glassy black eyes, missing lines of fur, and only half an ear. He laid the head down gently, pulled the hem of his shirt up onto his face and wept.

He coughed as he rose and set out for the docks. Confused by the dark, the familiar landmarks hidden, he held his side and slowed to a walk. The roar from behind reverberated within his chest cavity. Hide? Climb a tree? No, run! He broke into a sprint. From behind, trees rustled and swished - the animal wider than the path. Joe pumped his elbows and knees. Harder. Faster. His heart pounded. Adrenaline surged. Sweat stung his eyes. The roar came again. Louder. Nearer. On his heels? He heard the thumps in the dirt. Branches snapping. The trail curved. Forked into two ahead. The canopy blanketing all light. The forest black. Which one? Right. The opening led to the boat ramp. His sneaker slapped the decking. He hurdled the handrail, dropping onto the rocks. Skid, fell, but getting a palm out in time, pushing upward, righting himself. He looked back towards the woods. Through hazy, grayish moonlight, he saw its silhouette. Resting on its haunches, the beast was tall, broad, a mountain, the mass of three elephants. It looked up to the harvest moon and roared while making weird, circular, pedaling motions with its massive front paws. It roared again, the sound's deep, guttural reverberation seemingly coming from every direction. Joe stumbled over the gravel, the rocky sand. His legs struggled to run even as he found himself knee-high in the bay falling forward into the frigid waters, sloshing, slapping, arm-over-arm, swimming, moving away from shore. The beast bellowed as though in pain. Joe swam onward, not looking back, his attention focused on the endless, murky black span between him and the dark patch of land more than a mile away.

26

He wished he'd written a note before running away. Eventually, it would've found its way to his mom. He could've explained why he left. And told her how much he loved her and how sorry he was. Now, whenever his body washed up on shore, his death would be a mystery. People would stand over his bloated, discolored corpse and assume he'd fallen overboard. When the police determined he hadn't been in a boating accident, they'd rule it a suicide. Why else would somebody enter frigid waters alone at night while fully dressed? Nobody would guess he jumped into the bay to escape a wild beast as big as a house. No. People would say he cracked from stress and from being alone and wrecked a rental cottage and took his own life. His mother would be consumed by grief and guilt until she, herself, died. That's if they found his body before she passed away. If the currents didn't carry his corpse to land, he was already paddling within his final resting place. Zoe, Bill, and Eli would wonder what happened to him until enough time had lapsed and then they'd stop thinking about him, altogether. They'd go on to get married, have kids, move on to new careers and new homes, and Joseph Bustamante would become nothing more than an insignificant footnote in the biographies of their lives. It couldn't end like this. He had to try.

Joe was a half mile out, maybe more. He'd stopped swimming half an hour ago upon facing the futility of trying to make it to shore. Now, his chin rested on the water, his teeth chattering from the water's all-consuming coldness. His head bobbed like a buoy, his mouth and nose above the surface only by the uncomfortable tilt of his neck. Had the water not been flat calm, he'd already be dead. Even so, small waves periodically swept over his face, flowing into his ear canals causing pressure within. To remain afloat, he spread his arms wide and rotated his hands in small, slow circles. He pedaled lazily with his feet as if warming-down on a stationary bike. After some trial and error, he'd determined this was the best form to conserve energy. Once the adrenaline surge he'd experienced on the island had cut off, Joe became instantly fatigued - deltoid muscles strained, legs like sandbags weighing him down, and every cell within every vital organ starved for oxygen. Naturally, he knew he should try swimming again, though it was obvious he'd never make it to the other side. To not swim recognized the inevitable. Of course, he wouldn't make it back to Barrier Island, either. He'd gone too far out. How far, exactly, was hard to determine. At least the opposite coast had points of light emanating from it. The uninhabited island, on the other hand, was a desolate, black rock.

Another thirty minutes or so passed. The slow, low, unchanging metronome of the tide now sounded like silence. Rising…and falling…rising…and falling… The steady rhythm lulled him into near sleep, and Joe's conscious mind entered a trance-like state until a wave washed over his face, seawater flooding his mouth. Joe coughed out the water along with stringy spittle that stuck to his chin - too tired to wipe it away. The foul taste of bay water remained on his palate. A salt residue coated the sensitive areas within his cheeks and scratched within his throat. Perhaps for the first time in his life, he understood thirst. Why hadn't he helped people dig wells in poor countries? Because he hadn't cared enough. More time passed. Still, he paddled with hands and feet. He considered how much water was beneath his leaden sneakers. The bay was known to be relatively shallow. But what did that actually mean? Twenty-five feet? Forty feet? Who knew? Didn't matter, anyway. One inch over his head would be too much. If he couldn't stand on the bottom, a sandbar or whatever, eventually he'd tire and sink below the surface. How long could a man stay adrift in a blackened sea? Nobody knew. This bay, oddly enough, was technically a lagoon - he remembered hearing that, though he had no idea what the difference was. Surely there was green, shiny sea lettuce and other darker, knotted rope-like seaweed stuck to him by now. In fact, his throbbing, splayed fingers were webbed with it. Strange the way things work. Three weeks ago he was teaching uncoordinated kids to use only one hand when dribbling a basketball. Now he'd morphed into the creature from the black lagoon. We make no choices, it seems. Life pulls you wherever it wants, like a current.

Joe had hoped a current would eventually carry him to land. Either shore on either side. Even the beach on Barrier Island would be OK. He'd be far from where he'd entered the water and wouldn't need to worry about the beast he'd left behind. But, sadly, he wasn't' being carried towards land, at all. The nearly indiscernible drift was dragging him sideways, towards the inlet. Joe knew how this would go once he rounded the tip of the island. He'd be pulled into the ocean where the waves and riptides wouldn't be as amenable - he wouldn't survive ten minutes in the open ocean. The only hope was to last in the bay until daybreak. Maybe someone on a fishing boat might spot him, though the odds were slim. He was nothing more than a pumpkin seed floating in an Olympic-sized swimming pool. Unless a search team was specifically combing the area for him - which they weren't - he'd never be spotted.

How many hours to dawn? With exhaustion overtaking him, even the small hand movements required Herculean effort. How long could a big man tread water? Not long enough, apparently, for Joe now sat lower in the water, only able to keep his nostrils above the surface.

It wouldn't be long. The blurry balls of illumination coming from the docks would be the last thing he saw. Yes, the faraway lights would send him off...and the nearer one, too, the clear blinking one…the closer one. What the… Joe thrashed in the water. He didn't know if it was attached to a buoy or some type of marker for the boat lanes, but it was only two hundred yards away. And the current was pulling him towards it! At least in its general direction. If he could make it, he might be able to cling to whatever it was and gain some rest.

A second wind, a supernatural surge of energy, came into him. Joe mentally forced an arm to come upward, to break the surface, and curve down hard in an arc - followed by the other arm, the first, again. Initially, he seemed to swim in place. Soon, however, by bringing his body horizontal and kicking with his feet, he was propelled forward. He grunted with each stroke. But even as he found his form and moved better, more efficiently, the object did not appear to grow any closer. Was it an optical illusion? A hallucination or a mirage? Was he a dying man in a desert seeing an oasis up ahead yet always beyond reach? No. It was real. He had to keep faith. Of course, if he was wrong, he'd be a goner for he would've squandered the very last of his strength. Its outline grew more defined as he approached - a boat. The white beacon sat attached to the top deck. Jubilance mixed with fear; the vessel seemed impossibly far away. Joe anchored his gaze to it, cupped his fingers together and sliced through the water, stretching, reaching, and pulling his body along. Soon, it grew nearer. Then he was upon it.

He approached from the front and realized its engines weren't running. He slapped at the hull and yelled in a hoarse voice, barely audible. No lights, no movement came from the boat. While positioned next to the vessel, the water appeared rougher. The boat bobbed up and down and Joe's body struck hard against its hull. He slapped palms to it and moved himself around searching for a way to climb aboard. But there was none. Nothing to grip. No way to hoist himself out of the water. He cried out again - no response. The mental anguish became unbearable - he'd found a boat in the middle of an empty bay but there was no way to get on it! He felt his own bodyweight, his own meaty flesh pulling him under. There was no way up, the boat too tall. He worked his way further around to the opposite side where he found a cord dangling. The line wet up high above to a large, tubular, red canvas pouch. The reflective white lettering on the pouch said RESCUE. He yanked the cord. It pulled open a strip of Velcro and something rolled down - a rope ladder with aluminum rungs! Joe snaked an arm through the rope and held, not attempting to climb, simply drifting along, resting, now one with the boat.

Upon regaining strength, he tried to climb. The exertion required extreme upper-body strength, for the first rung only reached the water's surface. Joe would have to, at least initially, climb without the benefit of feet and legs. This proved to be brutally hard. How sadistic he'd been to make middle-schoolers attempt the peg board during gym class. His grip slipped from the third rung and he plunged, going under, sucked beneath the boat. He fought his way back to the surface, pushed his head and shoulders through and drew in a loud, painful breath. He found the ladder again and hung on, gasping...Time passed. Still no signs of life from the boat. Sleeping? Drunk? Joe gripped the rungs again. This time, he focused, pausing on each one before proceeding. On the fifth, he was able to get a foot on the bottom rung. From there, it was easier. At the top, he threw himself over the rail, rolling onto his back on the ship's deck. He breathed hard and laughed and cried simultaneously. Then shivered uncontrollably, the night air unbearably cold.

He rose and slid open the cabin door. He opened a lid to a bench seat where he found a stack of green army blankets. He removed three and wrapped himself head-to-toe like a mummy. He sprawled out as best he could on the too-short bench, body shaking, teeth chattering. Pain came to his feet and hands as he warmed up, his palms, especially raw and sore. The undulating boat swayed him gently like a baby cradled in a rocking chair. The old wooden vessel creaked and groaned in a melodic manner, singing a soft, long-forgotten lullaby. Within minutes, he was asleep—a sleep as deep as the ocean itself.

He woke to the sun's rays coming through the cabin windows and warming his face. He rose to a seated position and rested hands on knees. Standing would be a task he needed time to prepare for - every muscle ached, his entire body tender to the touch. It seemed, during the past few hours, he'd become one big bruise. He stood up, clothes heavy, sneakers saturated, squishing as he moved about the cabin. No. It wasn't possible...but, yes—the life preserver hung on the bathroom door. The hard, wooden benches bolted to the floor. The large windows with the dirty glass he'd peered through many times before.

The boat rose up - way up - and dropped. To keep from falling, Joe grabbed the center pole and circled around it. The water had grown incredibly rough. He'd have to find his sea legs quick. Joe slid the cabin door open and walked the skinny lane towards the bow. The line of orange life vests...the railing...every rusty cleat was familiar.... He knew this old trawler. Been aboard many times. Including that day the storm hit. Yes, by the most improbable of coincidences, Joe stood within the salty breeze on the bouncing bow of All My Glory.

He looked up the steps to the second deck for the mates, but the landing was empty. He presumed the captain was above aluminum rungs, perched within the small enclosed third deck. At least, he hoped so. Maybe there was no captain or crew, at all, and he was simply adrift on a ghost ship. Joe went to the tip, leaned over the rail, and scanned left and right. They'd traveled a vast distance while he slept. Perhaps they'd drifted, for he hadn't heard the engines run. This far? Through the inlet and out into the ocean beyond sight of land? Didn't matter. The vessel had proven sea-worthy and he was safe. So, despite the giant swells raising and dropping the bow, the water was no longer foreboding in the immaculate shine of daylight. True, the sea wasn't as fearsome and menacing when viewed from above. In fact, it really was quite beautiful. Majestic and grand. Without boundary…but why would the captain venture so far out alone? Eventually, he'd have to go up the steps to the second level and then climb the rungs to the third in order to rouse him from his slumber and introduce himself. For the moment, though, he'd admire the view. And what a gorgeous vista it was...

The shadowy form deep below the surface lay only thirty yards from the starboard side of the vessel - four times the length of the boat and twice as wide. A shipwreck or a reef? No they were out too deep to see bottom. Besides, it was moving. A whale? No. It came nearer. Within twenty feet. It swam no more than thirty feet down, lazily, effortlessly circling the boat. Joe darted from one side to the other, watching. With each revolution, it ascended higher, nearer the surface. The trawler rolled side-to-side.

"Hey!" Joe yelled up towards the third deck. "There's something by the boat!"

It rose higher in the water, only ten feet down. Joe could see its reddish purple coloration; the white barnacles attached to its hide, the large scales, each an armor plate. It continued the slow circles. He ran to the port side, looked up to the sky instead of the sea - darkness. He stood stunned, paralyzed by disbelief. Where the sky had been a clear cerulean, an inky cloud, the storm approached like a colossal balled fist. The creature beneath the waves swam faster, pulling the sea in its wake, a whirlpool forming. As it rose and fell on the swells, the ship simultaneously began turning on an invisible axis, slowly at first, but then faster, faster as the creature increased its speed. Joe looked down and up and down again. The storm spun in a cyclone, the wind crossing the deck, blowing his body as he clutched the railing. The beach chairs and deck chairs were sent skittering across the deck, clanging against the rails. The storm moved closer, enveloping the ship in darkness. Fear gripped Joe hard - he couldn't think, couldn't breathe. The creature's humps crested the surface, its broad back an island in itself. The boat spun in slow circles while moving in the way the earth goes around the sun. The wind spun in-sync with the water. The sea washed over the deck up to Joe's knees. Wood planks cracked, glass shattered, and the boat listed to one side.

"Captain! Captain! Save me!"

No response came.

Joe made for the steps but was flung back into the railing, toppling halfway over but catching himself.

He looked to see the head emerging from the deep - a triangular skull, mouth long like a crocodile's. Eyeballs black, its neck long and leathery, rising... Mouth opening to reveal doubled rows of pointed teeth. The neck unfurled, the head looming high above. Smoke plumed from its nostrils. It threw its head, opened its mouth wide, and shrieked. The shrill sound cut through the wind. It's forked, flat tail rose high above the surface, coming down, smacking the surface, sending a tidal wave. The boat turned on its side. Joe toppled, slid across the deck, and banged an elbow against the bait box – hard, only to slide back in the opposite direction as the vessel dropped and righted itself. He squirmed on his back, clutching for something, anything, but finding only air while icy, frothy seawater rushed over him. He looked up and became frozen by fear, awed by the size of the sea monster, its head looming high above. Unable to stand, unable to speak, he recognized he would die...until a bald-faced defiance settled upon his spirit, and he fought against the wind and the rushing water and stood. He gripped the railing with one hand. With the other, he raised and pointed a single accusing finger toward the upper deck and shouted.

"What the hell kind of captain are you, anyway? Show yourself, coward!"

No response came.

Joe mustered more courage. His voice cracked through tears of fury, his voice heard over the shriek of the creature and the force of the wind.

"Always hiding. Always invisible. Never taking responsibility. Come and explain yourself! Are you even up there? Who's steering this lousy ship, anyway?"

No response came.

Joe choked on raw emotion. His shoulders shook as rage boiled his blood. His hands tightened into stones. His throat constricted as he screamed.

"Show yourself, damn you!'

From the whirlwind came a deep, booming voice. "Does the one who contends with the Captain believe he can correct Him?"

The words resounded as thunder. From right, left, up, and down, inside his head, everywhere… Joe B. cupped a hand over his mouth and looked up in awe and fright. The wind stopped. The whirlpool stopped. The boat slowed and stopped. The captain's door creaked open. He stood as a backlit shadow on the top deck. The tone angered, sharp and forceful. A spear to the chest.

"Let the one who accuses me answer me!"

Joe silently pleaded by shaking his head no. He'd changed his mind. He'd prefer not to meet the captain, but it was too late. The figure climbed down the rungs to the second deck. From there, he bellowed once again. "Grab hold and brace yourself. I shall question you!"

He came down the steep steps, and paused at the bottom. "Answer me, this," he said. "If you know all things, please tell me how deep the sea is? Describe what creatures flourish at the bottom of its icy depths where no light reaches? And inform me, where were you when the clay bowl was made and filled with the water? And what of the stars and the wandering stars? Were you present when they were set in the heavens? Can you use them to navigate your way? Who is the one who questions the course I've set? Who is this who questions my plans without knowledge?"

Joe gaped, lips parted but unable to speak. Petrified, yet unable to look away. His face… The captain's face was...familiar. Joe recalled the wispy, reddish hair and the broad, bulbous nose and ruddy complexion. He recognized the folds of brownish skin above the cheeks below those alert, twinkly, hazel eyes. He knew this short man with a barrel-chest and bulgy forearms.

"You're the bartender," Joe said, voice breathy, more to himself. "From Steeples."

The captain tilted his head but said nothing.

The realization left Joe dumbstruck. He didn't know the bartender had a side-hustle. That the man moonlighted as a fishing boat captain, or maybe it was the other way around. Either way, the brave barkeep remained oblivious to the sinking ship and the sea monster lurking about for he continued, unconcerned.

"Do you believe you could steer the ship? Then take my coat and my place at the helm."

Though it was a really cool wool coat with big gold buttons, not the dingy apron he was used to seeing him wear, Joe declined with a humble shake of his head.

When the captain seemed to wait for a response, Joe answered verbally. "I'm not capable," he muttered. "I'm not worthy to..."

"Do you know how big the earth is? Have you stretched a tape measure? Have you calculated its vastness?"

The captain paused before continuing. "Do you know where the lightning comes from? How about the wind? And the rain? Can you have it come down in torrents? Do you know where snow and ice are stored? Can you whisper and tell the seasons to come and go?"

He took a step towards Joe. His voice stern, deadly serious. "And what of all the creatures of the earth? Do you know where the mountain lions give birth? Or where your doe will bear her fawn this spring?"

But…Van Gogh was gone he wanted to say but didn't. The captain took another foreboding step forward.

"Can you take the sting out of your aunt's bees or the bite out of a wild dog? Will the tiger sharks consent to serve you? Can you have a seagull lay her eggs in the sand and have the sun warm them?"

The captain took another step. He intended harm - it was in his eyes. "Does the hawk fly by your wisdom? Does the cow make milk at your command? Does the horse credit its strength to you? And what about the behemoth? You met him on the island. Why didn't you simply put a ring in his snout and lead him back to marshy lands and feed him some grass? And what of Leviathan?"

At the mention of his name, the sea-beast emitted a high-pitched yodel, its head swinging wild on its long neck, to and fro, like a pendulum.

"Well?" the captain said.

Joe remained silent. The leviathan bared its teeth, its long, bluish tongue poking out.

"Can you catch him with your fish hook? Cook him on your grill and serve him with a slice of lemon?"

The leviathan screeched in protest. It swung its head downward, quickly, directly towards Joe - to devour him in a single snap of its mighty jaws. The captain signaled the monster with a small, downward motion of his palm. The creature stopped, reversed direction, and slowly lowered, submerged into the sea. The boat rocked, and then steadied.

Gone. The monster had gone. For a moment, Joe couldn't move. Then, in a display of retroactive fear, he scuttled backwards on his butt, pushing with his heels, sloshing in the water-covered deck in order to put distance between him and the crazy captain.

The captain's march continued with another lone step. His countenance showed indignation. He spoke words of iron. "Let him who accuses me answer me!"

Joe grabbed the metal rails, struggling, slipping, but ultimately pulled himself to his feet, and braced his back against the banister. He held both palms outward.

"Hey, hey…wait!" he said. "Stay away! I didn't do anything. I'm innocent! Don't! I never deserved any of this."

The captain took another step, eyes fiery with emotion. Then another step. Joe begged.

"Please…. Please. I didn't do anything! I never wronged you. You know that's true!"

The captain stopped short, boot heels snapped together. His visage turned down, profoundly saddened. "Yes,' he said. "This is true. You are innocent. You did everything right. You never wronged me in any way, but you never knew me."

When he raised his face, Joe saw a single tear rolling down the captain's craggy cheek. Wide-eyed, stunned, he stared into the forlorn face. Joe ruminated upon what he'd just heard. It was true. As many times as the barkeep had served him, he didn't know him, at all. Terror became displaced by grief. A feeling far greater than those spawned by Rebecca leaving him, his friends rejecting him, his boss betraying him…sadder than even learning of his mom's cancer… He had never made the effort. None, at all. He never knew he was supposed to know him…he never knew he wanted to be known. Joe hadn't given it a thought. As he'd served, all-the-while, he'd thirsted.

Compelled by regret, by longing, by a deeper more meaningful love than he'd ever felt, Joe lunged forward, wrapping the captain, the bartender, in a tight embrace. He craned his neck downward and buried his face into the powerful shoulder and sobbed.

"I didn't know...I'm so sorry," he said. "I'm so very sorry."

The captain rubbed Joe's back. For a while, no more was said until he spoke softly, a mere whisper. "It'll take time," he said. "But you'll come to know me. And, eventually, you'll grow to trust me. C'mon, son. I'll bring you home."

Joe wiped the tears from his cheeks, nodded and smiled. The captain winked, turned and slowly went up the steps and up the rungs to the third deck. At the top platform, he gave a little wave before opening the door and entering. The engines rumbled to life.

Joe remained on the bow overlooking the sea. The storm had passed and the sun dried his clothes and warmed his muscles and bones. All My Glory cut through the water, sending waves churning on each side. The wind blew Joe's hair, which hadn't happened in some time, and it felt good. He thought about how big the sea was. How there was a definite number of fish and squid and urchins and eels and what have you, and how that number could be known - astounding. He thought of all the fish he'd caught recently. Considered how after he'd hooked them and pulled them from the water, they'd squirmed and flopped about surprised. It was as if they hadn't known they'd been immersed in water until being yanked out of it. Only then did they appreciate the water. Only then did they miss it. Of course, a lot of the skates and the sea robins - the ones people called garbage fish - knew about the water surrounding them. They're the lucky ones that get unhooked and tossed back. Joe wondered if the garbage fish thought about it and communicated it to the other fish. He hoped so. Otherwise, their suffering wouldn't amount to anything. It would've been for nothing. But if they did share their hard-earned wisdom - who knew? Good things could happen. Many might even come to realize the purpose of their pain.

The boat puttered along, slowing while moving through the inlet. Joe saw the fishing boats and sailboats and motorboats going out for the day. He smiled as a fine mist of salt spray caressed his face. Happy people wearing reds and whites and canvas shoes waved to him. He waved back. The canal and docks up ahead were a familiar, welcome sight. The bay itself appeared different, however. Where it had been a formless, black void only hours before, it was now emerald green and glinting and teeming with life. Everything renewed, all corrected and made perfect. Each coming day offered the possibilities of a new beginning, he supposed—the water patiently bringing about birth and death and rebirth. What a glorious thing to witness. What a lucky man he was.

Epilogue

Joe left the bar at the stone patio carrying a white wine spritzer by the stem. His shoes made foot-prints in the lawn as he said hi to three pretty ladies, their hair and makeup done, not exactly sure who they were as he passed. More people had come than ex-pected. He walked on. Joe knew the ones at the gazebo. He especially knew the one in the yellow sundress. Her sisters, mother, and two best friends surrounded her, all in brightly-colored outfits with big, floppy hats. She'd fretted about the possibility of rain, but he'd told her not to worry. The house could hold dozens of guests, if nec-essary. As it turned out, she needn't have given it a thought. The sun shone bright, the slight breeze was warm and hospitable. Not a single cloud obscured the heavens on this wonderful summer afternoon.

"Yes, I can believe it's been a year," she said, and threw her head back and laughed. "A year isn't long enough for me to forget. They say a woman has to or she'd never have any more. But I'm tellin' you, I ha-ven't forgotten. Not after sixteen hours spent pushing out three duplicates like a copy machine... Tell you what I do forget is how it happened. All from one tipsy night in the Bahamas? Twins don't even run in our family, let alone triplets. Right, Mom?"

"Pardon me," Joe said, extending an arm through the ring, his wife receiving the wine glass. Attempting to make a quick getaway, added, "Here ya' go."

"Oh, don't try to make it up to me now," Rebecca said playfully. "Here's the man who's responsible."

She pulled him by the hand, making him join the group before continuing. "It's always the shy ones you gotta watch. He bought me countless Pink Ladies on the beach during our honeymoon and then coaxed me back to the villa."

"I coaxed you?" Joe said, and the women chortled. One poked Rebecca's shoulder. Another fussed with her hair. She took the teasing in good spirit.

"Well, six in one, half dozen in the other," she said. "Point is; you made it happen. I knew it to! I peed on the stick as soon as we got home and it turned blue - royal blue! Six months later, I was a house."

The girls pinched her forearms while saying it takes two to tango and asking if her arm had been twisted... Rebecca's cheeks shined with embarrassment and delight.

"You're all no good," she said. "You're supposed to be on my side."

"I'm on your side," Joe said.

He kissed her cheek and everyone went aww… He took her in a brief moment before moving on. She truly was beautiful. The few extra pounds she hadn't lost manifested as thicker upper arms and a small, fleshy wad beneath the chin only made her more so. To think he'd almost missed out on a life with her. How he'd foolishly chucked his cell phone into the bay without checking the number as she called. She'd wanted to tell him she'd changed her mind about going away with Dr. Spiera. Rebecca had wanted to say how seeing Joe in the parking lot at her garden apartment made her realize what a huge mistake she'd made. Specifically what she'd said after agreeing to meet at a corner booth in Steeples was this:

"Ever since I was a little girl, my mom and dad and all my aunts told me you can fall in love with a rich guy as easily as a poor one - why make your life hard? What they said made sense. So, when I realized I'd never be a success on my own, I went husband shopping for a doctor… And I found one. A nice one. A good one. But I didn't love him… Lucky me, I fell head-over-heels for a poor gym teacher. And I think you feel the same about me. I know life is going to be a little harder - for both of us. And I know it really doesn't make any sense - but, hey, who says love is supposed to make sense?"

Naturally, Joe asked how she could say she didn't love him. She became teary-eyed.

"I was lying to myself, crushing my own heart and yours – I am so sorry, Joe. I wanted… I thought if you just went away, things would be better for both of us. I thought we could just move on. But I was wrong. True love doesn't let you move on.

The doctor took the break-up fairly well. After being served the restraining order, he stopped calling. Eighteen months later, Joe and Rebecca had a big church wedding. Nine months after that, a trio of children to call their own.

"Don't listen to her complain, ladies, we're going to have seven more," Joe said. "I always told her I wanted ten, a nice round number, and she agreed."

"I must've been out of my mind. Three's a round number," Rebecca insisted. "Draw a three. Numbers don't get more rounder! The only one who'll get rounder is me."

"Then we'll adopt," Joe said.

"We'll talk," Rebecca said, waving him off.

Joe took a step back as Rebecca delighted their guests by the mere power of her personality. He listened to the lovely tone of her voice, that of a lyre or a harp, as he moved further into the backyard.

"Seriously, if I didn't have the nanny and the cook, I don't know what I'd do. Who knew Joe was loaded? I don't know how you managed it, Ma, way back when. Of course, sometimes I wish I didn't have Rachel. She's keeping me so fat..."

Joe tucked his hands into his sports jacket and walked on. He never imagined he'd be marrying into such a big family. There were so many kids having fun, and the joy he shared with them ballooned inside his heart. There were younger ones running barefoot with water pistols and splashing in the pool, screeching in glee while the teens hung out by the deejay booth. Oh, how he wished he could be a kid again. Most of the adults were standing around holding cocktails or waiting in the line leading to where the caterers were serving hamburgers, hotdogs, clams and lobster tails, and some type of shish-kabob with meats and veggies. Then again, being grown-up wasn't too bad, either. The smoky aroma almost made Joe want to join the line right behind Nicky Diamonds.

"Hey, big guy," Nicky said, putting up a hand for a high-five. "This is some shindig you've put together. If you feel like throwing my next B-day party, I'm down with it. You remember Clarabella, right?"

The woman standing in front of Nicky Diamonds turned to grasp Joe's hands. Joe leaned and kissed her on the cheeks.

"I don't think we'll ever forget one another," Joe said. " Hello, Clari. You brought the kids, I hope."

"Hola, Mr. B. Oh, they here, somewheres. They not stop moving. So much food and fun. Gracias."

"My pleasure," Joe said. "I'm happy to have you here."

He and the cleaner had become better acquainted since his return to work. Showing up at the administrative hearing, she'd dropped a bombshell by initiating an unprecedented, one-hundred and eighty degree legalistic turn; Clarabella had withdrawn her complaint alleging discrimination and harassment. Apparently, she'd had a dream where she was told to do so. When questioned by members of the panel, Clarabella refused to elaborate any further than saying it was good and brought her peace. Naturally, Principal Shelley expressed reluctance to reinstate Joe in his teaching position. But after three days and a particularly pointed letter from the tenacious Nicky Diamonds threatening a lawsuit, Joe was back at work in extra-white knee-high socks blowing a shiny new whistle strung around his neck.

"Enjoy, guys," Joe said. "Don't eat too much, Nicky."

"But that's my whole plan," Nicky Diamonds said. "To eat too much and crash on your couch and wake up and eat some more."

Joe smiled. "That's fine," he said. "But I'd hate to be your cardiologist."

"Hey, you only live once," Nicky said.

Joe nodded in agreement, though he didn't necessarily agree. He continued on, coming to the bouncy house, a giant inflatable thing with a blue and yellow canopy pyramid top and mesh walls. The little kids had played within it for an hour before losing interest as soon as the man with the pony arrived. Since then, it was home to three bigger kids - Bill, Eli, and Zoe.

Joe pulled the flap open and popped his head in. Zoe and Eli were seated Indian-style with Bill lying flat, hands cupped behind his head.

"Hey, guys," Joe said. "Why you hanging in here?"

"'Cause this is way cool," Zoe said.

"Yeah, look what you can do," Bill said.

With difficulty, he rolled onto his knees, stood, and began jumping. He purposely dropped onto his butt, springing back to his feet. Then repeated it again.

"I want to try," Eli said, and he stood and bounced.

As did Zoe. Soon, all three were bouncing off their butts and laughing.

"Hey," Zoe said. "I got an idea. Tonight we should all get drunk and do this in the nude."

"Not now that you're my girl," Bill said, the tone becoming stern. "You need to straighten up and become proper. I can't marry a girl gone wild. Not, me. I need a girl gone mild."

Yes, it had finally happened. Zoe and Bill had begun dating, had fallen in love, and were now engaged to be engaged, whatever that meant.

"Oh, so we're going to get married sometime during this millennium?" Zoe said.

"You're damn right we are…and Eli, here, is going to be the best man."

Eli stopped bouncing, and waited to be wounded by a zinger that never came.

"I'm gonna be your best man?" he asked, cautiously.

"Damn, right. Who else? Joe? His leash is too short. What kind of bachelor party would he throw? A night at the bingo hall? I need to go out with a bang. You're the man, dude. Besides, you're my best bro."

Taken aback, Eli fell silent, emotional, and almost teary-eyed. Zoe tried to save him from embarrassment.

"Hey, nude bingo doesn't sound too bad," she said.

"What is it with you and taking your clothes off?" Bill said. "What am I signing up for?"

The three laughed. All friends, again. The bad feelings in the bar long forgotten.

"So when is the big day going to be?" Joe asked.

"Shooting for next summer," Bill said. "Just got to get a couple bucks together. I want to give this one the kind of ceremony she deserves. A big one with all the bells and whistles like the one you and Rebecca had."

And now it was Zoe's turn to be caught off guard. She stared at Bill with such unspoken affection. Joe knew they'd have a good marriage.

"Joe B had a royal wedding," Eli said. "You'd better hawk more shoes."

"God knows I'm trying," Bill said, and sighed. Then, becoming lighter, asked, "So where's my beer, Joseph? The one I asked for half an hour ago?"

"Plenty up at the bar."

"You mean I have to hustle my tired ass all the way up there? Your yard is a friggin' public park."

"Your skinny butt could use a workout. And you'll get a chance to meet the bartender."

"The one in the vest?" Zoe said "Isn't he from Steeples?"

"Yep. And he's a really cool guy. Take the time to get to know him. The more you do, the more you're gonna want to... Nothing will ever be the same, because nothing is more important."

The three looked at Joe curiously.

"Um...did you drink my beer?" Bill asked. "Along with a few others?"

Joe smiled, stepped back, and closed the flap. He continued on towards the rear side of the property.

Bill was right. The grounds of the estate and the house itself were enormous. The realtor needed to show aerial shots from high above. The main house, not to be confused with the servants quarters or the pool house, was a grand, beautifully-restored stone mansion with steeply pitched roofs, a turret, moss covered blocks, and huge French doors opening to ornate, wrought-iron balconies. The estate was pricey, but Joe had been sold upon pulling up the circular driveway next to the fountain - he'd always liked fountains. It's a vampire's castle, Rebecca bemoaned upon removing the blindfold as they'd first arrived at the big reveal. Of course, during the past six months, she'd grown to love it. Not too shabby for a starter home, she'd become fond of saying.

Naturally, Joe would never have been able to afford such a place - perhaps the most desirable in the Land of Uz - on a teacher's salary. He'd paid cash having sold his shares of Pillbox Pharmaceuticals after their value rocketed. It seemed the unflappable CEO, Mr. Stephanie LaPlace, had a few more moves in his shell game. With some minor tweaking, the formula for the Starfish eyelash pill turned out to be a spectacularly good topical cream for bald men's heads. The result was often better than their prior, long-lost, natural hair. Most men and a small percentage of women users developed full, shiny, jet-black pompadours. One guy applied it to the scalp of his pet spider monkey, and it, too, grew a pompadour. The monkey, which already had a penchant for grinning and banging the bongos, made a big splash on the daytime talk show circuit. Pillbox shares soared. The Hong Kong giant Brighter Tomorrow acquired the smaller company as originally planned and the shares split. Unlike most investors, Joe hadn't sold when the stock initially tanked. He'd been alone on a deserted island. His investment doubled from its value before the collapse.

Here at the party, Joe noticed one of Rebecca's great uncles, a skinny, pasty-white octogenarian sporting a cane and the tell-tale Elvis mane. Everyone, including those with decent coifs, craved the new look. Joe sold-off before the situation could get...um...hairy.

Even after voluntarily paying double for the damages to the Barrier Island cottage, he was now, possibly, the wealthiest man in Uz. His own hair, of course, had been fully restored without the use of drugs. He enjoyed combing and slicking it back in the mornings. He had a bit of a dollar-store Elvis thing going on, himself.

Joe continued on, towards the rear of the property beneath the birch tree. His three boys played in the grass. All wore identical outfits of red and white striped shirts and denim shorts with suspenders. The diapers beneath the shorts padded their bottoms to comical proportions. All three sat in the grass as did Aunt Edna. David gripped a dandelion. Samuel stood and tried a shaky step and fell forward onto his elbows, surprised by what just happened. Solomon pointed at nothing in particular and chatted away, having a long conversation in his own secret language. Lord, Joe loved them so. Seemed his heart might burst just for seeing them play in the grass.

"Hey, here they are, the three musketeers," Joe said. 'Why are the guests of honor missing their own party?"

"They wanted to get away from all the fuss and commotion," Edna said.

"Did they?" Joe said, and smiled. His aunt was never one for crowds.

The three boys grew excited at the sound of their father's voice. Samuel clapped hands, missing only a few times. Solomon pointed and muttered some sort of salutation. David lifted and shook the dandelion within his chubby fist.

"For me, handsome?" Joe said and leaned over and accepted it but handed it back when the child immediately started whimpering and making opening and closing motions with his tiny fingers. "Here ya' go. I didn't mean to steal your flower."

"This one doesn't like to share," his mother said. Gladys sat legs tucked beneath her in her good Sunday dress without concern of wrinkles or grass stains. "But they all love a nice lawn, just like your father did."

"He liked it too much," Joe said. "Let's hope they develop some important interests. Like football and baseball."

"Or maybe art and dance," Aunt Edna offered.

"Yep, those would be fine additions to a solid foundation of football and baseball," Joe said, which made the two sisters laugh.

"I think you like sports a little too much."

"Nah…I have other interests. I also like cake. Which reminds me of why I trekked back here. We'd better get the birthday boys to the patio. They're telling me it's almost time to blow out the candles."

"Help me up, wise guy," Gladys said.

Joe gently reached and held his mom's wrist and elbow as she rose to her feet. She had gained weight since finishing chemotherapy. Her hair had regrown, too. Changing her mind and continuing treatments turned out to be a good thing, even though Joe didn't attribute the remission of her cancer to the treatments. He credited his mom's recovery to a miracle, nothing less—one that he neither asked for nor deserved yet was deliriously happy to receive.

"Can you handle Hughie, Dewey, and Louie by yourself for a few minutes," she said to her sister.

"Not a problem," Edna said. "I'm sure I can juggle my three boyfriends."

Joe walked hand-in-hand with his mom to the sycamore tree.

"You know, kiddo," Gladys said, "I never thought I'd meet my grandchildren, let alone attend their first birthday party. So, I just wanted to say I'm sorry. You know, for everything I put you through. Your mother's a fool."

"I was the one who ran away and left you," Joe said. "So I guess your son's a fool, too."

"Well, we're a pair then," his mom said. "And maybe it's like playing cards. A pair of twos will beat an ace every time."

"And a full house is one of the best hands you can get," he said.

"Joseph, will you stop already," Gladys said and playfully slapped Joe's shoulder. "You have three. That's enough. I'm too old to babysit more than that. You and your ten kids - you're crazy."

"Crazy about you," he said and he squeezed an arm around his mom's shoulder, happy to feel more than bone.

"You know, Joe," she said, "I'm proud of you. I know I don't tell you that enough, but I am. And your dad would be too, if he were here."

Joe nodded and looked at his feet. He wanted to tell her his dad was here. Instead, he shuffled shiny shoes. His mom let him off the hook.

"Now let me go so I can save your children from hearing about Karl Marx or Carl Jung or some other Carl your hippie aunt will go on about."

She stood on her toes and kissed his cheek.

"Make sure you tell them about Carl Yastrzemski."

"I don't even know who that is and I don't want to know," she said and walked away, waving him off with a flick of her wrist. "Let's get some cake. Not too much for you, however. You're getting a little pudgy. Life has been too good to you."

Joe smiled. He sure loved his mom. And he loved that his boys would get to love her as well.

Suddenly alone for the first time in a long while, Joe crossed his arms over his chest and surveyed his property. But not only his house and lot, he look across his whole life, really, for all his family and friends were here. His mom. His wife. His children. His three best friends. All the people he loved. Some eating. Some drinking. Some talking. Others dancing, singing, shouting, running, playing, swimming, splashing… All these funny and quirky and beautiful and kind and generous and caring souls, each a unique creation. All these very different people coming together out of love. All wanting to be a part of something bigger and more glorious than themselves. All seeking something more but not knowing what it is. And the barkeep in his blue vest with the big gold buttons patiently overseeing it all, serving. Waiting for someone to say hello—thirsting for someone, anyone, each and every one, to come to him.

Michael James Winn is an author and a born-again believer in Jesus Christ. He lives in Long Island, New York with his wife and two children. He now writes stories as a way to serve our Lord, and he's never been happier. You can visit him at **www.mjwinnfiction.com**.

CPSIA information can be obtained
at www.ICGtesting.com
Printed in the USA
FSHW020623170819
61127FS

9 780984 026975